1994

She was an Amazon!

Her hair was the color of a roaring fire, and her eyes were like slanted marquise-cut turquoises in the oval of her face.

Alaistair's voice was husky when he said, "I'm here to see Baron Stone on a private matter."

Liza's eyes narrowed. "A private matter? Would it have to do with money?"

"Yes. Not a matter to discuss with a lady. This is a matter between Stone and myself."

"You're mistaken," she said. "Michael may have gambled away the money, but I'm the one you will be dealing with. 'Tis only normal that I should be in charge of things until he comes into his majority."

Alaistair looked at her sardonically. "Somehow, I don't believe anything about you is 'normal,'" he murmured.

ABOUT THE AUTHOR

Georgina Devon began writing fiction in 1985 and has never looked back. Apart from her prolific writing career, she has led an interesting life. Her father was in the United States Air Force, and after Georgina received her B.A. in social sciences from California State College San Bernardino, she followed in her father's footsteps and joined the USAF. She met her husband, Martin, an A10 fighter pilot, while she was serving as an aircraft maintenance officer.

Georgina, her husband and their young daughter now live in Tucson, Arizona.

Georgina Devon

Untamed Heart

Harlequin Books

TORONTO • NEW YORK • LONDON
AMSTERDAM • PARIS • SYDNEY • HAMBURG
STOCKHOLM • ATHENS • TOKYO • MILAN
MADRID • WARSAW • BUDAPEST • AUCKLAND

Published October 1994

ISBN 0-373-31215-6

UNTAMED HEART

Copyright © 1994 by Alison J. Hentges.

PROLOGUE

MICHAEL JOHNSTONE, Baron Stone, swallowed hard. The murmur of aristocratic male voices was a buzz in his ringing ears. Cheroot smoke almost obscured the cards in his hands. All the wrong numbers stared at him.

As nonchalantly as he could he raised his sight to the man sitting across the table from him, the man who was the Faro bank at Brooks's this night and doing well at it. Lord Alaistair Gervase St. Simon...or "Saint," as the Polite World called him— looked more like a demon to Michael. The second son of the Duke of Rundell, Lord Alaistair had eyes the color of gunmetal and hair shot with iron, though Michael knew the man to be no older than thirty. He was also reputed to have the coldest heart in the ton. Seeing the hard glint of Lord Alaistair's gaze as it settled on him, Michael could well believe it.

Sweat trickled down his back as he made himself meet that uncompromising stare, but he couldn't suppress his stutter. "I—I've lost."

He laid down his losing hand and forced a twisted grin to his stiff lips, knowing it must look sickly. Liza told him that when he was upset he looked like a whipped puppy.

"Your luck is out, Stone," Lord Alaistair said, his voice a lazy drawl that crawled down Michael's back. "Why don't you call it a night?"

Michael drew himself up with all the pride of his twenty years. "I—I believe I—I'll d-do one more hand, my lord."

The older man's teeth glinted like polished sword blades in the light from a nearby brace of candles. "Suit yourself." With a studied casualness, Lord Alaistair rose. "However, I find that the game has lost its allure."

Desperation quickened Michael's heartbeat and moisture began to soak his shirt beneath the fashionable jacket he'd purchased only that day. He couldn't stop playing now. He had to win back his losses. He had to. He couldn't face Liza if he didn't. Not that she'd scold, but the sadness in her eyes would chastise him more than any words.

"I say, S-Saint, just one m-more game." His hands began to shake and a flush mounted his downy cheeks at his daring in using the older man's nickname. But he needed desperately to keep playing. Every bone in his body screamed that he could win. Lord Alaistair's luck had to turn. No one was so blessed for an entire night.

Lord Alaistair's broad shoulders stiffened in his loosely fitted gray coat. "It's Lord Alaistair St. Simon."

"Y-yes, yes, Lord A-Alaistair," Michael said, not mistaking the iron will under the soft words. "One m-more game?"

Lord Alaistair's lips thinned. "My answer is no. I've seen my fill of boys still wet behind the ears who didn't know when to stop. Most of them died at Salamanca. I've no interest in seeing you dig yourself deeper."

Even Michael, new to London the week before, was familiar with Lord Alaistair's war exploits. It was said that King George had offered him a title. It was further said that Lord Alaistair had turned the offer down, commenting that he wouldn't ridicule his family name of Rundell by accepting a title that would be a paltry thing in comparison to the one his father held. A proud, hard man, and Michael owed him a great sum of money.

Lord Alaistair raised one black brow, a silent inquiry that Michael couldn't misinterpret. His palms were clammy as he clasped his fingers tightly together to stop their shaking, and stood. He forced himself to meet the other man's gaze.

"I—I don't have the f-funds on me. W-will you accept my v-vowel?"

Lord Alaistair's lips curled derisively. "A puppy who plays where he doesn't belong is soon torn apart by the dogs."

Michael gulped, feeling the color drain from his face. He couldn't think of a reply, short of falling on his knees before this arrogant man and begging his forgiveness for being so presumptuous as even to be here at Brooks's. He wouldn't do that. Instead, he signed the paper on which he had voweled his debt and handed it to Lord Alaistair.

"How much of your inheritance have you lost tonight?"

The harsh words cut into Michael. Half? All? He had no idea.

Before he could prevaricate, Lord Alaistair addressed him again. "See that you are at my home by noon tomorrow to determine your methods of payment," he said curtly, then nodded and turned away. Without a backward glance, he strolled off until his tall figure was lost among the gaming tables.

Michael slumped back down into his chair, his chin trembling. He ran slender fingers through his hair, negating his valet's efforts to coax his curls into the semblance of a Brutus, the most fashionable style for young men about Town. It didn't matter now.

What would Liza do when he told her? She would look at him for a minute with her solemn blue eyes before turning away so he couldn't see the hurt his gaming caused. His mouth quivered at the mental image.

Pulling himself up, he quickly left Brooks's very exclusive gaming rooms before he disgraced himself. Once outside, he waved down a hackney coach and gave the driver his direction. The sooner he got home the better. Liza would know what to do. She always did.

In the east, the sun was rising. He'd gambled the night away, as well.

The mellow beige of the Town house Liza had rented for them here in London during the Season came into sight, and with it came renewed hope. The situation couldn't be as bad as he imagined. Liza would make everything all right.

With a lighter step than when he'd entered the carriage, Michael exited and ran up the steps to fling open the door. Liza would be in the small breakfast room she'd converted into an office.

Michael pushed into the room. "Lizabeth," he said, feeling relief ease the ache in his shoulders. "Lizabeth, I need to..."

He looked around the sunny room Liza had preferred over the library, which she found dark and depressing. Near the wall of windows was the massive cherry desk she'd had moved in here, ledgers stacked neatly on one of its corners. But Liza was nowhere to be seen.

Anxiety clawed at Michael's stomach. Sweat popped out on his upper lip, the light fuzz of a fledgling mustache glistening like golden drops in the sunlight coming from the open window. He had to tell her. Until she made everything right, he would not be able to rest.

In the hall, the clock struck seven with a light chime. He relaxed. She was still on her morning ride. She'd be here within the hour. All he had to do was wait until eight o'clock. At eight, Liza would solve everything. She'd tell him there were funds to pay his gambling debts. She'd take care of everything as she always had.

Feeling like a rag doll that had been squeezed until the stuffing fell out the sides, he collapsed onto a well-worn leather chair. In spite of all that had happened, sleep overcame him and he welcomed its oblivion. Slumber was the escape he sought whenever things went wrong.

The hall clock chimed the half hour, waking him from his doze. A serving girl was starting the fire.

When she had finished and turned to see Michael rising, she bobbed him a curtsy and quickly left. Michael only knew she had gone because the sound of the heavy oak door closing penetrated the melancholy that wakefulness had brought rushing back.

The sound of the door opening and his sister's light tread on the tattered carpet caught his attention. He rose to greet her. "Oh, Liza," he said, "I— I thought you'd never get b-back."

Liza lifted one auburn brow, her blue eyes lighting with pleasure and a hint of amusement as she noted his dishevelment. It was a look he knew well— her maternal look, somewhat incongruent with the flame-colored hair tumbling about her shoulders and the voluptuous curves of her statuesque figure. No mother he'd ever met looked like Liza.

"Michael, it appears from your person that you made a night of it."

Dull red suffused his face. Doubt nibbled at him, but he pushed it away. "Y-yes, I did." He forced a smile to his face. The shadow of alarm that clouded Liza's eyes told him the smile had been more of a grimace.

She strode over to him and put her arm around his shoulders. She was just shy of his six feet in stature. She scanned his countenance for signs of strain, her face on a level with his. "Something is wrong," she stated, her rich contralto voice laced with concern.

She led him to the chair by the fire and pushed him into it. Kneeling at his feet, she said, "Tell me about it, Michael."

Michael gulped, the air entering his lungs in a huge painful lump. *Liza will make it right,* he told himself. "Y-you'll know what to do. I-it isn't as bad as i-it sounds." He beseeched her with his eyes.

Liza lifted one long-fingered hand and stroked the fine brown hair back from his face. She had taken care of him since their parents' death in a yachting accident eighteen years ago.

"What happened, Michael? It can't be so bad." A slight smile curved her generous mouth, but her eyes remained clouded with worry.

Michael pulled himself up straight. "I—I lost a lot of money last night."

The bald statement hung heavily between them. Michael watched Liza swallow slowly, the smile leaving her face. Her thick auburn brows drew up into two inverted Vs.

"How much?"

"A lot." He couldn't quite screw up the courage to tell her exactly. He'd never had difficulty laying his troubles at her feet before, but this was different. He was sure she could find the money, but he feared that it would make them paupers.

Putting both hands on his shoulders, she shook him gently. "Michael, don't prolong this. How much?"

He whispered the answer with stiff lips, his eyes fixed on her countenance.

Liza squeezed her eyes shut and her fingers dug into his shoulders. "Oh my God," she breathed.

When she opened her eyes, they were an opaque blue, hiding her emotions, but Michael knew. Even the forced laugh that seemed to catch in her throat couldn't negate the fact that she was trying to keep from him the enormity of what he'd done. She was protecting him, just as she always had. Only this time Michael knew it. The last hours had aged him as the twenty preceding years had not.

"We can pay it, c-can't we?" he asked, beginning to shake. Liza had always taken charge when he'd gotten in a fix. Always. Had he gone too far this time?

Her gaze slid away from his. "Of course we can."

It was what he wanted to hear, wanted to believe. "And it won't be too hard on us?"

Her eyes were riveted on him. The angles of her high cheekbones were sharply pronounced in the sun streaming in from outside. Her voice was harsh.

"Michael, that's more money than the estate produces in twenty years. Of course it will be hard. We'll have to sell everything."

Never in his life had she spoken to him like this. His eyes watered, making her image blurry and disgusting him with his own weakness: first gambling away his inheritance, and now crying over it. He despised himself.

She must have seen the misery in his features because her face softened and her lips eased from the hard line of seconds before. "You're old enough, Michael, that I won't lie to you and tell you it will be easy. But we'll manage."

He heard the attempt at reassurance in her voice and saw the love in her eyes. But he also saw the resignation she tried to hide by lowering her lids. He knew he'd ruined not only himself but her. With all their capital gone, she would never find a husband, never be anything but a poor relation at best, a governess at worst. It would be easier for him. He could join the army, though not as an officer, since there was no money for a commission. But it would still be better than the path open to her.

Liza broke his thoughts by rising. "Why don't you go to bed, Michael," she said, her voice weary. "You look as though you could sleep for a week. I'll take care of this."

He watched her leave the room, her black riding skirt swishing over the worn carpet that she'd refused to change. She'd said a London Season was too exorbitant as it was, and that she was damned if she'd replace the carpet in a rented house, as well. Now he'd pauperized them, gambled away his entire inheritance and hadn't even realized it.

Shame rolled over him in hot waves, bringing with it guilt and regret. His stomach cramped and sweat bathed his face. How could he live with what he'd done to them . . . to her? What kind of man was he?

A bitter croak escaped him. He wasn't a man. Never had been. Liza was the one who managed the estate and saw to it that everything got done. Without her he wouldn't have had an inheritance to gamble away.

Remorse sapped his strength and he sank down into the worn leather chair. He leaned his forehead against his knuckles, his elbows digging into his knees. What good was he? To her? To himself? He'd done nothing but bring them ruin.

Liza was the one who had cared for him. When he'd been too sickly to attend Eton, she'd arranged for him to have a private tutor. When the croup took him, she had nursed him herself, not trusting anyone else to care for him as she would. All his life

Liza had been a mother to him. She'd never failed him. And this was how he had repaid her.

He didn't need her to tell him the ramifications of his weakness. He'd seen them in her tense shoulders and the blank look in her eyes. He knew all too well what he'd done. The question was, now that he knew, how could he ever live with himself?

CHAPTER ONE

LORD ALAISTAIR GERVASE St. Simon reclined in the heavy oak chair positioned in his dressing room so that the maximum amount of sunshine shone on his face.

His sleeping chamber was large and well lit, the beige damask curtains pulled back from two floor-to-ceiling windows. The room was paneled in rich walnut, not as modern as the Oriental paper that was all the rage, but it appealed to him. His maternal grandmother had left him this Town house in Grosvenor Square, and he had no intention of changing it to keep up with fashion.

The sound of his valet, Rast, sharpening the shaving razor was a soothing lull after a morning spent in Marie's arms. A sardonic smile curled Alaistair's lips. Marie was a demanding creature, the most voracious mistress he'd ever had.

A jaunty knock on the door interrupted his considerations. ''Come in,'' Alaistair said at the same moment that Tristan Montford entered the room.

"Wondered when you'd return from the Malicious Marie's tentacles, Saint," Montford said. A man of taller than average height with blond, almost white hair and piercing blue eyes, he was Alaistair's closest friend.

"Being provocative again, Tristan?" Alaistair drawled through the lather Rast had just applied to his jaw.

Opening one eye, he watched his friend sprawl on the nearby bed, his booted feet hanging over the edge. Tristan and he were as tight as two men could be. They'd grown up virtual residents in each other's north Yorkshire homes. They had attended Eton and Cambridge together and served in Salamanca under Wellesley, now the Duke of Wellington, together. Both were confirmed bachelors and both were determined to enjoy their freedom.

"Now, Saint, you know Marie is a forked-tongued viper. I'll be damned if you don't. And she'd stop at nothing to snare you in parson's mousetrap."

Alaistair cast his friend an oblique look. "Marie is an entertaining companion, but not a female I would trust to be my wife and bear my heirs."

Tristan chuckled. "I doubt if bearing heirs is what Marie has in mind when she thinks of you."

"You are undoubtedly right," Alaistair said dryly.

The valet had finished his ministrations and Alaistair sat up. Instead of allowing Rast to wipe the lather from his face and neck, he did it himself, then handed the disgruntled valet the towel.

With a grin, Alaistair said, "I know how painful it is, Rast, to have me clean up after your inestimable efforts, but I just can't help myself."

"Yes, m'lord," Rast replied with ill-concealed dissatisfaction. "'Twas those years as a soldier, if you don't mind my saying so."

Alaistair's smile widened. "Quite all right. After all, you were with me the entire time. So you also know I'm perfectly capable of dressing myself now that Tristan is here to help with my coat. Why don't you go down and see if Simpson needs your help with the household accounts? I trust you implicitly with my wealth."

The manservant's scowl lightened slightly. It was no secret that Rast had his employer's absolute trust. But to leave before his lordship was dressed... Still, he went without a word.

"What a trial I am to him."

Tristan ran his fingers through his thick blond hair, cut short as befitted a Corinthian. Both he and Alaistair were relentless sportsmen and noted for their prowess, thus earning them that title, favored among the aristocracy.

"You tease him beyond bearing, Saint. Luckily for you, Rast would die for you."

"Just so."

Alaistair dressed. His clothing was well-tailored, but looser fitting than his peers deemed appropriate. In no time he was deftly tying a simple knot in his first pristine cravat.

"Wish I had your knack with those," Tristan said.

Alaistair smiled at his friend. "Don't. 'Tis a skill that does no one any good."

"Mayhap, but it certainly enhances a chap's reputation with the ladies when he has a cravat style named after him. Everyone says the 'Saint's Simplicity' is brilliant. Even Brummell wears it."

Alaistair laughed outright. "George Brummell is a singularly unusual man." He finished the knot and smoothed the edges into crisp lines. "But my cravat-tying skills can't be what has rousted you out of bed this early. Why, it's barely afternoon."

Not as imperturbable as his friend, Tristan reddened. "Heard you won a fortune last night." His clear blue eyes looked directly into Alaistair's cool gray ones. "I thought you didn't game with green boys from the country who are still wet behind the ears."

Alaistair met the censure in Tristan's eyes calmly. "There's always a first time. And the boy was so easy. It was like guiding a baby around by the leading strings."

Tristan raised one almost white brow. "You've never been interested in innocents before. Why, you won't even look at the young chits trying to attract your attention, and I'd say dallying with them would be more entertaining. You say it's too much trouble to teach them how to make love like a woman. So why play cards with a boy who doesn't know a spade from a club? You certainly don't need the winnings."

The last word was just out of his mouth when Tristan noticed the gleam in his friend's eyes as Alaistair buttoned his waistcoat. Tristan shook his head in resignation. "Got me again."

"For all your savoir faire, Tristan, you can be remarkably gullible."

"Yes, and you're always there to exploit it." But there was no anger in the words. Tristan was glad Alaistair was once more beginning to joke. The years since Salamanca had been hell on his friend.

Alaistair sauntered to the walnut commode and picked up a silver pearl tiepin, which he positioned in the snowy folds of his cravat. "How did you find out this early about my exploits last night? Marie you could surmise, since that's my usual activity, but how did you hear about Stone?"

"My valet told me. It's all over Town. It's completely out of character for you. Or, if anyone is stupid enough to listen to Bent, completely in character with the man you really are." Tristan gave his friend a searching look, which was met with a grim smile.

"A piece of advice, Tris. Never best an older man. They're notoriously ill-natured about it."

"You had provocation," Tristan said flatly.

"Perhaps." Alaistair shrugged into his coat, his eyes inscrutable. "But enough of the past. Do you have Stone's direction? I'm beginning to think I need to hunt him out. He should have been here by now, and being the young fool that he obviously is, I don't want him doing anything rash. The whole purpose of this boring activity was to teach him a much-needed lesson about gaming, not to have him do something else equally crackbrained, such as blowing his brains out or running from his obligations—which it's obvious the puppy hasn't been taught to fulfill."

Tristan rose from the bed and followed his friend from the room, their Hessian boots ringing on the polished wooden floors of the hall. "Stone has rented lodgings in Mayfair. He also has a sister." He glanced slyly at his friend.

Alaistair grinned. "I'm not in the market. As you said yourself, milksop maidens aren't in my line."

Tristan chuckled. "No, but I've heard Stone's sister is out of the ordinary. An amazon."

Alaistair glanced at him with interest. "From whom?"

"Westford. He sat next to her last week at an informal dinner held by one of his aunts. The one that hails from near Romney Marsh. Seems Stone and his sister have come for the Season."

Alaistair yawned. "Everyone comes for the Season, Tris. You'll have to do better than that."

Tristan shrugged. "Can't. Westford didn't know any more when I picked his brain at Gentleman Jackson's. And you know how devilish hard it is to concentrate on anything when Jackson is aiming his fists at you."

"Don't I just."

"Don't you," Tristan said, a tinge of sarcasm lacing the words. "You're the only man I know who can beat him in the boxing ring."

Reaching the foot of the polished oak staircase, Alaistair picked up his silver-handled cane. "It must be my clean living."

Tristan laughed outright. "Must be your phenomenal luck. Everyone says you lead a charmed life—had to, to have come through Salamanca without a scratch."

Tristan regretted the words instantly. Alaistair's face darkened and his lips tensed in what his friend recognized as his "war look." Whenever the Peninsular Wars came into a conversation, Alaistair drew inward.

In an attempt to lighten the mood, Tristan blurted, "Why don't you come to White's with me for a bite first? Let Stone stew in his juices a while longer. 'Twill teach him a lesson all the better."

"I'd like to," Alaistair said, nodding to the footman who held the front door open, "but I've a feeling that Stone is too impulsive. It's not a good sign that he hasn't come for his appointment. Most gentlemen meet their debts of honor punctiliously."

"From what you've said, Stone is a boy." Tristan positioned his curly-brimmed beaver hat on his head. "But have it your own way. I'll be at White's when you're through."

Alaistair waved away the hackney coach that stopped to give him a lift. The pale February sun felt good, and in spite of incessant coal fires that gave the air the metallic odor of soot, he would walk to the unfashionable area of Mayfair, where Stone had rented a house.

Upon reaching the address, Alaistair handed his card, one corner turned under to indicate he was calling in person, to the very decrepit and very bent butler. The man, his brown eyes framed by deep wrinkles, showed Alaistair to the drawing room without uttering a word. Perhaps Stone had reason for his impulsiveness if he was surrounded by servants who moved as though they had one foot in a sepulcher. A man would need to liven things up.

Alaistair glanced around the dark room, taking in the heavy brown velvet drapes, the massive oak furniture that looked as though it had been found in some country-house attic and the threadbare rug that might once have been a burgundy color but now almost matched the drapes. There was no doubt this was a rented house and no doubt that the current occupants hadn't spent any money to improve its condition in preparation for entertaining. He did not know anyone who would invite company to so ramshackle a place.

And yet last night Stone had handed over a personal vowel for a sum of money that would buy this house and everything in it twenty times over. Had the boy failed to show for his appointment because he couldn't pay his debts? Alaistair was beginning to think so.

DOWN THE HALL in the breakfast room, Lizabeth Emily Johnstone lifted her head and rubbed her aching eyes. Minutes before, the sound of the front door closing had given her a much-needed excuse to look away from the columns of figures that represented the fruits of her life's work—fruits that were about to become someone else's marmalade.

Who could be calling? They had only been in London two weeks and knew precious few people. Mrs. Snowdrop, the vicar's sister, had had them to dinner once, but other than that... And no one bothered to visit because no one else knew them. Mrs. Snowdrop said she would introduce them to Society, but Liza had already concluded that a vicar's sister did not have an entrée into the ton. For herself it didn't matter, but Michael wanted so badly to make a name for himself.

She sighed, her gaze traveling to the portrait on the wall. She'd brought it from Thornyhold, their estate in Romney Marsh, because she couldn't bear the thought of leaving it behind. It symbolized everything she had had to become: mother, sister, estate manager.

Painted by Sir Thomas Lawrence, it showed a small family, the mother and father smiling happily at the artist while a chubby blond baby boy cooed contentedly in his mother's arms. To the mother's right, staring stolidly forward, was a little girl of six, her red hair caught back in a braid. They were a family, and that's what Liza had striven to maintain after her parents' death. She'd tried to become the protective mother and the shrewd investor and estate-manager father in one person. Somehow, she'd failed.

A knock heralding the appearance of Timmens, her decrepit butler, ended her fruitless reminiscing. She pushed the sense of failure caused by Michael's gambling to the back of her mind and focused her attention on Timmens instead.

White hair fell over the old man's creased forehead and he moved with more of a shuffle than a walk, but he'd been with the family since her father had been a boy and had comforted her when her parents died. Nothing would make her retire him until he was ready.

"Miss Liza," he mumbled with the liberty of a servant who used to dandle her on his knee, "there's a gentleman to see Master Stone."

Even though Michael had been Baron Stone for eighteen years, Timmens still called him Master Stone. She had never had the heart to correct him.

He handed her a white card, the corner turned down. In bold writing it stated Lord Alaistair Gervase St. Simon. The name was familiar somehow, but she couldn't place it. She thought she might have heard it before coming to London, but what sort of man would have a reputation that could penetrate the wilds of Romney Marsh?

Her curiosity piqued, she asked, "Have you notified my brother?"

"No, ma'am. The master isn't in his rooms and no one knows where he went."

Liza swallowed an exasperated sigh. It was so typical of Michael to disappear after making a botch of things. Only this time, there was nowhere to run. They would be lucky if they managed to keep even a single cottage on their estate.

But she was being disloyal. Michael was only a boy. He didn't really understand the magnitude of what he'd done. It was her duty to protect him.

Timmens's cough interrupted her bleak thoughts and she focused back on him. "Did the gentleman say why he's calling?"

"Didn't ask," the butler replied, no hint of chagrin marring his features. Timmens was a law unto himself.

Liza glanced at the ledgers open on the desk. She needed to calculate just how badly Michael had positioned them, but until she received the latest figures from the solicitor on her venture into shipping, she couldn't be exact.

And besides, Lord Alaistair Gervase St. Simon was beginning to intrigue her. Little snippets of memory were returning. It had been at the vicar's dinner party several months ago, when she and Michael had first mentioned their plans to visit London, that she'd heard about the man now in her house. If she remembered correctly, and her memory was very good, he was a much-decorated war hero, as great a hero as Wellington.

It was too interesting to resist. She would just have to take Michael's place and see what Lord Alaistair wanted. Perhaps it would be a moment of enjoyment in a day that had otherwise been a sojourn in hell.

Only as she stood outside the drawing-room door did she regret her impulsive action. She hadn't returned to her room to tidy up after hearing Michael's news, and her hair floated around her face in red tangles from her morning ride. For the first time since reaching London, Liza regretted not having had her hair cut fashionably short. Nor was her clothing appropriate for entertaining guests. A black riding habit was suitable only for riding.

But it was too late now, and she really did want to meet this man. He was said to be a very magnetic personality as well as a soldier without peer. Squaring her shoulders and lifting her chin, she entered the drawing room.

And stopped dead in her tracks.

He was magnificent. The light from the window limned his head and shoulders, glinting on the silver that was shot through his ebony hair. His eyes were like dark shadows, accentuating high cheekbones, and a long, patrician nose that would rival any of Elgin's Greek marbles led to a square jaw and full, sensual mouth. Liza's mouth suddenly felt parched and she quickly ran her tongue over her lips.

He shifted, drawing her attention to the lean lines of his body, the broad shoulders and narrow waist, the well-muscled thighs. The understated elegance of his dark clothing and the loose fit of his coat fairly screamed wealth and attention to detail. Even his boots gleamed.

He was unlike any man Liza had ever seen—a fallen angel, sent to tempt unwary females and make them feel the first warm tendrils of desire. For that was what she felt, a tight ache in her abdomen that was both pleasurable and frustrating.

There was no point in denying it. She was twenty-six years old and had spent her life in the country. She'd seen animals mating and humans courting. Once she'd even stumbled upon a serving maid being fondled by one of the stable hands. Liza knew that the same heat that flushed the serving maid's cheeks now stained her own.

"Lord Alaistair St. Simon at your service," he said, a mocking invitation in the sardonic curve of his lips.

The sensual drawl imbued his words with a double entendre that sent chills down Liza's spine. But the dispassionate gaze of his gunmetal eyes saved her from making a fool of herself. The man was physically without a fault, but she could see only mocking derision in him. At himself or at her, she couldn't tell.

"Pardon me," she said calmly, the blush receding from her cheeks as she moved farther into the room until they stood within feet of each other. "I know you were expecting my brother, but he is unavailable. Perhaps I can help you."

Alaistair watched her walk toward him, her hips swaying slightly in the unfashionable black riding habit. She moved gracefully and confidently, her shoulders straight and proud. In his experience, tall women—and this one must be close to six feet—

slouched to hide their height. She was an amazon, all right, with hair the color of a roaring fire and eyes the bright, clear blue of the desert sky at sunrise.

They were startling eyes, set like turquoise marquises in the oval of her face. Burnt brown eyebrows slashed across her forehead, their straightness at odds with the delicate curve of her bones. Full, wide lips, sheened with moisture, balanced the arresting beauty of her eyes. A tight sensation of desire shot through Alaistair.

He was glad when she impatiently tucked several wisps of unfashionably long hair behind her ears. The action drew his attention to a less volatile area of her anatomy. Her fingers were long and slim, the nails buffed a soft pink. They were elegant hands. The women he knew would have worn many rings to emphasize their beauty. This woman wore none and was seemingly unaware of the ink stains on the index finger and thumb of her right hand.

His voice was husky when he turned down her offer of help. "I don't think you can. I'm here to see Baron Stone on a private matter."

Her eyes narrowed and her hands stopped their attempt to tame her wild hair. "A private matter? Would it have to do with money?"

An intelligent woman. He nodded agreement. "Yes. Not a matter to discuss with a lady."

Her eyes flashed and she took a step closer. "So you are the one."

Amusement curved his mouth. "Perhaps. But this is a matter between Stone and myself."

She jutted her chin. "You are mistaken. Michael may have gambled away the money, but I'm the one who will pay his debt."

Mild surprise lifted his raven brows. "I knew Stone was a puppy, but I never imagined he was brought to heel by a woman." He gave her a curt bow. "I'll speak with your brother."

Peach tinted her cheeks. "Michael is twenty. I'm twenty-six. 'Tis only normal that I should be in charge of things until he comes into his majority."

Alaistair took in her blazing eyes and heaving bosom, and his blood felt hot. She was a magnificent creature. What a bloody shame that his errand today would stand between them. Under different circumstances, he would be tempted to break his own rule of leaving untried chits alone.

"I don't believe anything about you is normal," he murmured. The glacial glare she raked him with only increased his interest. A very unusual woman.

She drew herself up haughtily. "In that case, you will not be at all surprised when I ask you to leave.

If you insist on speaking with Michael, I'll arrange a meeting for the three of us."

"I'm here to speak with Stone—alone," Alaistair said softly, holding his budding irritation in check. Unique she might be, but that didn't mean he was in the mood for confrontation. And he didn't think there was much time left. Where was her brother? Stone was not only impulsive but immature. There was no telling what the boy might do.

She took a deep breath. "Michael isn't here."

Alaistair's gut jumped. "Where is he?" he demanded.

She was beginning to look agitated now, her cheeks flushed deeper. He saw the shadow of worry mute the turquoise brilliance of her eyes.

"I don't know," she said, barely above a whisper. "I haven't seen him since this morning... when he told me about his losses."

Alaistair frowned, saw her flinch and realized that his own anxiety was feeding the apprehension she was starting to feel. He'd seen it in Salamanca. One man let his emotions get out of hand and the rest followed suit.

"Have any of the servants seen him?" He kept the words free of inflection, speaking to her as he would have spoken to one of his men in the heat of battle, calmly and authoritatively.

She shook her head. "He's not in his room. Probably he's gone out somewhere. He always leaves after doing something like this."

"Always?" He didn't like the sound of that. The boy hadn't been brought up to take responsibility for his actions. Such people often did the unpredictable. "Have you searched the house?"

"Of course not." Her voice sounded strained. "This is not unusual for Michael. I tell you, he's gone off somewhere to forget what he's done."

He studied her, taking in the delicate fingers that shook ever so slightly and the flicking tongue that moistened her trembling lips. Stone might disappear after each escapade, but she was frightened this time. Undoubtedly, this was the worst thing her brother had ever done, and there was every likelihood that Stone would realize it.

Just then the door opened and in a rasping voice the wizened butler said, "Miss Liza, we've found the master. In the library."

She cast an agitated glance Alaistair's way as she sped from the room. He followed her, marveling at the grace of her movement even when fear drove her. Knowing instinctively that there was only one course of action open to a boy like Stone after what he'd done to his family, Alaistair hastened after her.

He caught her just as she pushed open the door.
For an instant he considered restraining her, then
decided against it. The sight would help her grieve.
Even here, on the threshold, he could smell the
stench of death. He looked at her face and saw realization, followed quickly by denial.

"Michael," she said, her voice higher and louder
than before. "Michael," she repeated, a shrill demand as she moved toward the still figure slumped
down in one of the two chintz-covered chairs.

From his vantage point near the door, Alaistair
saw the pale, waxy hand that hung down from the
arm draped over one side of the chair. Two booted
legs stretched toward the fireplace, the feet splayed
outward from the heels. Had he shot himself?
Alaistair strode into the room, determined to be beside her when she found out.

For an instant she stood still, frozen in horror, her
face contorted in disbelief. Then she flung herself
forward.

"Michael! Oh God, no. Please." The high, tight
words streamed from her. Grasping the cold body,
she tried to pull him into her arms. "Oh God, oh
God," she moaned.

Alaistair watched, careful not to touch her. It was
too soon. She wasn't crying, but he knew that would

follow. Later. Once the realization set in that the boy was truly dead. She'd cry then. They always did.

Pain creased her forehead and her eyes were glassy with shock.

"Michael. My baby. Oh my God, Michael. Why? Why? It would have been all right."

She held the body in her arms, rocking back and forth, holding him to her breast as she would a baby. The bloody head stained the black bombazine of her bodice a dark rust. At least she wasn't afraid of death. Some people were.

Alaistair remembered one incident while fighting on the Peninsula. Two brothers were in the same battle. One of them had been hit by a French bullet. In the head. The other had been beside him during the fighting. Even though the two had been inseparable in life, the living brother hadn't been able to bring himself to touch his dead brother. This woman wasn't that way. She was clasping her brother's body to her as though by strength alone she could give him her warmth . . . her life.

"Oh, Michael," she moaned. "If only I'd thought. If only I'd told you it would be easy. I spoke too soon. I should have given you more time before telling you it would pauperize us. I should have known better. My God, my poor baby, no one even heard you. . . ."

Words tumbled over one another as she continued to rock her brother's body, smoothing the
brown hair from his forehead. Alaistair listened to
her blame herself for everything. Soon she'd be
blaming herself for the way she'd raised him. The
living always felt guilt. He knew all about that.

He watched horror and despair mar the delicate
perfection of her features, contorting them into a
mask of pain as she gazed down at the lifeless head
held to her bosom. Then the tears came, and her
entire body shook. Alaistair knelt beside her and
pried her arms from around Stone's body. Standing, he yanked her up and into his embrace.

When she tried to pull away, he tangled his fingers in her hair and held tight. "Cry it out," he
commanded, feeling the silken weight of her hair
like rope around his hand. He slid his other hand
down to the small of her back and pressed her close,
sharing his body's warmth with her.

She struggled against him, but only for a few
moments. Then she clung to him.

"Cry it out," he repeated, his hand stroking up
and down her back. "That's it. Let the grief out."

He knew it would be a while before she was able
to stop crying. It would be days before she would
think of anything but her brother sprawled in the
chair, a bullet hole in his head. And months, maybe

years, before she'd be able to remember it without breaking down.

When the sobs racking her slender frame subsided and he heard her sniffling, Alaistair released her and gave her his handkerchief. She took it and blew her nose without regard for appearances.

When she looked at him, her turquoise eyes shimmered with the residue of tears. "Why did you gamble with him?"

His face inscrutable, he stepped away from her. Now wasn't the time to tell her the reason for his call. "Because he was there and he wanted to."

Fiercely she wadded the used handkerchief in her hands. "That's all? Nothing but a diversion?" She swallowed hard. "And now he's dead. He's dead and to you he was nothing more than an evening's entertainment."

CHAPTER TWO

MARIE HARDCASTLE picked up a strand of her chestnut hair and trailed it down the long line of Alaistair's hip and thigh. She followed it with her tongue, not stopping until she saw him clench the muscles of his leg tightly. He was insatiable tonight, as though devils drove him deeper into desire, as though he were trying to forget everything else. She'd never seen him like this before, but she intended to enjoy every second of this mood.

When he'd arrived on her doorstep two hours earlier, she'd been dressed to go to the opera, having given up on his coming tonight. He didn't appear every night, and when he did it was usually after going to White's or the gathering of some London hostess. Last night it had been gambling at Brooks's. He made sure she never forgot they weren't engaged to marry.

Like a cat who has spied a mouse, Marie licked her lips in anticipation of what she would do to him. This time she would mount him. She would control their lovemaking. The thought made her body turn to liquid.

Her green eyes glowed as she moved to straddle him. In the dim light from two nearby candles, his eyes seemed black, and sweat beaded his brow. His sensual lips were pulled back from his teeth in a grimace of harsh sexuality as he positioned his hips beneath her.

"You're an animal tonight," she murmured, leaning down to bite his nipple. "You've never been this voracious."

His eyes shut, he muttered, "Be quiet, Marie."

Marie froze, a tiny frown marring the smooth perfection of her brow. He was speaking to her as he would to a whore, with words of contempt.

She realized he was upset over something; that was why he'd come to her so early. Even so, his words were an insult. He was using her, and while she didn't mind using him, she didn't want the same done to her. She had plans for Alaistair St. Simon, plans to marry this man the ton called Saint. And she knew him well enough to realize that he wouldn't marry a woman he didn't respect.

Marie moved with the intent of getting off him, but his hands gripped her hips and pulled her down hard. He slid into her warmth and began to thrust inside her. He felt delicious. He always did. All thought of denying him—of denying herself—fled.

Later, she watched him dress while she reclined on the green satin sheets she'd bought to complement her eyes. All her lovers admired her eyes, at least before the Saint, that is. She'd been faithful to Lord Alaistair—or almost. It was a deprivation, of course, but one she tolerated because of his skill in bed and his wealth. A slow smile curved her lush mouth as she admired his firm buttocks and broad shoulders while he pulled on his shirt.

"Did something amuse you?" he asked, his deep voice a drawl.

"No," she purred. "It pleases me." She reached for the candelabra on the nearby table and rose. Padding silently on the thick bronze carpet, she swayed toward him. Her hips undulated, and she watched his eyes take in her full-blown femininity. "Do I please you, Saint?" she asked, knowing that she did.

She didn't stop until her breasts grazed his lawn shirt. Reaching down, she cupped him, enjoying the feel of his fullness in her hands.

A look of boredom crossed his features and his mouth took on the hard line she knew too well. She'd seen it directed at others too often not to recognize it. It meant he'd had enough of her and was ready to be on his way.

"Not now, Marie," he said, exhaustion scoring lines around his eyes.

She held on to her temper. He was in a dangerous mood and she didn't want to risk losing him. Not after all the work she'd done to keep him this long. He might be the second son of the Duke of Rundell, but he was rich in his own right and a war hero to boot. Once they were wed, she'd convince him to accept the peerage he'd turned down. After all, she didn't want to be simply Lady Alaistair. But for now she must bide her time.

Letting him go, Marie backed away and donned a green silk robe. "Will you be at Lady Cowper's ball this Friday?"

He gazed at her with a total lack of interest, and a feeling of unease began to snake through Marie.

"Probably not. Perhaps Wright will escort you." He finished buttoning his shirt and pulled on his breeches.

"Wright?" she asked with a nervous laugh. "You know he only dallies with women he beds."

Alaistair sat down on a nearby chair with lacquered legs, a fashion all the rage. "Then share your bed. He'll treat you well."

Her eyes narrowed into slits. "What exactly are you saying, Saint?"

He looked dispassionately at her. "Thank you for the lovely night, Marie, but I think it's time we parted ways."

The cold glitter of his eyes did nothing to cool the hot anger flowing through her veins. "You can't do this!" She lunged at him and grabbed his arm with both hands, falling to her knees before him. "You can't just come in here and *use* me all night and then tell me it's over."

He glanced down at her fingers digging into the muscle of his forearm. When his eyes shifted to hers, they were bleak and devoid of warmth. She felt a sudden panic but she held on to him. She had too much to lose if she let him go.

She forced the hysteria and anger from her voice. "You can't mean that, Saint. We've been together a long time."

One by one, he pried her fingers from his arm, then moved out of her reach. "Too long."

The sheer boredom in his tone, the utter ennui, confirmed the finality of his decision. She had nothing left to lose, so she let her fury rage.

"You bastard," she spat. "You came here to use me, knowing all the time that when you were done you were going to leave me." Her long red nails snaked out to gouge him, but he neatly sidestepped the attack. "Well," she said spitefully, "it doesn't matter. It doesn't mean a thing to me. I was never faithful to you anyway. Wright has been my lover for months. Do you *hear* me?"

"The whole household hears you, Marie. And Wright's been your lover for more than a year. It's only been the last several months that he's been paying some of your debts."

She blanched. All this time he had known. She watched as he pulled on his boots, her mind working frantically. He'd stayed with her a year even though he knew Wright was also enjoying her favors. That wasn't like Saint. He had a reputation for being faithful to his mistresses and for not sharing their company. Still, he'd shared hers. Perhaps he had feared to lose her if he hadn't. Perhaps all wasn't lost.

Her tongue flicked over her red lips as she sauntered toward him, allowing the neck of her gown to gape open. She knew her breasts were fully visible in the golden light from the candles.

When he had finished with his boots he glanced at her coolly. "I'll have my secretary pick out a suitable bauble and get it to you today." Picking up his coat, he shrugged it on. "I'll tell him money is no object."

Marie stopped in midsway. "Bastard."

The word didn't faze him. Picking up his silver-tipped cane, he bowed curtly. "Adieu, Marie."

Heart pounding, breath coming fast and furious, Marie grabbed the first thing available. The candelabra hit the closing door with a resounding thud.

Alaistair shook his head at the sound as he headed down the stairs. Marie's temper was her worst trait. He remembered when she'd thrown a kitten against the wall because it had had the temerity to climb up her gown and pull several threads. That had been a year ago, about the time he'd decided she was suitable as a mistress but never as a wife.

It was also the time he'd decided he didn't care if she took another man to her bed; he was using her, and he wouldn't begrudge her the opportunity to find someone else. As the widow of an earl's younger son, she was marriage material for someone who wasn't too particular about the woman to whom he allied himself for life.

As he stepped out the front door, Alaistair drew in several deep breaths of the cool dawn air. It smelled of the pasties being hawked by a man on the nearest corner. His stomach growled, and for the first time in the last twenty-four hours he felt hungry. Taking several coins from his pocket, he bought two of the thick, rich meat pies. As he bit into one, brown juice trickled down his chin and he licked it away, savoring the flavor.

He ate quickly and strode on. A cool breeze caressed his cheek and lifted the hair from his brow. To the east, the sky was tinted pink and amber. It felt good to be alive.

Alive.

The thought was like a punch in the gut. God, why hadn't he just given Stone the vowel before the young fool left Brooks's? Why had he decided to teach the puppy a lesson?

Not since Salamanca had he felt such despair, such guilt. There he had watched men die all around him while he lived, the French bullets miraculously missing him. He'd had two horses shot out from under him and been decorated with every medal the British Crown boasted. He was one of Britain's most celebrated war heroes. None of it mattered in the face of the carnage he'd been part of.

But the guilt he carried from Salamanca was nothing compared to what he felt now. War was an atrocity he couldn't prevent. He could have prevented this. He should never have let Stone leave Brooks's thinking his debt would be called. He'd tried to teach the boy a lesson. Instead, he'd caused the boy to kill himself.

His jaw hardened. He would make retribution as best as he was able; he'd make sure the sister took back the vowel. But yesterday hadn't been the time. Lizabeth Johnstone had been too distraught. She needed time to grieve, time to come to terms with her brother's suicide.

Soon he would call on her and relieve her of the debt. And never again would he try to be his brother's keeper.

LIZABETH EMILY JOHNSTONE, the last of her line, had inherited the title Lady Stone by special writ. She rubbed her aching temples. All she wanted was to go to sleep and forget the past months; first the funeral, then the meetings with the solicitor telling her what she already knew—that paying the vowel to Alaistair St. Simon would require selling the estate and all the investments.

It had hurt her to realize that the inheritance she'd worked so hard to maintain for her brother's coming of age was to be sold for something as fruitless as gaming debts, but it had to be done. She had ordered the solicitor to begin the transactions. She didn't want the money. To her tortured mind, it was blood money.

God, she wanted to go to sleep and wake up to find all this was a nightmare. A strangled laugh escaped her trembling lips. So much had happened.

So much. She would go crazy. Even Bedlam—the insane asylum—would be preferable to this.

She gazed up at the portrait above the fireplace, the one she would have to sell. Her mother and her six-year-old self looked reproachfully down at her. Liza turned away, but the memory came.

When she was eight, both her parents had died in a yachting accident in the North Sea. No one had survived. She and her two-year-old brother were at home with the nanny and governess.

Liza remembered it as though it were yesterday. She and Michael were playing in the enclosed garden when the governess told them what had happened. Michael was too young to comprehend, and Liza hadn't fully understood herself.

For days she spoke to no one, until finally Timmens, their faithful butler, had told her to cry out her pain. That night, when the household was asleep, she'd sneaked down to the drawing room, where the family portrait hung. Staring up at it, memorizing every line and curve of her mother's face, Liza had vowed to care for her tiny brother. She would commit her life to Michael as her mother would have wanted. And she'd kept that vow.

Until now.

No mother would have let her son shoot himself over something as trivial as a gaming debt. A true mother would have realized the depth of his despair. She hadn't, but she should have.

Instead of staying with him and reassuring him, she'd told him to go to bed. She should have encouraged him to talk about what had happened. She should have acted as though his gambling away a fortune were nothing, as though it didn't matter... because it didn't when compared to his life.

But she hadn't. And now he was gone.

Liza lowered her head onto her forearms atop the oak desk. She'd been sitting there, staring at nothing, since the night before. Suddenly she began to shake in spite of the roaring fire in the grate, the bright sunshine spilling down her back and the paisley shawl pulled tightly around her shoulders.

A wisp of hair, come loose from her chignon, waved across her eyes. She caught it and began twirling it in her fingers. It was a soothing, calming reflex that she'd had since that fateful day eighteen years before. But today it didn't ease her tension because it couldn't numb her pain.

With a sigh, she rose and crossed to the crackling fire, sinking into the closest chair. She had to put her own pain aside for a while. There was so much still to do. She had yet to notify their nearest relatives, unless they had already seen the news in one of the London papers.

There were the servants to consider, as well. She had very little money, but she would provide for them. Somehow she would manage to find the funds to pension off the older ones, even if it meant selling every piece of jewelry she owned and every picture gracing the walls of Thornyhold. She twirled the piece of hair faster.

It was almost too much, losing Michael and now losing everything else she cared for. For years she had managed the estate and invested the profits. It was a job she had taken on the day she found the estate manager embezzling their funds. She'd fired him on the spot and had learned all she could about Thornyhold. That knowledge had paid off, and there would have been a sizable fortune for Michael when he came of age. It was gone now, just as he was.

Grief washed over her, threatening to paralyze her, but she straightened her back resolutely. There were still the younger servants to consider. She would provide them with recommendations.

And lastly, she would find herself a position as a governess. It was the only thing she was qualified for and was better than being a poor relation. At least a governess earned her keep and a salary and kept her self-respect. A poor relation earned her keep and not much more.

In spite of her determination to put these past months from her mind, her thoughts led back to the reason for all her plans...Michael's untimely death. When would she be able to think of it without having to fight off tears?

Her stomach knotted, and it was all she could do to stand and walk back to her desk. From its polished surface, she picked up a heavy sheet of vellum.

The cream-colored stationery was thick and rich, covered by a maze of black lettering. She stared at the writing—Michael's sense of failure and remorse scrawled for the whole world to see. For her to see. Her fingers trembled at the remembered agony of finding him. Nausea threatened to overwhelm her.

And even at his death she had betrayed him. How in God's name could she have sought comfort from Alaistair St. Simon? She shouldn't have been able to even look at the man, let alone crumple in his arms and cling to him as though he were the only one sure mooring in a sea of wild emotions.

Lord Alaistair St. Simon—Saint, as Michael had named him in the note still dangling from her numb fingers.

Liza dragged air into her lungs, fighting for control. She wouldn't cry. Not again. Crying did no good. It hadn't brought her parents back. It wouldn't bring Michael back.

A knock on the door startled her, making her jump and drop the note.

"Miss Liza," Timmens said, entering and closing the door behind him, "Lord Alaistair St. Simon is asking to see you."

Liza clenched her hands at her sides, the nails digging into her palms. "Tell Lord Alaistair I'm not at home." She bent and picked up her brother's suicide note.

"Best see him, Miss Liza," Timmens said, his rheumy eyes meeting hers without flinching.

"Don't push me, Timmens. I won't see him. Tell him I'm in mourning."

Timmens tsked. "As you wish." With little more than a bow of his head he left.

Liza twisted around to stare at the flames dancing in the grate. London was warm with June's summer sun, but chills racked her body. She felt as though she might never be warm again. Hunching forward, she extended her hands to the fire, rubbing them together.

A commotion sounded on the other side of the heavy oak door. Liza spun around just in time to see Lord Alaistair St. Simon push Timmens out of the way and enter the room in spite of the butler's at-

tempts to block his path. Alaistair St. Simon. Saint.
An angel of death. Michael's murderer. The man
stood in the middle of the room, his feet planted
widely apart.

Seeing that to do otherwise would be futile, Liza
said, "It's all right, Timmens. Since Lord Alaistair
has barged in, he may stay—for the moment. I'll
ring when he's ready to depart."

Timmens bowed, then cast an "I told you so"
look at Liza and an aggrieved look at the intruder
before closing the door behind him.

Liza, hands pressed tightly together behind her
back to keep them from shaking, studied the inter-
loper. He held himself with assurance, but his full,
well-shaped lips were set in a grim line. In the mi-
asma of her misery, she'd forgotten how handsome
he was, how potently masculine. In spite of herself,
her pulse quickened.

Fleetingly she remembered the warmth of his
arms around her, and the chills that had consumed
her like the ague ceased. It didn't make her any
fonder of her guest that his presence could ease the
pain of Michael's death, however slightly.

"To what do I owe the dubious pleasure of this
visit?"

Heedless of the disdainful look she cast him, he
studied her as a hawk might study its prey. When at

last he spoke, his voice was low. "I wish to express my condolences for your loss and to give you this. I never intended to keep it and my solicitor informed me that yours has already attempted to redeem it."

Her attention flicked to the sheet of paper he held then back up to his solemn face. It was the vowel. It had to be. He was giving it to her because of guilt, because Michael had killed himself over it.

"It's covered with Michael's blood," she whispered, the color draining from her face. "I've no use for it. Now, please go." Her voice was harsh as she fought the grief that squeezed the breath from her lungs. "You've already brought enough misery."

His eyes clouded and his lips thinned. "You've no reason to like me, and I don't ask it of you. For what it's worth, I'm sorry. I never intended that he should act so drastically."

Fury blazed through Liza, burning away all previous feelings about this arrogant man. He'd ruined her world and then excused his own part in it. "Michael was only twenty. Twenty, do you hear? He had his whole life ahead of him and you took it from him. You snuffed it out like a candle." Her voice rose in pitch. "Oh, you didn't pull the trigger. You didn't have to."

He remained mute, his eyes watching her warily, as though he thought she might launch herself at him. His impassivity infuriated her all the more.

"You think that because you're the son of a powerful duke you can do as you please. That you can ruin another person's life on a whim. Well, you can't. I'll see that you pay."

Her hands shook and her chin trembled, but she stood her ground. She wouldn't break down. She wouldn't disgrace herself again in front of this man who stood before her as cold and motionless as a Greek statue.

He took a deep breath and for an instant Liza thought she saw regret blur his perfect features. Then it was gone and she knew she was mistaken.

"Naturally you're overwrought, and you've every right to condemn me." Again he held out the paper to her. "But take this. I don't want your money."

"It's a sop to ease your conscience. Well, I won't let you take the easy way out. I won't dishonor Michael by doing so. And I don't want your charity."

He sighed, his fingers tightening on the sheet. "It's not charity. I'm merely giving you back what is already yours."

"Mine?" Hysteria bubbled up in her. "Take Michael's vowel? Take the sheet of paper he ended his life over?" She laughed, the sound echoing eerily in the room. "It's a little late to return it, wouldn't you say?"

He flinched, then his features smoothed out and he stretched his hand closer to her.

Liza backed away until the heat of the fire beat at her back like a vengeful sprite. "I don't want it. It's worthless now. Michael died because of that. I won't besmirch his name further by reneging on his gaming debts. He wouldn't thank me for it. I'd never forgive myself if I did so."

"I have no need of your inheritance." His voice was low and calm.

She stiffened her back to keep from succumbing to his will. "Keep it. Michael's honor is more important than money."

He frowned, his black brows angling down. "If you pay this, you'll be penniless."

"If I don't, I'm faithless." Her gaze didn't waver from his, and she detected a look in his eyes that hadn't been there before. She could almost mistake it for an understanding of her plight, but she knew better. It was only the memory of the comfort he had offered at Michael's death and the unwelcome feelings it had evoked that now muddled her thinking. Nothing more.

Twisting away from him, she seized a sheaf of newspapers. "See these," she demanded, spinning around and waving them in his face. "Each one carries the story of how Michael gambled and lost to you. Each one says he was too weak to face the ruin he'd brought on his family. And each one tells how you've never gambled with a young boy fresh from the country." The words rushed from her trembling lips, a bitter purge that left her feeling no better.

In one swift motion she threw the papers into the fire, wanting to destroy the scandalous gossip that tore her brother to shreds with each vile word. They burst into flames, sparks flying. She stepped back, head bowed as she fought for calm.

Finally, the white-hot fury in check, Liza lifted her head in disdain, her eyes bright turquoise chips. "If I took that vowel, I'd desecrate my brother's death. I'd take away his honor—what little the scandalmongers have left him—and I won't do that. I won't sully his memory that way." She shook her head vehemently. "No, I want none of it. I'd rather ply my wares in Covent Garden than take it from you."

Lord Alaistair's jaw hardened. Liza could have sworn she heard his teeth gnash. But he said nothing, and just put the paper back into the pocket of his jacket.

With a curt bow to her, he let himself out of the room. Before the door closed, she said loudly and clearly, her voice vibrating with the intensity of her emotions, "I hate you, Alaistair St. Simon. I'll destroy you as you destroyed Michael."

She sank onto the floor, the dingy carpet spreading around her like mud. With tear-filled eyes, she stared up at the portrait of her family, everyone dead but her. "I failed, Mother," she whispered hoarsely. "I promised you I would care for Michael and I've failed. Please forgive me, for I can't forgive myself."

CHAPTER THREE

"COME IN," Alaistair called without glancing up from the account books he was studying.

Light streamed in from the tall French windows behind his desk and fell on the carefully organized papers. Although he was a younger son, he'd inherited several very profitable estates and a considerable amount of money from his maternal grandmother, who had been an heiress. Managing them consumed a large portion of his time.

"'Arternoon, guv'nor."

A thin weasellike man with a long face stood in the doorway, his felt hat held deferentially at his side. He had large blue eyes, a beak of a nose and his chin was pointed.

Alaistair smiled. "Winkly, it's a pleasure to see you."

"Same."

A rare smile revealed two missing front teeth in the man's mouth. Alaistair remembered how Winkly had lost them in a fight over a pretty Spanish seno-

rita. But that was years ago. Winkly was a Bow
Street Runner now, and a good one.

"Have you managed to find her?" Alaistair
asked, rising and going to a side table. Without
asking, he poured Winkly a tumbler of good Scotch
whiskey.

"Thanks, guv. You always remembers me likes,
you does." He took a long swig, downing half the
liquor. "I found 'er right and tight. But it don' bode
well. No, it don'."

Alaistair poured himself a finger's width of the
fiery Scotch. It wasn't a gentleman's drink, but he'd
grown to like it in the years since Winkly had first
introduced him to it. He sipped his to enjoy the
strong flavor. "Where?"

"She be in the Earl of Bent's household." Winkly
shook his head before finishing the drink. "Even the
likes o' me knows that gent's reputation don' bear
lookin' into." He looked at his employer out of the
corner of his eye.

A low whistle escaped Alaistair's compressed lips.
"Damn. Bent, of all people." His knuckles whitened around the glass. "And to think I worried
when she worked for Ravencroft. Ravencroft's a
veritable monk compared to Bent."

"Right-o," Winkly seconded, before finishing his Scotch and wiping his mouth on the back of his hand.

Alaistair slammed his glass down so that the table swayed precariously and the whiskey sloshed out. He knew too well what the man was capable of. "I can't let her stay there."

"Reckon not, sir," Winkly agreed, his head swiveling around to watch Lord Alaistair exit the room. "Bent'll 'ave 'er before she knows what got 'er."

LIZA FOLDED the linen for her young charge. She'd been in the Earl of Bent's employ for one week and already knew her duties were not limited to teaching the earl's motherless son conversational French. She was also the boy's nanny and housemaid.

But she didn't mind. Her heart went out to the little boy, who was only ten. In many ways he reminded her of Michael at that age: adventurous, yet wanting the security of a mother to run to.

Liza smiled wistfully, simultaneously dashing her sleeve across her eyes. *Michael*. The memories of him still hurt, bringing pleasure mixed with pain.

She took a deep breath and finished folding the sheets, pushing the disturbing recollections aside. There were other drawbacks to being a governess besides caring for a little boy who evoked bitter-sweet memories. She'd think about them instead.

One employer had already let her go because she refused his son's advances. And here she was noth-ing but a drudge. She'd have been no worse off if she had become a companion to some moldering old dowager.

Arms laden with sheets and clean towels, she left the laundry and made for the back stairs. Adjust-ing her burden so that one hand was free to hold up the skirts of her black bombazine mourning dress, she started up. This and one other mourning gown were the only luxuries she had allowed herself after the sale of the estate and payment of Michael's debt.

She was halfway to the third floor, where the nursery was, when a sound caught her attention. She stopped in her tracks. A few steps above her stood the Earl of Bent, legs apart, hands on hips.

His blue eyes were red-rimmed from too much drink and too little sleep, and his full mouth was pursed. The scandalously tight yellow pantaloons he wore could scarcely contain his very generous paunch. Some of the older servants said he hadn't always been this way, that a woman was responsi-ble. And Liza thought she could make out a glim-mer of handsomeness in his square jaw and the cut of his cheek, but it was now submerged beneath the damage caused by too much licentious living.

Well, disappointment in love might be the cause of his decline, Liza thought, eyeing her employer with as much sangfroid as she was capable of, but it was still no excuse for wallowing in depravity. She'd heard—and even seen—the women he had here every night he was home.

And now her. She might be twenty-six, on the shelf and never kissed, but she knew what Bent wanted. Oh yes, she knew what Bent intended. She could see it in the glitter of his eyes as he looked down at her, and it sent a chill along her spine.

She had to escape before he did something irreversible. Glancing behind her, she saw empty stairs. It was her only chance.

Slowly, keeping her eyes on him as one would a dangerous animal, Liza began her backward descent. A sob of frustration escaped her when Bent followed, step by step.

This was nothing like Ravencroft's heir trying to put his hand up her skirt. That incident had involved a young man no older than Michael had been, and she'd simply slapped his hand away and then packed her bag when told to leave shortly afterward. This was different. Bent was stalking her and would stop at nothing less than her ruin.

What a fool she'd been. No wonder the woman at the employment agency had smirked as she handed over the letter of introduction to this household. No wonder the wages were so generous. She should have investigated first. But it had seemed the only alternative after Lord Ravencroft let her go with no reference.

She had to stop Bent.

"My lord," she said, her voice a croak, "how... how interesting to meet you this way. Why, I was just on my way to the nursery. Johnny will be expecting me. I daren't disappoint him."

Bent's full lips stretched wide, dwarfing and dominating his double chin. "Little Johnny can wait a while longer, m'dear. I've been meaning to, shall we say, converse with you." His grin widened obscenely.

The linens fell from her arm as she clutched the smooth mahogany banister. Her damp hand slipped and she lost her balance, flailing wildly. Only the narrowness of the servants' stairs saved her from a nasty fall.

A shrill, desperate laugh escaped her as she steadied herself. "I—I don't believe we have anything to—to discuss, my lord."

Bent's tongue snaked out and licked his lips until they shone. "Oh, but we do. Unless you want to be out on the streets by evening."

Liza's breath caught. There it was, bold as brass. Bed him or leave. Disgust lent her bravado. "I would rather starve than participate in the activity you have in mind." She intentionally left off the honorific "my lord." Such a contemptible person didn't deserve a title.

His mouth twisted and his double chin jutted out. "We shall see about that, m'dear." And he darted forward like the reptile his actions emulated.

A sharp scream escaped Liza as Bent's hand grabbed for her wrist. She had no recourse. Putting all her strength behind it, she swung her other arm at him. Her fist caught him squarely in the lips, making a squishy sound. She turned and raced down the stairs two at a time.

Panting, she reached the back hall and spun around, making for the foyer. Her feet slipped on the polished marble and she slammed into a gentleman the butler was in the process of ushering inside. The man wobbled slightly but held firm under her onslaught.

Strong arms encircled her shoulders and held her to a hard chest. The slow beat of the man's heart was oddly reassuring. It returned a measure of calm to her. Intending to thank the gentleman for his concern, she pushed herself slightly away from him and looked up.

Clear gray eyes, with silver striations radiating out to a black rim, caught and held her attention. Alaistair St. Simon. She'd gone from bad to worse.

This was the second time his arms had surrounded her and made her feel warm and comforted. This had to stop. Twisting around, she tried to escape from the allure of his closeness, to flee from her reaction to him.

A large, warm hand closed over her wrist like a manacle. She was pulled up short.

But what horrified her more than the restraint was her body's reaction to his touch. Heat, insidious as smoke, drifted up her arm and a corresponding heat unfurled inside her.

"Not so fast," his hated voice said.

Liza shivered as the rich baritone combined with the smoldering touch of his fingers to send frissons across her skin. She loathed this man, yet her flesh responded to him against her will.

"Let me go," she demanded, completely forgetting Bent, who was now stepping onto the last stair.

"Tut, tut," Bent drawled, his oily voice sliding like a knife between Liza and Lord Alaistair. "It would seem that the very plain Miss Stone has a savior." He leered at her. "Such a pity that she's damaged goods."

Liza's mouth dropped open as she stared in horror at the beastly man. "That's a lie and you know it."

"Do I?" Bent asked, his voice innocent but his bulging eyes hard and appraising. His gaze shifted to the man standing beside her. "And Alaistair St. Simon, no less. Quite a catch, m'dear."

"That's enough from you, Bent," Alaistair said, "or I shall be forced to clean up a mess that should never have been allowed to proliferate."

Bent yawned. "I believe I've heard those very words from you before, Lord Alaistair. Or something tiresomely close."

Alaistair's smile was deadly. "Perhaps something permanent can be arranged this time, Bent."

Liza didn't understand, but she sensed the tension throbbing between the two men. She watched as Lord Alaistair's eyes turned icy and his mouth curled in contempt. The two had a past, of that she was certain.

"Are you calling me out?" Bent bluffed, his face reddening.

"Someone must endeavor to rid the world of vermin."

Liza couldn't believe her ears. St. Simon, the man she'd vowed to hate, was offering to fight a duel over her.

Bent's face went from red to purple. His smile was sinister as he shifted his attention to Liza's still figure. "I don't believe I shall give myself the pleasure of putting a bullet through you, Lord Alaistair. No, I have better ways of dealing with you. Ways that not even the feted son of the Duke of Rundell will be able to deflect."

Without another word, Bent turned on his heel, but his raucous laughter rang in Liza's ears. All she wanted was to escape this house.

Before she could act on that decision, Lord Alaistair yanked her through the nearest doorway and into a small room that held two ladder-back chairs. It was the waiting room for tradesmen who futilely came to call on the Earl of Bent for monies owed them. It was where the Earl of Bent's housekeeper had interviewed her for the position of governess.

"Whatever possessed you to work for that worm?" he demanded angrily, his eyes smoldering.

Liza blinked in surprise at the fury he made no attempt to blunt. It raised her hackles and reminded her of how much she was supposed to despise this man. "I didn't know what he was like. And besides, it's none of your business."

She turned her back to him, hoping that her rudeness would make him take his leave. Instead, she found herself being spun around, his large hand on her upper arm. His touch burned into her nerves.

"Everything about you is my business," he replied grimly. "You're my responsibility now."

The man was crazy. "I most certainly am not your responsibility! Now let me go."

He shook his head, the heavy waves of blue-black hair falling roguishly over his high brow. "Someone must take responsibility for you. It's patently obvious you have no idea of how to go on. Even a chit fresh from the schoolroom would know better than to take employ in Bent's household. He's the most hardened, depraved rakehell in England." His fingers tightened on her arm. "And where do I find you?"

Liza turned her head, unable to continue defying the intense scrutiny of his eyes. "If it's any comfort, I intend to leave as soon as you release me and I can pack my belongings."

His fingers loosened and she was able to free her arm. Not giving him a chance to say more, not wanting to stay any longer in such dangerous proximity to him, she skirted around his muscular body and bolted like a fox from a hound.

Fifteen minutes later, portmanteau in hand, she descended the stairs, determined to go out the front door like the lady she was instead of out the back door in disgrace. Lord Alaistair stood waiting, his broad shoulders propped against the foyer wall, his well-shod ankles negligently crossed. Power emanated from him as he plucked the portmanteau from her fingers.

"Persistent, aren't you?" Liza said, ignoring the flutter in her stomach.

But his closeness made her feel safer. In spite of her bold words earlier, she'd feared that Bent would do something to prevent her leaving. Now he would be forced to let her go without argument. She owed Lord Alaistair that. Never having been one to refuse to give credit where due, she added, "My thanks for staying."

He nodded curtly. "At least you have *some* sense."

Not deigning to answer, Lizabeth preceded him out the front door held open by the impassive butler. Neither of them spoke as Lord Alaistair accompanied her to the corner of Grosvenor and Charles Streets.

Planting her feet firmly, Liza turned to her escort. "I've no need of your further companionship. I thank you for getting me out of Bent's clutches but I wish to go on alone."

Instead of answering immediately, he studied her, taking in the determined line of her jaw. "What do you intend to do next?"

She drew herself up, the strange flutter in her stomach intensifying. At one point she'd wanted revenge on this man, but now she only wanted to get away. She had many things to consider, not least of which was her body's traitorous reaction to him.

"I have thanked you as best I can for your protection. As for my plans for the future, they are of no concern to you. The minute you won my brother's fortune at Faro you ensured that our paths would cross only for revenge."

His eyes darkened to the color of thunder clouds, and his voice was low and hard. "You don't mince words. Then neither will I. The vowel is still yours. Just say the word."

Liza's face flushed and her shoulders stiffened. "How dare you continue to insult my brother's memory? How dare you insult *me* by assuming that I'd take back something Michael lost in gaming? I may be a woman, but I know something of honor, and I will not take Michael's from him."

Lord Alaistair's shoulders stiffened. It gave her a fleeting sense of satisfaction, but one that was short-lived. No matter what she said about revenge, she knew it was a luxury she couldn't afford. Somehow she had to find work, and she had to get away from this man's disturbing influence.

Seizing her portmanteau, she pivoted on her heel and hurried away. Better to work for another Bent than accept Michael's vowel from Lord Alaistair.

St. Simon watched her stalk off, an appreciative smile taking the edge off his temper. For a long Meg, she moved with a flowing grace that would be the envy of any ballerina. Were her legs equally grace-ful and attractive? It was a tantalizing consider-ation, but one he had no intention of pursuing.

"I say, m'lord," Winkly muttered, appearing suddenly at Alaistair's side, "she do be a looker—if a fella can get past the carrot top and ain't too par-tic'lar about who stoops to do the kissin'."

Alaistair's smile widened. Winkly didn't quite reach his shoulder while Liza came up to his chin. "I suppose at your height, that would be a consider-ation."

"Right-o." Winkly chuckled.

Liza disappeared around a corner, and Alais-tair's ease of mind evaporated with her. "She's left Bent's, but he's a nasty character and there's bad blood between him and me. He thinks I'm interested in her and will make trouble for her to get at me. Keep close to her. I want to know her next employer as soon as she does."

Winkly nodded before disappearing into the growing number of people in the streets. Alaistair settled his beaver hat firmly on his head and strolled off toward St. James's Street and his club. Fleetingly, he thought of beckoning for his coachman to pull up, but even with the afternoon fog rolling in off the Thames, he preferred walking to being cooped up in a coach.

WHEN SHE WAS SURE Lord Alaistair was far enough away, Liza took a deep breath of relief and looked around her for the first time. Either by chance or by unconscious thought on her part, she was on the same street as the employment agency.

Well, she would make a call on the woman who had sent her to Bent. Perhaps she hadn't known about Bent's reputation, and besides, Liza needed another position. This time she'd agree to be someone's companion.

She didn't have long to wait before seeing the same woman again. Taking a seat on the straightbacked oak chair indicated, she said, "I've just left the Earl of Bent's employ and wish to find another position." The other woman's eyes held a knowing gleam that told Liza she certainly knew the reason she'd left. With great difficulty, Liza managed to swallow back the anger beginning to percolate in her stomach. "This time, I'd like to be a companion to a dowager, if possible."

"I wish I could offer you employment, Miss Stone," the woman replied, using the false name Liza had given. "But now that you've worked for the Earl of Bent, no decent household will have you."

Liza glared at the poker-faced woman, whose devastating statement had been made in supercilious tones. "You're to blame, madam. Had you told me the reason no one would accept the position of governess with Bent, I would not have done so, either. Instead, you let me take it so you could get your commission."

The woman's long nose quivered. "You forget yourself, miss." She took a calming breath, her bony chest rising and falling. "But it does not matter. There is nothing for you here, or at any other agency. I dare say your sojourn with the Earl of Bent will be all over Town by now."

Liza clamped down hard on the urge to reach across the wide oak desk and throttle the woman. Instead, she settled her straw bonnet on her head and picked up her portmanteau.

"In that case, good riddance," she stated plainly, before sailing out of the stuffy little room.

Outside the sun shone fitfully through the gathering gloom, while around her, merchants hawked their wares. A milkmaid passed by on her way to deliver her produce, and a flower girl called out to passersby by urging them to purchase nosegays of pansies, the last of the season. In all, it was a scene of bustling activity and on another occasion would have interested Liza. Today it only emphasized her plight.

Setting the increasingly heavier portmanteau on the sidewalk beside her, Liza considered her choices. Unconsciously, she separated a wisp of hair and began to twirl it around her finger.

She could perhaps try the other agencies, although she thought that would prove fruitless. After spending only one week under the Earl of Bent's roof, she was sure his reputation was black enough to be known throughout fashionable London—and probably unfashionable London, as well. It would be impossible for her to find respectable work as a governess or companion.

She couldn't sew a straight line, so working for a modiste was out, and she was too tall and ungainly to go on the stage. Besides, she'd always been the worst at charades, not to mention the well-known fact that most actresses were men's mistresses. She might threaten to follow that trade in order to get back at Lord Alaistair, but she truly didn't think she could actually bring herself to pursue it.

She could go to the vicar's sister, who had been their one acquaintance in Town, and ask for a loan, though the very idea caused a sour taste in her mouth. She'd only contacted the woman in the first place because the vicar had asked her to visit his married sister, and when she had then invited Michael and Liza to dinner, they couldn't politely refuse. No, better that she go door-to-door on the London streets than admit to anyone the situation Michael's gambling had left her in.

Perhaps she should write to Sarah. Dear Sarah, her closest childhood friend, now expecting her first child, would surely send her the funds to get back to Romney Marsh.

But what would she do then? She couldn't live with Sarah for the rest of her life. Her pride wouldn't allow her to.

No, she had to find employment. It was the only thing her pride would permit.

Liza stopped twirling her hair and dashed away the moisture blurring her vision. She took several deep breaths and looked around. Across the street was Hatchard's book shop, its clientele coming and

going in a steady trickle. She enjoyed books and she
knew all about them. Perhaps she could get a job at
Hatchard's. She'd been there only once since coming to London and it had been like coming home.
With a jaunty step, she started toward No. 187 Pic-
cadilly.

Two frustrating and disappointing hours later she
emerged. Disappointment dragged her step. Hatchard's wasn't hiring anyone—most particularly not
impecunious females.

At four in the afternoon the shops were full of
people. Liza was jostled numerous times as she
stood lost in contemplation. Beside her was the now
ponderous portmanteau. Any more rejection and
she feared the luggage would become impossible for
her to tow. However, her search for a position was
finished for today.

Stepping back into a doorway, Liza opened her
reticule and counted her funds. Four pounds, two
shillings, and two pence. If she were careful it would
keep her for days. Her accommodations couldn't be
luxurious, but she could afford a roof over her head
until she found work.

Squaring her shoulders, she put the money back
in her reticule and pulled the strings tight. Just then,
a house of a man rammed into her, slamming her
back against the closed door.

Indignation overrode the pain of her shoulder being jammed hard against the wood and brick. "How dare you?" she exclaimed, pushing her hat out of her eyes.

Before she could do more, she felt a sharp tug on the arm that held her reticule strings. There was a loud snap and burning pain circled her wrist.

"What . . . ?"

She glanced down. Simultaneously, a hand shoved her back against the door. She stumbled and fell to her knees. Struggling to stand, she heard a grunt and then nothing more.

Liza cradled her aching wrist against her waist and stared dazedly about her. The huge man who'd plowed into her was gone, taking her reticule. She was destitute.

"Bloody bas—that is, are ye a'right, milady?"

She focused in the direction of the voice. A thin man with blue eyes and a beak of a nose watched her anxiously.

Still in a daze, Liza hastened to reassure the stranger. "Yes, yes, I'm fine. Just . . ." She gulped as the full realization of her predicament struck her. She had nothing but the clothes on her back and the meager possessions in her portmanteau. "I'm fine. Everything's going to be just fine."

It was all she could do to keep the tears from falling. Never had she felt so defeated . . . except when she'd found Michael. And she'd survived that. The knowledge gave her strength. No matter how bad her situation appeared, nothing could be as devastating as Michael's death.

"Yer don' look fine ter me," the man said, worry creasing his narrow forehead.

Liza forced herself to concentrate on him. When he spoke, she noted that his two front teeth were missing. It gave him an almost gamin look, as if a little boy peeked out of a man's face.

"I'm just unsettled. I don't often get mauled, particularly not in broad daylight. Thank you for your concern." She smiled at him to show that everything was under control.

"Mightn't I take ye 'ome, like?"

Apprehension darted through her, drying her mouth. Not another one! How many times was she to be molested today? It seemed as if she was ricocheting from one man's unwanted advances to the next.

Maybe she should just give up and accept Lord Alaistair St. Simon's offer. That would be the easiest.

She grimaced. She couldn't betray Michael's memory. She had to be strong. Something would happen to improve her situation—she would *make* something happen.

"Are yer in pain?" the thin man asked anxiously.

"No, thank you. I need to be on my way." He reached for her and she flinched, her eyes darting to his. But there was no hunger or evil in his gaze, and she relaxed. "Thank you for your offer to escort me, but I don't want to put you out."

Then, before he could protest or suggest differently, Liza skimmed past him and sped into the crowd. She didn't know where she'd go now, but she certainly didn't want a strange man following her trail.

Anxiety gave her the agility to weave in and out among the people, despite the weight of the portmanteau. Somewhere there was work she could do. She simply had to find it.

CHAPTER FOUR

"SHE'S WORKING IN A tavern? Bloody stubborn woman!" Alaistair wished he'd never set Winkly to following Lizabeth Johnstone, but he knew he couldn't have done otherwise.

"Right-o, guv," Winkly concurred. "My sen'iments exactly."

Alaistair paced the library twice, wondering what he was going to do with the creature. She was a thorn that was starting to draw blood. More than ever, he regretted keeping that blasted vowel overnight. Somehow he would force her to take back the money, even if it killed him.

Irate to the point of wanting to punch something, Alaistair strode past Winkly. Not waiting for the butler to bring him his hat, he stalked down the front steps and made his way to Gentleman Jackson's.

Tristan found him there two hours later.

"Been enjoying yourself, Saint?"

Alaistair glanced around. Jackson chose that instant to throw a punch. It landed with a resounding *whack* on Alaistair's jaw. Staggering backwards, rubbing his red skin, he growled, "Next time, Tris, why don't you just hold my hand?"

Tristan shrugged. "Thought you were sensible enough not to look away from Jackson when you box."

Alaistair knew when he was defeated. Recently it had become an all-too-familiar experience. With a nod to Jackson, he took the towel Tristan was now holding out to him and rubbed the sweat off his chest and arms, careful to avoid his rapidly swelling jaw.

"What brings you here, Tris?"

"Came to see if you're game for dinner at White's and some whist later. I've got Buckley and Carruthers interested."

Alaistair grinned, and immediately winced. "Damn, but that's sore. You plan on a lucrative night, I take it."

Tristan smiled, his blue eyes dancing. "If you can bear to spend one night away from the opera dancer that rumor says will be Malicious Marie's replacement."

"You know I never let a woman tie me to her apron strings. Particularly one I pay to entertain me."

Tristan gave his friend a knowing look. "You're as touchy as a baited bear today."

Alaistair didn't deign to answer. Tristan might be his closest friend, but he didn't need to know everything. While boxing with Jackson, Alaistair had reached the decision to let Lizabeth Johnstone work in that tavern for a few days. After several episodes with the rough men and women who frequented such places, she'd be more than willing to take that blasted money.

Shaking his head to clear it of the infuriating thoughts about Lizabeth, Lady Stone, Alaistair made short work of dressing. When he finished, his cravat was slightly less perfect and less starched than when he'd left home. It didn't matter. He'd never been a slave to fashion.

Together they strolled to White's. Entering the gaming room, they were met by Buckley and Carruthers, who'd already had their meal and were eager to start the game of whist.

Buckley, a man of similar age to Alaistair and Tristan, frowned as though remembering an unpleasant thought. He drew Alaistair aside and whispered, "Before we get started, Saint, I think you'd better look at the betting book. There's an entry that I vow will make you see red.''

Alaistair gave his crony a searching look. Buckley was dead serious, and for a man known as a practical joker, that meant the wager in the book was incendiary.

With a wistful sigh for the entertaining night he saw fast dissipating, Alaistair went to the book. On the last page in bold lettering was a wager: *Will Lord Alaistair St. Simon or the Earl of Bent be first to sample the wares of a certain lady whose brother shot himself over gaming debts?*

Fury raged through him like wildfire. Bent had been active. The bloody cur would pay for this.

''Saint,'' Tristan said quietly, taking the book from his friend's hands. He whistled low. ''Nasty business, but you can do nothing about it without further sullying the lady's name.''

Alaistair looked at his friend without seeing him. With an extreme effort he checked his temper, but when he spoke, his voice was dangerously low. ''Bent will regret this. Five years ago I let him go with only a whipping. This time I'll put a bullet through his treacherous heart.''

''Easy,'' Tristan soothed, placing a restraining hand on his friend's tense shoulder. ''The best you can do for Lady Stone is to pretend it doesn't matter. Play whist tonight and plan what you'll do to-morrow."

"After I get her out of that place," Alaistair muttered, deciding to cut her stay down to two days and one night.

"What?"

"Her latest position is in a tavern." He ground his teeth in frustration. "That woman has done nothing but make my life miserable. She once vowed to destroy me, and I swear that she's succeeding."

Tristan shook his head as he led his friend to the table where Carruthers and Buckley waited. They played into the small hours and followed the game with a hearty breakfast of kidneys and eggs washed down with ale at Alaistair's Town house.

After the other two left, St. Simon rose and beckoned Tristan to follow him into the library. Feeling as though he carried the weight of the world, he sat in the chair behind his desk. "Take a seat," he said, undoing his cravat and opening the top button of his shirt. He was procrastinating, and he knew it. But damn, this wasn't easy.

Opening the bottom drawer of the desk, he drew out a metal container. From it he took a sheaf of bills and carefully counted out one hundred pounds. He handed it to Tristan.

Tristan raised his blond brows. "What's this? You've already paid your debt to me."

Alaistair grimaced, unable to smile at Tristan's lighthearted needling about the money he'd lost that night. "And if I hadn't, I wouldn't have had to go into my reserves. Please take this and keep quiet about what I'm about to ask you to do."

Tristan's quizzical look became a frown as he took the money. "Not something illegal?"

It was an attempt at banter, but it fell flat. Alaistair rubbed the back of his aching neck. "Worse. I want you to obtain a Special License."

"What?" Tristan rose from his seat, realized what he'd done and sank back down. "For whom?"

Alaistair steadily met his friend's questioning blue eyes, but the tension in his shoulders and neck were giving him a headache. Not since Salamanca, not since his mother's elopement with Bent, had he felt this on edge.

"For me," he said flatly.

"You! Never say you're going to marry that opera dancer. Marie would be better." Tristan's eyes narrowed. "Are you drunk?"

Alaistair sighed and stood up. He paced to the fireplace, where he gazed into the empty grate. "No. And I'm not marrying the opera dancer. Or Marie."

"Then who?" Tristan rose and walked over to join his friend. Putting a hand on Alaistair's shoulder he asked again, "Who is it?"

Alaistair directed a cautionary look at him before returning his attention to the blackened fireplace. "Lizabeth Johnstone." Tristan's hand involuntarily squeezed hard. Alaistair forced himself to smile at his friend's reaction. "You'll give me a bruise."

Tristan let his hand drop and stepped back. "You've gone mad."

Alaistair shook his head, one thick lock of black hair falling onto his forehead. He brushed it back impatiently. "No. I *shall* go mad if I don't marry the blasted woman. It's the only way I can relieve her of her brother's debt."

Tristan folded and unfolded the money he still held, his attention never wavering from his friend's agonized face. Softly, he observed, "I thought you wanted to marry where you had affection."

Alaistair glanced at him, his gray eyes almost black. "It's a stupid notion. People in our circle don't marry for love, they marry for financial gain . . . or expediency."

"Like your parents?"

Three simple words, but they drove the knife home and twisted it. "Yes, like my parents."

Tristan stepped back from the pain flashing in his friend's twisted features. "Your parents made a mistake. Don't do the same thing."

Alaistair clenched his hands into white-knuckled fists. "I . . . don't . . . have . . . a . . . choice. I can't let her work in a tavern. I can't let her do something worse. This is the only way I can provide for her." He stared into Tristan's widened eyes. "Don't you see? I owe her this. If I hadn't kept that vowel overnight, she wouldn't be destitute." His voice became a whisper. "And her brother would still be alive."

"You're not responsible for that puppy's action."

Alaistair turned away. "I know. It's the girl I'm worried about. She deserves better than she's getting, and this is the only remedy I can think of. As it is, I'll have to force her into it."

"Force her? You could have any female you wanted. Just give Lady Stone back the money and rip up the paper. Don't ruin your life."

"I've already tried. My solicitor called on hers and was told that under no circumstances would the vowel be taken back. That everything she owned was on the auction block." Alaistair smacked his fist into the mantel, trying to relieve some of the tension drawing him up tight. "I bought it all and hold it in trust for her. I intend to give it back to her." He turned to watch Tristan's face for a reaction, his own a mask of self-derision. "So far, I've been unsuccessful."

Tristan looked skeptical. "Never known a woman to tell you no."

Alaistair's lips turned up sardonically. "Believe me, it's been a novel experience, and one I don't wish to keep repeating."

"I should think not," Tristan replied, folding the hundred pounds into a neat rectangle and putting it into his pocket.

Alaistair smiled for the first time since they'd entered the library. Tristan would do as he asked. "Thanks. Meet me back here at midnight. I'll have her with me."

Tristan shook his head. "I know I'm fighting a losing battle. Once you make up your mind, there's never any changing it. I remember when you fell out of the apple tree and broke your arm. I told you the top two limbs were weak, but oh, no. You decided to climb to the top of that tree and nothing I did or said would deter you."

"Just so."

St. Simon watched his friend leave. When the door was firmly shut behind his co-conspirator's back, he moved to a side table and poured himself a full glass of whiskey. It was more of the strong liquor than he normally drank, more than he poured for Winkly. He downed it in three gulps, reveling in the burning sensation that coursed down his throat and exploded in his gut.

Damn. He didn't want to marry Lizabeth Johnstone. But then he hadn't wanted to fight in the Napoleonic Wars, either; it had simply been the right thing to do. Nor had he wanted to be his mother's savior when she fled with Bent. But he had. His father and older brother had been out of the country, so the responsibility had fallen to him.

Responsibility. It was a weighty word, but one he lived by.

He set his empty glass down and crossed the room to the mantel, where he took down a smooth mahogany box. Setting it on a table, he opened it and stared down at the elegantly formed dueling pistols.

This was the first time he'd looked at them since returning from the wars. Pistol shots made him nervous, a legacy of his time in battle. He'd have to exert tight control over himself when he used these.

He took one out and sighted down it. Then he weighed it in his hand for balance and feel. Grimly he returned it to its box and set the box on his desk.

He would soon need these.

THE WORK Liza had found was not what she would have chosen, but it was honest labor, she told herself as she straightened up from wiping a recently vacated table. Frowning, she rubbed her aching back before pushing a thick lock of red-gold hair off her forehead. She would have to stop and redo the bun to keep her vision unimpeded.

She'd learned within minutes on her first day that it didn't do to take her eyes off this crowd. The customers were forever pinching her or trying to pull her down onto a more-than-ready male lap. The life of a tavern wench was challenging, but somehow she'd survived two days.

A sigh escaped her pinched mouth. It was work, and the landlord gave her room and board. He'd hinted there was more than one way to earn a wage, but he hadn't pushed her.

And if she continued to carry half a dozen tankards of ale every fifteen minutes, she would develop arm muscles that would floor any man who tried to press her. Her mouth curved upward at the ridiculous thought, and she made her way back to the bar, where her next order sat. Four tankards this time.

"'ey, you!"

The raucous voice rose above the general hubbub, catching Liza's attention. Turning around, she saw a thick, muscular man beckoning in her direction. She glanced behind to see who he was yelling at.

"Yeah, I mean you, copper'ead." A huge grin split his face and large yellow teeth gleamed in the smoky atmosphere created by the sputtering fire and too many cheap candles.

He was new here. Liza decided to ignore him. Turning, she continued to the bar and got her mugs. Careful to dodge any wandering hands, she delivered the ale.

A sharp yank on her skirt pulled her off balance and her empty tray clattered to the floor, accompanied by loud guffaws from the mass of patrons. Liza landed with a thud on the big brute's lap.

Her eyes widened as she realized just what a mountain this man was, and all of him appeared to be muscle. Her gaze traveled up his rough shirt to his bearded face and the lecherous gleam in his brown eyes. Was it her fate these days to be mauled by brutish men? Was there no one who would help her get off this lout's lap?

She scanned the crowded room, but from the grins of envy on the men's faces and the looks that said "She's gettin' her comeuppance" on the faces of the few women present, she knew no one would speak up for her. The men assumed fondling was what tavern wenches were for, and the women were hostile because she was different from them, not welcoming male advances or using coarse language.

Liza swallowed hard. Wheedling would get her nowhere, so she took the bit between her teeth. "Let me go this instant," she demanded in tones a drill sergeant would be proud of.

The big man smirked. "Ye kin call me Tommy, copper'ead."

His endearment for her drew more guffaws from the crowd. Apprehension began to tinge Liza's anger. There was every possibility that this situation might worsen to the point where her honor was in danger. No one here would object if Tommy dragged her upstairs to one of the small, dingy rooms available for such a purpose.

She had to move quickly. With all the strength she could muster, she shoved hard against her captor's massive chest, at the same time swinging her legs to the side in an attempt to slide off his lap. Startled by her actions, Tommy loosened his grip.

In a flash Liza was free. She lunged into the crowd, aiming for the door, only to find a phalanx of burly male bodies barring her escape. As she staggered backward, she was all too aware of the leering faces of the men hemming her in.

Fear twisted her belly into knots. Not even when the Earl of Bent had waylaid her on the stairs had she felt such danger. These people were like spectators at a bear baiting, eager for blood.

Frantic, she whipped her head from side to side looking for help. There had to be a way out.

Just then a commotion arose near the tavern's door. Through the smoky haze, Liza glimpsed a tall form draped in a bottle-green greatcoat. The newcomer held himself with an air of authority that was palpable.

A gentleman. Hope leapt within her. Surely no gentleman would let these ruffians bespoil her.

As he approached, the man stooped to keep from hitting his head on the ceiling beams. An ominous silence fell over the crowd as one by one the men blocking Liza's way fell back. Relief buckled her knees—and was immediately supplanted by shock as she got a good look at her savior. Alaistair St. Simon.

From wind-tossed hair to mud-spattered boots, he exuded a deadly power. Much as she might dislike the man, Liza couldn't be anything but thankful for his uncanny timing.

He jerked his head in the direction of the door. "Go on, *Miss* Johnstone." To the dark shadow moving beside him, he said, "Winkly, make sure no one tries to stop her."

Liza's attention shifted to the weasel-faced man next to Lord Alaistair. He was the one who had tried to help her outside of Hatchard's. Tonight he was in a coat too large for his scrawny frame, and it gave him a hunched appearance. Dimly, she remembered noticing a man similar in silhouette who had slid into a shadowed corner of the room earlier in the evening. Had he been following her? Had St. Simon told him to?

But those questions could be answered later, when she was safely away from here. Lingering would jeopardize them all. Lord Alaistair and his companion were only two, after all, and they didn't appear to be carrying weapons.

She scurried to the door and didn't stop until her back was firmly planted against the solid wood. Wide-eyed, she watched Tommy rise up, both hands clenched into ham-sized fists.

"'ere, wot you think yer doin'? She's *my* fancy piece. I saw 'er first."

Lord Alaistair's eyes were burning coals as they raked down the man's form. When he spoke, his voice was dangerously soft. "I beg to differ with you."

Tommy licked his thick lips, his bravado slipping. "No swell cove'll be takin' 'er wi'out a fight." His eyes darted round the room looking for support. When he got several assenting nods, his chest puffed out like a bullfrog's.

Slowly and deliberately, St. Simon reached into the two pockets of his coat and withdrew a pistol from each. He aimed one at Tommy, the other at the room in general.

"If any of you has an objection, please let it be known." He scanned the faces, stopping at Tommy's mottled purple countenance. "I see you all agree that the lady comes with me."

Not taking his attention from his adversary, Lord Alaistair slowly moved toward the door. Winkly hustled ahead of him, a pistol appearing in his hand as though by magic.

"We'd best get outta 'ere," Winkly said, taking Liza's arm in his free hand and pulling her through the door.

She went with alacrity. Much as she disliked being in Lord Alaistair's debt again, the thought of being ravished by Tommy was even less appealing.

St. Simon moved with a studied casualness until he was in a position where Winkly could cover his back. "The first person who sticks his head out this door will get it blown off." He looked around the room. "Is that clear?"

Several people nodded, but most just stared at him. Tommy took a menacing step forward then stopped when Lord Alaistair angled the pistol barrel his way.

A menacing smile thinned St. Simon's lips, and Liza, seeing it, began to shiver. This man might be the younger son of a duke and steeped in the fripperies of the ton, but she had no doubt he was dangerous. Oh yes, Alaistair St. Simon was very dangerous. But he would never intimidate her as he had the occupants of the tavern.

Alaistair slammed the heavy door behind him. Gesturing for Winkly to start off down the road, he said, "Hurry up, man. They won't be long in deciding that twenty of them outnumber two men with guns."

Neither Liza nor Winkly needed encouragement. They ran as though the hounds of hell were at their heels.

Liza heard the light tread of Lord Alaistair's boots ring against the dirty cobbles. She felt Winkly's bony but surprisingly strong fingers dig into her arm. And she tasted the bitterness of her own fear. The skirts of her well-worn black bombazine dress flapped against her straining legs, hampering her speed.

Her clog-covered foot caught on a dislodged cobblestone and she stumbled forward, jarring loose Winkly's fingers. Liza raised her hands to break her fall just as an arm circled her waist. Her headlong plunge stopped with a jolt that shook the breath from her exhausted body.

Even as she tried to regain her footing, she was set upright, but the arm remained around her, burning through the layers of material to her flesh.

She didn't need to look to see who held her. It could only be Lord Alaistair.

The three of them burst around a corner onto a wider street where a chaise waited. Lord Alaistair motioned the driver to stay seated. Then, without asking permission, he lifted Liza up and tossed her into the dark interior. She landed on a soft velvet squab. It was the first time since her brother's death that she'd felt such luxury.

The two men followed immediately. Not wanting to feel Lord Alaistair's strong body beside her, Liza shrank into a corner. She didn't have to worry; he sat opposite her.

The carriage lurched into motion as St. Simon lit one of the two lanterns inside the vehicle. Through half-closed lids, Liza studied him in the flickering yellow light. His high cheekbones and square jaw were harsher than she remembered, and his mouth was set in anger.

"What the hell possessed you to work *there?*"

Liza bristled, the gratitude she had felt toward him all but gone. "It was honest labor."

"M'lord—" Winkly interposed.

"Stay out of this," Lord Alaistair growled at him. His eyes pinned her to the seat. "You don't have the sense you were born with. No woman is safe in a place like that during daylight. And after night falls she might as well hand out a red light."

"Don't cast your moral judgments on me," she declared, not caring that there was a witness to their unseemly dispute. "I went there because I had no place else to go."

"Bloody blazes, woman." He was holding fast to the leather strap set near the ceiling of the coach to keep from careening into Winkly during the rapid turns of the vehicle. In his anger, he ripped the strap from its moorings. "You could have come to me. I've already told you the damn vowel is yours. I wish to heaven I'd never seen it. Or you."

Liza blanched as he tossed the leather strap out the window. He was a strong man and furious at her. "We've plowed this ground before. The vowel is a debt of honor. I won't take it."

His eyes became slits glinting in the flickering light. "You leave me no choice. You'll bloody well marry me. I'm not going to allow you to continue this path of self-destruction just because you hate me and have more honor than sense."

Liza felt as though the seat had fallen away from her, lodging her stomach in her throat. "*Marry* you? I can't bear the sight of you!"

"Ahem, if I—" Winkly tried again.

"Shut up," Lord Alaistair snapped at him, his attention remaining on Liza. "I don't give a tinker's damn what you think of me. I didn't beat your brother at gaming so he'd kill himself and you'd sink into a life of sin. And I don't intend to continue living with the worry your rash, ill-considered actions cause me."

Liza gasped, her ire matching his. "I'll *never* marry you. I'd rather rot in hell."

The coach bolted around another corner, sending Liza flying to the opposite side. Before she could right herself, they stopped.

"You have no choice," Lord Alaistair said in a forbidding voice that caused the hair on her nape to rise.

"The hell I don't." Any other time Liza would have bitten her tongue before cursing, but things were out of hand. She was at his mercy and she knew it. Never had she given up without a fight, and she wasn't about to start now.

Lord Alaistair swung open the door before a footman could and took hold of her. He dragged her out and up a set of stone steps to a large, two-doored entry. As he stalked into the well-lit foyer, Liza dug in her heels behind him.

The butler and several footmen scattered out of his way. "Prepare a room," he ordered.

Liza twisted like a wild animal in his merciless grip. "I won't marry you."

He turned on her, his hands digging into her shoulders, his face so close she could see the individual thick black eyelashes. "I've had enough of you and your blasted honor. No one will take you into their home, and you don't have any marketable skills or you wouldn't have gone to work in that vile establishment."

"How dare you," she gasped, trying desperately to put some distance between them.

"I might say the same of you." He glared down into her upturned face. "How dare you drag me through the mess you insist on making of your life? If I didn't feel responsible for you, I'd leave you to rot. But, God help me, I can't."

Liza bit her lip. What did he intend to do now? Imprison her?

He stared at her for a long moment. This time he spoke calmly, as though the emotion of seconds before had never been. "Do you know your name is in White's betting book? *Someone* wonders who'll be your lover first—Bent or me."

She drew back in shocked revulsion. Even she had heard of White's betting book. The vicar's sister had mentioned it that night at dinner, her voice making it sound like a spawn of Satan. Liza knew that to have her name bandied about in that manner was almost as bad as having the actual event occur.

"Who would do such a horrible thing?" she whispered.

He sneered. "Certainly not I."

"Bent," she said softly. "He's the only one who would do such a dastardly thing."

"You're quite perceptive when you choose to be."

She ignored his sarcasm. "How dare he! Not only does he insult me, but he disparages my name." Liza gnashed her teeth. "If I were a man, I'd call him out."

"And confirm to Society that what he implies is true—that you're a loose woman."

That drew her up short. "I'll leave London. That will stop the rumors."

"And how will you travel?"

The sardonic gleam in his eyes made her bristle. "I don't know, but I'll manage. Just release me and I'll be gone."

He laughed, the harsh sound ringing out in the marble-tiled foyer. "That's rich. If you had the funds to leave London, I'm sure you would have done so before now." He sobered. "No. I'm through with this nonsense of yours. I vowed to make things right and I shall. You're going to marry me."

"No!"

"Yes," he said, his eyelids slipping down to conceal any emotion in his eyes. "Definitely yes. It's extreme, but it's the only way. You've left me no alternative."

Lord Alaistair glanced around the foyer. Nervously, Liza did the same. Surely someone would save her. But there was no one to be seen.

"Simpson!" Lord Alaistair bellowed, his fingers keeping a strong grip on her shoulders. When that worthy showed, he gave him orders. "Simpson, escort Lady Stone upstairs. Put her in the room adjoining mine—the one I had you prepare earlier—and see that all the exits are locked." He eyed Lizabeth knowingly. "She'd tie the sheets together and go out the window if she could."

"You can't do this," Liza protested, becoming increasingly frantic as her captor became calmer and more methodical. "You can't force me to marry you."

"Can't I?" he asked, one black brow raised.

Liza gulped. It was patently obvious that he intended to go through with this wild scheme.

"Take her, Simpson," he said, handing her over to the butler.

With a look of extreme unease, Simpson clasped her wrist. Liza knew that if she struggled, the servant would very likely release her, but what good would that do? Alaistair St. Simon would simply seize her and take her to the room himself, and a lot less gently, she was sure. She didn't want to provoke him to violence, and she sensed that he was on the edge of losing his temper completely. She would think of something else to stop this madness.

Head high, she allowed Simpson to escort her up the stairs to her prison. The door was shut and the key turned in the lock before she allowed herself to wilt. But she pulled herself up sharply. She had to find out if all the exits were barred.

Both doors, one of which led to Lord Alaistair's bedchamber were secured. And the windows were locked and planks of wood hammered over them. She was trapped.

There was nothing to do but wait, and she had never been good at that. She caught a loose strand of hair and began to twirl it furiously.

CHAPTER FIVE

ALAISTAIR ABHORRED waiting. Another legacy from Salamanca. The constant waiting to attack or to be attacked. The long vigil by a sickbed, waiting for a friend either to live past the danger of infection or to succumb to it. No, he preferred action.

Consequently, he paced the library as he waited for midnight. At any minute Tristan would be here with the Special License. The rector was already waiting in the drawing room, licking his chops at the promise of a large donation to his parish, in return for performing a marriage of convenience.

"Bloody hell."

Alaistair spun around, the ball of his boot gliding on the highly polished wood floor. He didn't want a marriage of convenience. He'd decided that five years ago when his mother tried to run away with the Earl of Bent. No, he didn't want this union with Lizabeth Johnstone but he wouldn't—couldn't—add to his burden of guilt by being responsible for her ruin. And no one married for love, in any case.

He frowned as he strode to the window and threw it open, the cool night air filling his lungs. A noise in the foyer interrupted his melancholy musing.

"Tristan!" he bellowed, pacing to the library door and swinging it wide with such force that it struck the wall. "I thought you'd decided not to do it."

Tristan shook his head as he assessed his friend's demeanor. "You're a mess, Saint. Where's the impeccable nonpareil of London Society?"

"Stow it, Tris. I'm hardly in the mood."

"So I see," Tristan murmured. "I hear marriage does that to a fellow."

Alaistair could see that his friend still did not approve of his plan and intended to be difficult. Striding past him, he told Simpson, "Please bring her ladyship down."

The butler bowed his acquiescence, but his eyes were wary as he started up the stairs.

Liza, sitting tensely in one of the chairs placed on either side of the fireplace, jumped at the knock on the door. "Come in."

The butler stood in the doorway, his features morose. "You are requested below, my lady."

This was the moment, Liza thought. Nervously she patted her hair into place. Then, lifting her chin, she followed the servant down the stairs to meet her fate—or to thwart it.

Alaistair St. Simon waited for her, with another gentleman at his side whom he introduced as the Honorable Tristan Montford. She nodded perfunctorily, her mind racing in circles, trying to find a way out of this untenable situation.

"Have you come to your senses, Lord Alaistair?" she inquired coldly.

He stared at her, making her flush. She wasn't a diamond of the first water even when clean and welldressed, but he didn't have to look at her as if she were vermin. Her chin rose defiantly.

"I'm afraid not," he replied dryly, distaste evident in the tone of his voice.

Liza's mouth tightened as his disparaging perusal continued. She couldn't help that her black bombazine dress was wrinkled and soiled. Nor could she do anything to straighten the disarray of her hair. Her hairbrush was back on the rickety table in the room above the tavern. She shuddered at the memory of that hellhole. What a close call she had had, and she owed thanks to the arrogant man in front of her. But now was not the time—not until she had convinced him that this marriage he kept discussing was absurd.

Forcing herself to take a calming breath, she said, "You do not desire this union any more than I do."

He shrugged, his broad shoulders flexing beneath the fine wool of his gray jacket. "A marriage of convenience to you or to another woman is all the same. At least this way I'll be able to help you."

Her straight auburn brows drew together. "That's a dreadful reason, and utterly wrong. I'm perfectly capable of taking care of myself."

He looked at her skeptically. "Is that what you were doing in that lout's lap? No." He shook his head slowly. "This is the only way."

His voice was low and resigned. More than anything else it spoke of finality. He truly did intend to wed her and no amount of reason would sway him. The false calm deserted Liza and she felt a rising panic.

"But I don't want to marry you! I hate you!"

He studied her for a long, unnerving moment. "Come along," he ordered abruptly. "Tristan has the Special License."

When she stood frozen in place, watching him, her turquoise eyes wide with alarm, he took her arm and pulled her.

She twisted frantically, but his hold only tightened about her wrist. This was crazy. "I *won't* marry you," she insisted. "I'd rather starve. I...I'd rather prostitute myself."

His mouth became a derisive curl. "Don't worry. A marriage of convenience is merely a legal form of that activity."

Tristan, who'd been silent until now, suddenly spoke up. "I say, Saint, no need to be ungentlemanly. She *is* a lady."

Alaistair swallowed his exasperated retort and changed the topic. "The rector is here."

"Rector?" Liza's voice rose an octave, and she renewed her struggle to escape his grip. "Rector? You can't marry me against my will. This is 1814."

Lord Alaistair cast a disdainful glance at her. "In England, as elsewhere, money talks. You should have remembered that when you refused my offer of the vowel."

"I shall say no," she said desperately. "I'll tell how you abducted me—that you're forcing me."

Ignoring her, he turned his attention to Tristan. "Will you be the witness?"

Tristan looked with distrust at the struggling woman. "Yes." His eyes caught his friend's. "Are you sure you're doing the right thing?"

Alaistair sighed, his grip tightening on Liza. "She gives me no other choice. I found her just as some lout was about to make her his unwilling bedmate."

Tristan gaped at her, taking in her muddy dress and tangled hair. "I thought fighting with *you* had put her in this state."

Alaistair strode toward the double doors, towing Liza's resisting body behind. "No. I'm not such an eager bridegroom as to maul her before the wedding. Conjugal bliss isn't my reason for becoming leg-shackled."

His disparaging remarks only fueled Liza's determination not to wed him. He didn't want her, and she hated him. She had to do something.

She could agree to take the gaming voucher. Just a couple of words and he'd release her. But even at the expense of her own happiness, she knew she couldn't besmirch Michael's name. She would stop this farce of a marriage some other way.

Her mouth firmed. "I'll get an annulment."

Alaistair didn't even bother to look at her as the carefully expressionless butler opened the doors wide for them to pass through. "It won't be granted. As I said, money has influence."

"Not to mention your father's rank," she added bitingly.

"Just so."

"I say," Tristan interposed, having followed them into the drawing room, "it won't do any good to continue fighting him, Lady Stone. I've never known him not to get his way. And he won't abuse you, even though his current actions imply otherwise. I've never known him to beat a woman."

She glared at Tristan. "You, sir, are no better than he is. Rank and wealth don't make a gentleman."

Her cutting words caused Alaistair's shoulders to become rigid, but the expression on his face remained emotionless. "When we're wed, you'll learn to mind your shrewish tongue."

"Never." She glared at him, meeting his cold eyes with the heated anger of her own.

Tristan, face flaming, hurried ahead of them to the fireplace, where another man stood. Liza took the opportunity to look around her; there might be a way to escape yet.

The room they were in was large enough to be the ballroom in another house. Settees and chairs covered in straw-colored silk were scattered about, with richly inlaid tables interspersed among them. A games table, set up for the moment, reposed along one wall. Liza's lips curled derisively.

"I see that you even carry your gambling vice into your home," she murmured.

He clenched his fingers briefly, but it was the only satisfaction the situation afforded her, because at that moment the two men approached.

Tristan introduced the other man as the Reverend Darvey.

Lord Alaistair's nod was curt, his temper obviously held tightly in check. "Thank you for coming out at this hour, Darvey. As you can see, my bride is eager for our joining."

Liza gasped at the blatant lie. "I am not."

The rector looked from one to the other before addressing Lord Alaistair. "It's my pleasure to perform this small deed, my lord. Many's the time your father, the duke, has aided my parish."

Hearing him, Liza realized with a sense of impending doom that the rector would ignore anything she said. It was obvious that the man owed much to the Duke of Rundell and intended to repay him by helping his son.

Once more she toyed with the idea of accepting the voucher, but she could take the thought no further. If she besmirched Michael's memory she would never be able to live with herself. Dealing with Alaistair St. Simon would be easier.

From one of his pockets, Tristan pulled a large sheet of folded paper. Liza sensed that it was the Special License. Tristan handed it to the rector.

Lord Alaistair released her wrist, warning her with a look that if she tried to run away she would live to regret it. She frowned at him before turning away.

Surreptitiously, she rubbed at her wrist, which was sore from his grip. As though from a distance, she heard the Reverend Darvey begin to speak. When he asked if she took Lord Alaistair Gervase St. Simon for her wedded husband, she ignored him, looking beyond his shoulder at the flickering flames of the coal fire, her heart a heavy weight within her.

Shivers spread out from the small of her back, up her ribs and down each arm until her fingers shook so that she had to ball them into fists and hide them in the folds of her gown. From under her lashes she cast a glance at her soon-to-be husband. His silhouette stood out in stark relief, his silver-threaded hair swept back to accentuate his narrow, well-defined nose and strong chin. His mouth was a slash of suppressed dissatisfaction.

It gave her scant pleasure to know that he desired this union as little as she. The whole situation strongly reminded her of one of Fanny Burney's gothic romances. Only this one would not end on a happy note. No, she and Alaistair St. Simon loathed each other and would only make each other miserable.

"I now pronounce you man and wife." The words reverberated along her nerve endings as the reality of what had just happened rained down on her.

She was married. At twenty-six she was finally married—to the man who had killed her brother. The man she had vowed to destroy had destroyed her. For, as his wife, she had no legal recourse. The law would condone whatever he chose to do with her. For better or worse, she was married to the only man she'd ever hated.

A hoarse laugh rasped along her raw throat. "Married in black, my lord? It bodes ill for our future."

He turned an unreadable countenance to her. "You can always take the voucher."

Exhausted to the point of collapse, Liza murmured, "You're like a harp with one note. And I'm equally monotonous. No."

Alaistair shrugged. "As you wish. Tristan will take you back to your room."

"Me? Why not the butler?" Tristan asked, stepping away from the two of them. "Why not you?"

"Because she's damn likely to try and escape. She went with Simpson before because she didn't think I'd actually go through with this." He shot Liza a fulminating glance. "And I have other things to attend to."

Frowning, Tristan grumbled, "I don't want any part of this, Saint. I've already done more than a friend should have to."

Alaistair held his arms rigidly at his side. "Tris..."

Tristan sighed and ran his fingers through his unruly blond hair. "Oh, all right. But you owe me."

For the first time since she'd met Lord Alaistair, Liza saw him smile. He always exuded a masculine potency that put her nerves on edge, but now he also had an aura of warmth.

Unconsciously, she took a strand of hair and began to twirl it, contemplating the transformation wrought in her new husband by that one smile. She was surprised when a hand touched her shoulder.

"Lady Alaistair," Tristan said, taking his hand away as soon as he had her attention, "if you'll come with me..."

Tristan Montford's polite request broke the spell. Drawing herself up to her full height, which was several inches shy of Tristan Montford's, Liza said, "My name is Lady Stone."

Tristan took a step back, shot a quick look at Alaistair and bowed. "As you wish. However, as Saint's wife, the ton will call you Lady Alaistair... if they don't call you Lady Saint."

Liza stiffened at his levity. Neither name was palatable, since both implied ownership by the man she loathed. She glanced contemptuously at her groom. "His title is a courtesy, mine is not. I am Lady Stone."

Tristan's jaw snapped shut. It was the first time Liza had seen him look irritated. "Please follow me, Lady Stone."

"Best not to give in to her, Tris," Alaistair said from his position beside the rector. "It'll only set an example I don't intend to follow."

Not waiting to summon a footman, Tristan yanked one of the two doors open and held it for her to pass. He directed a defiant look at his friend. "She's right."

Liza, without a backward glance, sailed through the door and up the stairs. She knew where she was going, and there was no sense in fighting it. Not yet.

She could hear Tristan following, his tread heavy as though reluctance held him back. And well it might, Liza told herself. After all, he was only helping his friend, something she would have done for Sarah. If it hadn't been for Michael's urgent desire to come to London, she would have stayed at Romney Marsh to help Sarah with the birth of her child. But Michael had always come first. As it was, the thought of how much Sarah meant to her blunted Liza's ire at Tristan.

Reaching the doorway to the room she'd previously occupied, Liza stopped and waited for Tristan to catch up. She held her hand out to him and gave him a tentative smile. "I'm sorry for taking my anger out on you. You didn't deserve it. Lord Alaistair is your friend, and I respect your loyalty to him."

Taken aback, Tristan was slow in accepting her proffered hand. When he did, he raised her fingers and lightly brushed her skin with his lips. It was a fleeting touch, a token of acceptance, and did nothing to Liza's insides; no melting, no churning, not at all like the effect of Alaistair St. Simon's touch.

"Thank you for understanding, Lady Stone." Tristan's blue eyes were solemn as he released her. He didn't smile, but neither did he scowl. "This is a bad business, but Alaistair believes he's doing what is right. I've known him too long to think he would do something like this, otherwise."

Liza's back stiffened. Coldly, she said, "He would have done better not to have played Faro that night."

In the muted yellow light from the candles in the sconces on either side of the door, Liza saw Tristan's face redden. When he replied, his voice was equally frigid. "Better that your brother played with Alaistair than another. Alaistair had no intention of keeping your brother's inheritance. Many another man would only have counted himself very lucky."

"Lord Alaistair is most fortunate to have a friend such as you," Liza observed, even as she discounted the validity of his words.

"Alaistair is a very worthy man," Tristan replied, stepping back so that the shadows hid his expression. "Now, if you'll excuse me."

He didn't move away but stood watching Liza until she took the hint and backed into the room. As she closed the heavy oak door, she saw him still standing there, making sure she was secured. The latch clicked into place and she heard the sound of muted footsteps down the wooden hallway, then a man's voice. She recognized it as Lord Alaistair's but couldn't make out what he was saying. It was followed by the click of a key turning in the lock.

Once more, she was confined like a prisoner. A mirthless laugh was all she had the energy for.

TIME PASSED SLOWLY as she prowled aimlessly around the room. With time came honesty, and she admitted to herself that she had nowhere to go and no money to go with. For the moment she was stuck.

Demoralized and exhausted, Liza went to the nearest chair, her feet dragging on the richly colored blue-and-gold carpet. Sinking into the padded seat, she ran her fingers through her tangled hair and wished for the silver-backed brush she no longer had. Separating out a strand, she began to twirl it, her eyes closed.

Things were no darker than before, she told herself. She'd survived her parents' death and Michael's suicide, she could survive a short marriage of convenience and eventually outwit Lord Alaistair.

A measure of calm wafted over her and she opened her eyes to study the room where she was held prisoner. It was always best to know as much as one could about one's surroundings. She'd learned that while managing Thornyhold. Useless information today could be valuable knowledge tomorrow, and she hadn't really looked about earlier.

She noticed that the boards had been removed from the window. Her mouth curved sarcastically. Her husband must think she wouldn't try to escape now that the deed was done.

Queen Anne furniture filled the large room, yet it still retained an air of spaciousness. A bed, a wardrobe, a dresser, several chairs and tables all managed to find a place and still leave plenty of room to move around in. Two floor-to-ceiling windows flanked the four-poster, their drapes the same rich blue and gold as the thick rug underfoot. It wasn't a modern room, but it was beautiful. If circumstances had been different, Liza could have relaxed and enjoyed being here.

St. Simon had implied that this was the mistress's sleeping chamber and had a connecting door into his room. The possibility sent warm tendrils drifting down from her stomach to the place awakened by her first sight of the man.

A discreet knock on the hall door sent the blood pounding in Liza's ears. Was it *him?* This was their wedding night. Had he come to exercise his marital rights? She gulped hard.

"Come in," she said, her voice barely above a whisper.

"Milady," a young woman said, curtsying as she entered, her arms full of fresh linens. "His lordship sent me to help you prepare for sleep."

Liza's breathing returned to normal. The maid was little more than a girl, with brown hair pulled into a braid and dark brown eyes that smiled shyly. She was short and thin, and her shoulders and elbows jutted out at bony angles. Liza warmed to the child instantly.

"Come in," Liza said, rising and walking toward the girl. "What's your name?"

"Nell, milady," she replied, shuffling.

Behind the child, the door to the hallway was still cracked open. It would be so easy to get past this girl and be on her way to freedom. But what then? And what would happen to Nell for being the instrument of her escape? Liza sighed. She didn't know and didn't dare risk the maid's livelihood.

Putting thoughts of escape aside for the moment, Liza smiled at the young girl. "What have you brought?"

"Some clean linens, a brush and one of his lordship's nightshirts, milady." She blushed. "Beggin' your pardon, but there's nothin' else of quality."

His nightshirt! Liza felt her cheeks redden to match Nell's. "I understand," she tried to assure the girl, only to hear her own voice go deep and husky. She cleared her throat and tried again. "Thank you for bringing the items."

Nell bobbed another curtsy and set the things on a delicately carved cherry bureau. "If it please yer ladyship, I'm to help with yer bath."

"Bath?" Just the word reminded Liza of how dirty and sweaty she was. As a governess she wasn't often allowed the luxury of a bath, and as a tavern wench she had been lucky to find a pitcher of clean water to wash her face in. "Wonderful."

Nell smiled, revealing crooked front teeth and a dimple in her left cheek. "His lordship thought as how ye'd like it."

It was a considerate gesture, though most likely prompted by his wanting a clean bride when he came to demand his marital rights. Still, the bath was a pleasure she relished.

When the brass tub was filled with steaming water and set in front of the roaring fire Nell had worked hard to start, Liza turned to the young maid. "You may go now, Nell."

The servant turned a startled, then crestfallen, face to Liza. "I've done somethin' wrong. I ain't never been a lady's maid."

Liza's heart melted. She wanted to enfold the girl in her arms and reassure her that she'd done nothing wrong, but that would only embarrass the child. It would not be fitting for a mistress and a maid to embrace.

Instead, she put a hand on Nell's scrawny shoulder. "You've done everything perfectly. It's me." She smiled in self-deprecation. "I've never had a lady's maid. It never seemed necessary when I had Nurse." Liza's eyes clouded briefly at the mention of her old nurse, dead these last three years. "So you see," she went on, "I'm not comfortable having people around me. Please give me time to get used to it."

Nell's brown eyes were as round as saucers. "No need to be beggin' *my* pardon, milady."

Liza shook her head. In trying not to embarrass the girl with affection, she'd discomfited her by stepping out of the role of mistress. It was so hard to be the proper lady when the only family she'd ever known had been the people she'd employed, except for Michael.

Retreating into briskness, Liza smiled and said, "Now that everything is settled, Nell, you may go. I'm perfectly capable of taking care of the rest. When I'm done, I'll ring to have the water taken away."

Accepting her dismissal, Nell bobbed several times on her way out. Liza couldn't help but grin at the maid's exuberance. The feeling of contentment lasted through a long, hot soak, a good hair wash, and a brisk toweling dry.

After everything for the bath was removed by Nell and another servant, Liza sank onto the carpet beside the fire, a large linen bath sheet wrapped around her. Leaning toward the warmth, she finger-combed her waist-length hair. When it was almost dry, she picked up the brush Nell had brought.

It was a beautiful object. The back was made of mahogany wood, smooth and shiny from use. The bristles were boar. Only the master of the house would have so expensive a grooming aid, she realized, the thought confirmed by the few black hairs caught in the bristles. Her arm froze as she raised the brush to her head.

Alaistair St. Simon had sent his own hairbrush to her. What an incredibly intimate gesture, as though they shared the same room, the same bed. Heat mounted in her cheeks and her eyes strayed to the bed, where his nightshirt lay folded.

Putting the brush down, she carefully tucked the bath sheet around her breasts. Even though she was the only person in the room, her sense of privacy wouldn't allow her to walk about uncovered, and she was loath to put on her dirty clothes again. Satisfied that the sheet would stay in place, she rose and went to the large four-poster.

Her fingers trembled when she picked up the fine lawn shirt, its folds falling to the floor. The fabric was as smooth as silk. She rubbed it against her cheek and breathed deeply. It smelled of him, a heady blend of musk and sandalwood.

She dropped the shirt, stepping back as though it were a snake about to strike. Her reaction to just the scent of him was too intense, too frightening. How could she feel this way about a man who had forced her into marriage? She was supposed to hate him, not to swoon over something as trivial as a piece of his clothing.

"My God," she moaned, "what kind of woman am I?"

CHAPTER SIX

APPALLED AT HER reaction, Liza turned away from the bed and ran back to the chair by the fire. She sank into its upholstered comfort, burying her face in her hands.

Never in her life had she reacted to a man this strongly. Against her better judgment, she wanted to be near him. She felt more alive, more aware when he was around.

The memory of Alaistair's smile, given to Tristan Montford, surfaced. Briefly, guiltily, Liza wished it could have been given to her. She groaned and burrowed her face deeper into her hands.

An abrupt knock followed by the opening and closing of a door penetrated her confused misery. Her head jerked up. Her hands flew to the corner of the bath linen that tucked in at her breast. Just in time. Looking up, she met her new husband's inscrutable gaze.

Alaistair St. Simon stood inside her room, his back to the closed door that separated their apartments. His ebony hair swept back from his wide forehead and high cheekbones, the frosted temples a cold glimmer in the wavering light of the candle he held. A black satin robe, embroidered with exotic silver dragons, belted at his waist and fell to his knees. He still wore the black pantaloons and Hessian boots he'd been married in.

His eyes darkened as he watched her.

Liza swallowed, one hand holding the towel securely to her, the other splayed across her chest in an effort to shield as much of her nakedness from him as possible. Warmth, not of the fire's making, tinged her skin.

Shaken by her response to his presence, she went on the offensive. "Do you always enter a lady's room without waiting for permission?"

He took several steps toward her until she could see the dark hairs swirling on the visible portion of his chest. "I do what I wish in my home," he said, his voice deep and husky.

Anxiety mixed with anger. Her eyes flashed at him. "This may be your house, but this is my room. I demand privacy."

His eyes traveled over her, lingering on the expanse of creamy bosom visible above the sheet. A smile curved his full, firm lips.

"If you'll leave," Liza began, her voice breathless, which only increased her ire, "I'll get dressed and then we can discuss whatever has brought you barging into my room."

His smile turned wolfish. "Actually," he drawled, moving closer to her, "your state of dishabille is related to what I want to discuss."

Fearful of her own reaction to his nearness, Liza rose from the chair and retreated so that it stood between them. She couldn't allow him any closer. Her breath came faster. Both hands clutched the bath sheet.

"My dishabille?" She knew what he intended. "This is a marriage of convenience, my lord. It is not a love match."

He took another step toward her. His eyes seemed to glow with some emotion she was afraid to name, for to name it would force her to acknowledge the same emotion in herself.

"True. This isn't a love match. But even—" he paused, his hands going to the belt around his waist "—a marriage of convenience has its compensations."

Liza's throat constricted. "Not what you're thinking."

She stepped back, pulling the chair with her, her hands white-knuckled on the azure chintz. In her haste to put more distance between them, she let go of the towel. It gapped low over her full breasts.

His gaze burned her flesh. Slowly, suggestively, he sauntered nearer, his eyes wandering thoroughly over her.

Liza froze. She was trapped by the passion he made no effort to disguise and by her unwitting response to it. Her breasts tingled and ached. Her knees felt as if they would give out beneath her. *How can this be?* her mind cried, even as her body readied for him.

Desperate to stop her body's betrayal, she ordered, "Don't touch me. There are no compensations in this marriage, no matter what you may think." Still he continued his steady progression toward her, his eyes black embers. "How dare you expect me to welcome you in my bed—you who are responsible for my brother's death?"

At her words, he checked himself, his hands tight fists at his sides. "Michael killed himself. He was too immature to live with the consequences of his actions."

The harsh words buffeted her. "That's not true!"

His voice was deathly calm. "He didn't kill himself?"

"Cruel," she said, her lips trembling as she fought to banish the memory of Michael lying in her arms.

Not now. Not in front of this cold, domineering man. He'd already taken her life and arranged it to suit himself; she would not let him make her cry, too. She refused to give him that power over her. Anger strengthened her. "He was only a boy. You're a man. You should have known better."

His eyes turned to obsidian. He was on her before Liza knew he had moved, knocking the chair to the floor between them.

"Damn you." He spit out the words between clenched teeth, his fingers digging into her shoulders. "What do you know of men? What do you know of *me?* Nothing. Your brother was a boy, kept that way by you."

Liza gasped, trying to twist free of him, but he held her firmly.

She met his fiery look defiantly. "Go ahead, hurt me. Your words have already done more damage than anything you can do physically."

His face contorted into a derisive mask, but his eyes were bleak. "You don't know anything about physical pain. If you did, you wouldn't blithely compare it to my words. Words that tell the truth."

"They are lies," she cried. "Michael was only twenty. You're the one who should have been more responsible."

"Because I'm a man? Because I was in charge?"

The look on his face was demonic, and for the first time since he'd entered her room, Liza felt a premonition of real danger.

At her feet, the chair still lay on its side where it had fallen when he rushed at her. She tried to hook it with one bare foot and pull it between them. He kicked it away and sent it slamming against the wall.

She gasped, her pulse pounding painfully in her ears.

"Yes," he murmured, his face close to hers. "I'm a man. I know all about pain and death and responsibility, things you're only beginning to understand."

"Let me go," she commanded in a voice barely above a whisper, hating herself for the tingles that coursed through her arms in spite of all that stood between them.

His teeth flashed in a feral grin. "When I'm ready. When I've derived some small pleasure from this farce of a marriage." He lowered his voice threateningly. "When you've done your duty."

She tried to pull away, but his arms were around her now, one hand tangled in her hair, the other pressed to the small of her back. They were like burning brands against her skin, the linen sheet fallen to her waist.

"Open your mouth," he ordered.

Liza took a deep breath, intending to scream, when his lips covered hers, slanting across them in a hungry, demanding kiss that sucked the air from her lungs. There was nothing gentle in this, only passion and hunger and anger. Yet her body swayed into his, her hips moving where he guided them until she felt his arousal hard against her belly.

Soon, she thought, her emotions a murky haze of fear and anticipation. Soon he would take her, and she knew she had neither the strength nor the will to thwart him. A sob of frustration escaped her lips as she felt all her fine principles being swept away in a flood of unwanted passion for this man.

"Damn you," he suddenly growled, pushing her away.

Liza staggered, fighting to keep her balance on legs that were too weak to hold her. With trembling fingers, she raked the hair out of her face. He stood before her, feet spread apart, breathing heavily.

"Cover up," he ordered, his voice strained, "before I finish what we've started."

Only then did Liza realize that the bath sheet had fallen to the floor, leaving her fully exposed. Humiliation overwhelmed her. She'd been so caught up in the traitorous sensations of her body that she hadn't even registered her nakedness. Grabbing the meager covering, she awkwardly wrapped it around her.

It took all her pride to meet his eyes again. "Will you please leave now?"

He laughed harshly, but when he spoke his tone was conversational. "I almost forced myself on you. And I came here only intending to discuss our situation rationally."

As the strong emotions driving him eased, the hard angles of his face relaxed. Liza recognized that the crisis had passed. "Then let's do so. I have no desire to spend any more of this horrific night with you than absolutely necessary."

He made her a mocking bow. "I don't intend to drag you into the marital bed yet, but I must have an heir. In time, I expect you to fulfill that obligation. After my son is born, you may go your own way. But not until then."

Not waiting for her reply, he left the room. The hint of his sandalwood lotion lingered in the air.

Liza's cheeks flamed. She was from the aristocracy and knew how things were done. But still, his cold words left a hollow feeling inside her, a bleak emptiness, and no hope of ever having it filled with warmth and love. At least not by Alaistair St. Simon.

LIZA WOKE with a start. Sunlight streamed in dazzling rays over the bedspread, making it impossible for her to see clearly. Someone was moving in the room. She must have overslept and the other tavern woman was already up and about.

"Milady?" a soft voice asked.

Liza squinted, wondering who would be addressing her in such terms. Then memory returned with a jolt. The voice belonged to Nell, her new maid.

Sitting up, Liza rubbed her eyes and flipped the heavy copper braid over her shoulder. She was in the room set aside for Lord Alaistair St. Simon's bride. The same room he'd come to last night. The room in which he'd nearly made love to her.

Her cheeks turned crimson and she squeezed her eyes shut, trying to erase the image of the two of them by the fire. His arms...his hands...they'd been everywhere, and her body had come to life at his touch, aching for more.

Liza groaned and fell back onto the thick feather pillows. What would it be like when he made love to her completely? She groaned again and pulled the covers up to her chin.

"Milady?" Nell cast an anxious look at her. "Be you sick?"

Liza peeked over the top of the spread at her maid. Nell was as frail-looking as she'd been last night, but a soft light now shone in the girl's brown eyes. At least one good thing had come of her marrying Lord Alaistair. Nell would get the chance to be a lady's maid, which was a desirable position for a woman in service.

Nell's anxiety drew Liza from her disturbing thoughts. Sighing, she sat up once more, the covers falling to her waist. "No, Nell. I'm merely tired. I didn't sleep well." For fear of Lord Alaistair returning and finishing what he'd started, she added silently.

Nell gave her a knowing glance, her gaze traveling from Liza's flushed face to her chemise. Her brown eyes widened.

Liza looked down to see what had startled her maid. The heat from the memory of Lord Alaistair's kisses turned to the heat of chagrin, and Liza yanked the bedspread back up to her chin. In her anger at her husband and her confusion at her reaction to him, she'd kicked his nightshirt under the bed and donned her old, mended chemise. Nell, expecting luxury on her mistress, had seen poverty.

The young maid took several shuffling steps back. "I...I...beggin' yer pardon. I..." Her complexion, sallow from being indoors all day, reddened.

It was too much for Liza. What was she coming to, that being poorly dressed shamed her? This forced marriage was addling more than her body. It was affecting her character.

Carefully, she lowered the spread and got out of bed. "Don't be upset by my clothing, Nell. I've been many months living hand to mouth. Your master has remedied my plight by marrying me." There was no reason to disparage Lord Alaistair to his servant by implying that he'd done less than was proper.

"Corblimey." Nell spoke with hushed wonder. "His lordship married you for love." Her eyes sparkled and her mouth was a round O. "I heard Simpson sayin' the master had made a marriage of convenience and that his lordship was angry about it, seein' that he wanted to marry for love an' all…" Realizing what she'd just said, she turned beet-red. "Beggin' yer pardon. That is—"

Liza took pity on the child. "Don't worry, Nell. It's all right to speak your mind to me."

Still remorseful, Nell stuffed her knuckles in her mouth. "I'm ever so sorry. I weren't gossipin'. Jest that Simpson and Rast were talkin' and I couldn't help but hear. I niver meant to tell. Only… only if his lordship married for convenience, you'd be rich and all that."

The girl's discomfort was so pronounced Liza didn't have the heart to disabuse her of the fairy tale. The truth would come soon enough when word flew through the servants' quarters that she and Lord Alaistair had not spent the night together.

"Come help me unbraid my hair," Liza said to change the subject. "It's so long that without help it'll take all morning for me to brush it." That wasn't exactly true—under different circumstances she would have left it in the braid.

Nell worked with alacrity. When she had finished, the maid said, "Milady, Lord Alaistair had your things fetched."

She hurried away to the door and brought back Liza's old portmanteau. Liza just stared, trying to absorb the fact that her new husband had been considerate enough to do this. Grudgingly, she also had to concede that it was not the first thoughtful thing he'd done for her.

Nell was all smiles as she began rummaging in the bag. The smile slipped slightly when all she found was another tatty black bombazine gown, a threadbare chemise, a nightdress and a comb and brush.

"I'll have these pressed," Nell said, surfacing with the clothes in hand.

"That's fine, Nell." Liza smiled at the girl. "I'll wear what I had on yesterday."

Nell was buttoning her mistress into the same black bombazine dress Liza had been married in when a knock sounded on the door to the master's room.

Liza jerked upright, pulling the material from Nell's fingers so that the button ripped off. The tear was loud in Liza's ears as she watched her husband pause in the doorway, his cold eyes assessing the situation.

"You may go, Nell," he said, his broad shoulders leaning easily against the jamb.

Liza fiddled with the back of her dress in a vain effort to close the gap left by the torn button. Distantly, she heard the closing of a door and realized Nell was gone.

"What do you want?" she managed to utter through stiff lips.

He pushed away from the wall and sauntered toward her. She took a step back, wondering if they were going to reenact the scene from last night. She straightened her spine and stood her ground.

"Turn around," he said, halting a foot from her.

She stared defiantly at him, feeling the heat radiating from his body. "No."

His mouth curved sardonically. "I said turn around. I want to see how badly your gown is ripped."

Warmth flooded her cheeks. "It doesn't matter. If you'll leave, I'll mend it."

His brows drew together. "No, you won't. You're my wife now and I don't intend to see you dressed in rags beyond this morning. We are going to visit a modiste."

Liza gaped at him. "I'm not a charity case and I didn't ask to be your wife."

"True." He reached for her, but she sidestepped him. His frown intensified. "We've been invited to my parents' for dinner tonight. I won't have you looking like the charity case you deny being."

Liza flared at the insult, then realized what he had just told her. "I have no wish to dine with your parents. There's no reason for me to meet them. I'm not going to stay married to you that long."

She watched as Alaistair lounged into the blue chintz chair, his feet propped on the delicate Queen Anne table. The man's disregard for fine furniture was appalling.

"How do you propose to become 'unmarried'?" he drawled.

His eyes were half-closed, his chin resting on one raised fist. He might be reclining in the chair, but an aura of taut, controlled anticipation emanated from him. His shoulders were tense under the loose fit of his navy jacket, his thighs sinewy beneath impeccably fitted buckskins. Liza distrusted his seeming nonchalance, but neither did she intend to submit to him.

Lifting her chin, she moved far enough away that he wouldn't be able to reach her in one lunge. "I haven't decided yet, but there must be a way. I intend to find it."

He smiled, a cold flexing of his lips. "Then I must endeavor to prevent you, and I know of only one way to do that."

She panicked, knowing instantly what he referred to. He would finish what he'd started last night. "You're a libertine."

The fist he'd rested his chin on dropped to his side, and he spread his fingers casually across his muscled thigh. His eyes never left her face. "I'm a man—or have you already forgotten."

"No." How could she forget when her pulse quickened at the mere memory of his mouth on hers?

"And I have a responsibility to my name and to you."

The quietly spoken words hung between them. They were both a promise and a threat. Liza began to think it would be easier to accommodate him. For now.

Taking a deep breath to ease the constriction of her throat, she inched closer to the window and away from him and the large four-poster bed. "Since you put it that way, Lord Alaistair, I believe I do need several gowns."

"You may call me Alaistair," he said, rising and going to the door leading to his room. "And you need more than several. You need a complete wardrobe."

"No, I don't," she challenged, but he had already shut the door behind him.

Fifteen minutes later she still felt a simmering resentment but contained herself as she allowed her husband to wrap her ragged cape about her shoulders before departing for the modiste's.

Silently, he helped her into the carriage, the same one she'd traveled in last night. She cast a surreptitious glance at the spot where the leather strap had once hung. Sweat coated her palms in spite of the cold October air.

Settling herself as far from him as the interior of the coach allowed, Liza cleared her throat. "Thank you for having my things fetched from the tavern."

He turned a cool gaze on her. "Not at all."

"You needn't have," she continued, though she knew he would prefer her to be silent.

Instead of answering, he tipped his beaver over his eyes and slouched down into the gray velvet squabs. Only by gritting her teeth was she able to silence the words of outrage that danced on her tongue at his cavalier treatment. She wouldn't give him a second opportunity to snub her by continuing with her thanks. His acts of kindness must have been an aberration in his character, she concluded.

They made the rest of the journey to Bond Street in absolute silence. Liza cast covert looks at him, but he seemed perfectly relaxed, his body swaying lithely with each turn and jolt of the carriage.

It wasn't until they drew to a complete stop that he stirred. Then, like one of the great cats on display in the Tower of London, he sat up and stretched so that the muscles of his shoulders and legs flexed and rippled. An unwilling pleasure at the sight of such masculine grace suffused Liza, and she tore her gaze from him to stare out the window.

She caught a glimpse of a tall, well-endowed woman entering the shop. The satin-trimmed straw hat she wore was accented by several Pomona green ostrich feathers that exactly matched the color of her pelisse. Liza knew that if such a person frequented this modiste, the clothes would be expensive. She didn't want to owe her husband any more than was absolutely necessary.

"Lord Alaistair," Liza said, hanging back as he reached in the carriage for her hand, "perhaps we should go somewhere else for my clothing."

Seizing her hand, he dragged her unceremoniously out of the carriage. "I think not," he said.

Liza glanced around in desperation. Throngs of fashionable persons filled the street, strolling and pausing in front of shop windows to admire the wares. If she fought with him, she would only cause a scene, something she didn't want to do. She would have to ensure that he bought her only the absolute necessities. Straightening her shoulders proudly, she preceded him into the establishment.

Not more than ten feet inside they were approached by the same woman Liza had seen entering the shop, her gloved hands extended to Lord Alaistair. A radiant smile blossomed on her full, red lips, its sincerity belied only by the hard gleam in her green eyes.

"Saint," the woman gushed, taking his one hand in both of hers and clasping it to her ample bosom. "What brings you here?"

The woman acted as though Liza were nothing more than a servant. It was obvious by the way she cradled his hand so that his long, well-shaped fingers curved over the swell of her muslin-covered breasts that she was his mistress. Jealousy rose unbidden in Liza, even as she firmly admonished herself for the sensation. It was none of her business with whom Lord Alaistair chose to dally.

He freed his hand, too late for Liza's liking, but again, it was none of her affair. "Marie," he murmured. A wicked gleam entered his eyes. He glanced at Liza. "My dear," he said, taking her arm and tugging her closer. "I'd like you to meet Marie Hardcastle. Marie, this is my wife, Lizabeth, Lady Stone."

Feeling like a trapped animal, Liza nodded, her mouth frozen in a smile. "Pleased to meet you."

Marie Hardcastle turned eyes like chipped emeralds on Liza. "How interesting, I'm sure."

Liza blinked in surprise at the woman's cruelty. She had disliked Marie Hardcastle on sight, but she'd expected her to make the best of the awful situation Alaistair St. Simon was creating, just as she was trying to do.

Before fireworks could erupt, the modiste bustled up to them. "*Merci,* Madame Hardcastle. Your ball gown is ready." Clapping her black-gloved hands imperiously, she summoned a young woman. "Louisa, fetch Madame Hardcastle's gown." She motioned Marie to a chair before turning back to Lord Alaistair. "Milord, how may I be of service?"

Her dark Gallic eyes strayed only once in Liza's direction, assessing her worn attire, and she pursed her mouth as though tasting a lemon.

"Madame Celeste," he said, "I've come to place my wife in your capable hands. She requires a complete wardrobe."

The modiste's eyes lit up. *"Mon Dieu."* Her shrewd gaze darted back to Liza. "Milady, please turn around."

Liza, anger tightening her stomach, glared at Lord Alaistair. He frowned back at her, which she took to mean that she was to do as directed. Holding herself stiffly, she managed to turn without falling, all the while horribly aware of Marie Hardcastle's appraising gaze.

"Magnifique," Madame murmured. She addressed her words to Lord Alaistair, as though Liza was nothing more than a mannequin. "She is very tall. An amazon. But she has good bones and a figure many a young miss would envy—big-bosomed, and small-waisted." This time she circled around Liza, her eyes taking in every curve. "With her auburn hair and turquoise eyes, she will create a sensation." She cast a knowing look at Lord Alaistair, her head bobbing like a hen pecking at the ground. "And black is a very good color for her, too. It gives her skin the look of the finest magnolia."

"She's in mourning," Alaistair explained, "but may go into half mourning."

"Non, non," Madame said, continuing her inspection. "Black should be her signature. I can envision it all. She will become a darling of the ton. Everyone will try to imitate her." Her mouth turned up and she gave a shrug. "Very few ladies wear black well."

Liza couldn't believe it. They were discussing her as though she had no feelings. "I've had enough," she said, stepping away from Madame Celeste and toward the door.

Without seeming to hurry, Alaistair blocked her exit. "I think not, my dear. I begin to share Madame's enthusiasm."

Liza scowled at him. Under her breath, she said, "I agreed to several gowns. That was all. This woman—" she gestured in Madame's general direction "—is talking about a complete wardrobe, one fit for a Season. I didn't agree to that."

"I think you did," he said quietly.

"I did not," Liza reiterated. He was not going to coerce her into this. "All I need is one evening gown for dinner with your parents. Surely Madame Celeste has something already made that you may purchase and then we can be gone. The rest of the articles can be got at the Burlington Arcade."

He took her arm firmly, and Liza knew better than to try to jerk it away. Lord Alaistair might be called Saint, but he was the devil himself when his mind was set on something.

"No, Liza. You shall go with Madame and she shall take your measurements."

Liza tried to stare him down but in the end gave it up when a dowager and her pimple-faced daughter entered the store. She was in no mood to provide more grist for the ton's rumor mill. As it was, she knew Marie Hardcastle would not hesitate to spread this little tidbit about Town.

With a groan of frustration, she allowed the modiste to shepherd her into a back room. She vowed to herself she would be gone from Alaistair St. Simon's house long before the wardrobe was completed.

CHAPTER SEVEN

USING A KNIFE she'd slipped into her sleeve during breakfast, Liza ripped at the seam of her second black bombazine gown, the one Lord Alaistair had retrieved from the tavern. She fingered the material. The money was gone. The fivepence she'd sewn into the waist of her dress was gone.

Not much money, not enough to buy even the silk stockings she had on, but it had been hers, earned by serving at the tavern. She had hoped to add to it, little by little, until she had enough to escape.

Defeated, she slumped onto the floor, the torn fabric crumpled in her fists. The money in itself was not a great loss, but she felt as if one more door had been slammed in her face and she would never be freed from the gilded captivity of this farcical marriage to a man she despised.

"Can things get any worse?" she whispered into the bunched folds of the shabby dress.

The sound of footsteps, muffled by thick carpet, made her jump up, the wrinkled gown forgotten. In one short day and one interminably long night, she'd learned to recognize those footfalls. Her husband was in his own room, preparing to come into hers.

With her foot, she shoved the black bombazine under a chair; with her hands, she smoothed down the skirt of her evening gown, then fiddled with the bodice.

"The line is perfect without your meddling with it," Alaistair's deep voice said.

Liza's head jerked up. "'Tis none of your affair," she said, breathless with irritation, or so she told herself.

Even knowing he was coming, she hadn't heard the door open. He could enter her room at night and she wouldn't realize it until he was upon her. Shivers danced over her skin.

"Oh, but it is," he drawled, closing in on her. "I paid for it. Or have you forgotten?"

"Must you remind me?" She returned his scrutiny with pointed deliberation.

He was magnificent—as usual. Dressed all in black except for a white shirt and silver waistcoat, he appeared somber and brooding. His smile was laconic, as though he mocked not just her but himself, as well.

The scent of sandalwood wafted to her nostrils, making them flare. It was a scent she would never forget, no matter how long she lived.

He shrugged. "No. I've better things to do with my time. But after our contretemps this morning, it amused me to remind you." Liza opened her mouth to berate him, but he forestalled her. "I have something for you that will complement your gown."

It was a long, narrow blue velvet box. She eyed it with misgiving.

"Jewelry? I don't need any."

His fingers tightened on the box. "Then you haven't looked in the glass."

His clipped words brought the blood rushing to Liza's cheeks. "I'm not interested in how I look. I'm in mourning."

He laughed, a mirthless sound. "You're in a purgatory of your own creation. And God help me, I know what that's like."

She narrowed her eyes, not sure she'd heard him correctly. "You know about purgatory? The rich younger son of the most powerful duke in Britain? I doubt it."

His knuckles whitened and his mouth thinned. "Enough. Put these on."

Liza's resolve hardened, but the look in his eyes made her wary. He was like a stallion that has been driven too hard. Slowly she reached for the box. Inside was a triple strand of black pearls, held by a cluster of diamonds that circled another black pearl the size of a shilling. Nestled beside the necklace were matching diamond-and-pearl drops for her ears.

"They're beautiful." The words slipped out at the sheer magnificence of the jewels.

Alaistair watched her eyes widen. The dress she wore had been meant for another lady but he'd bullied Madame Celeste into adjusting it to fit Liza. The black silk of the gown accentuated her full, high bosom before falling in graceful waves to the floor. Yes, Madame Celeste was right; black was a very good color for his new wife.

"They were my mother's," he explained, "given to her by *her* mother. She gave them to me for my bride."

Regret turned the edges of her mouth down. "They're too valuable for me to borrow them." She closed the lid and handed the box back to him. "But thank you."

He couldn't believe he'd heard her correctly. They were the most perfect set of black pearls in existence, famous throughout Britain and the Continent. Marie Hardcastle had repeatedly told him she'd give her soul for those pearls.

"Put them on," he said again, more harshly than he'd intended.

She shook her head.

"Bloody hell." He growled the oath between clenched teeth. "You're the most stubborn female it could have been my misfortune to wed." Flicking the lid of the box open again, he took the choker out.

"What are you doing?" she asked, worry creasing her forehead.

Setting the box down, he took a step closer so that scant inches separated them. Slowly, enunciating every word, he said, "Either you turn around so that I can clasp these around your neck, or I'll call my valet and have him hold you while I put them on you anyway. The choice is yours."

Her mouth turned white around the edges and her eyes flashed anger. With a haughty toss of her head, she said, "You give me no choice. As usual, you have arranged things so that you get exactly what you want, like a spoiled child."

Alaistair smiled in spite of himself. The creature did not lack spunk. "You sound like my old nurse. Now turn around."

With ill grace she did as she was ordered, the faint scent of rose water wafting to his flared nostrils. Alaistair's smile widened, but was instantly wiped away as his fingers grazed the soft flesh of her neck. Her skin was smooth and faintly cool, and downy auburn hairs, so pale they were merely bronze glints in the candlelight, rose to meet his fingertips. The urge to undo the heavy chignon nearly over-whelmed him. He remembered how her hair had hung down her back last night, a fiery curtain that turned to liquid velvet in his hands.

Desire engulfed him, exploding in his loins. Pic-tures of her last night, naked except for the brilliant glory of her hair, taunted him. Her breasts had been full and tight with the arousal she denied. The tri-angle of red hair at the apex of her thighs had glowed hotly in the firelight.

He closed his eyes, trying to shut out the vision. Holding firmly to his self-control, he attempted to fasten the catch. Suddenly his fingers seemed to be all thumbs.

He took a deep breath and succeeded in closing the clasp. Stepping away, he took the eardrops out of the case and said huskily, "Here. Put these on yourself."

She turned to face him once more, her cheeks a deep coral. He noticed that her fingers trembled ever so slightly when she took the jewels from him, and it took her several attempts to put them on.

Her eyes shied away from his and he knew why.
She was reluctant to acknowledge the passion that
would be reflected in their gray depths—the same
passion he had fleetingly glimpsed in her own eyes.

"My parents will be wondering where we are," he
said, turning abruptly and striding to the door that
separated their rooms. "I'll expect you in the foyer
in five minutes."

The door slammed behind him and Liza felt as
though she'd just been rudely awakened from a disturbing dream, one she wanted to continue but knew
she shouldn't. She shook her head to clear it.
Somehow, she had to escape this marriage and the
very real danger of coming to care for the man responsible for Michael's death.

A WILLFUL, HANDSOME bunch, Liza decided an
hour later as Lord Alaistair finished his introduc-
tions. That was how she would describe the male
members in the Duke of Rundell's family.

The duke himself was a tall, slim, elegant man,
with blond hair, frosted with gray, swept back from
a high forehead and deep-set brown eyes. Jonathan, Marquis of Langston and heir apparent, was
the duke's duplicate. Even his voice was a replica of
his father's.

The youngest brother, Lord Deverell, was a paler
copy of father and heir, with sandy hair and hazel

eyes. But unlike the other two, who were languid
dandies, he had the bearing of a military man. He
reminded Liza of Lord Alaistair, even though their
features were completely dissimilar.

"Liza—" Alaistair's voice intruded on her mental meanderings. "I'd like you to meet my mother."

Only then did Liza realize that she hadn't been
introduced to his mother. The men of the family
were so overpowering she hadn't noticed the duchess's absence. She turned to greet Alaistair's mother.

Alicia, Duchess of Rundell, was startlingly beautiful. She was also the parent Lord Alaistair favored. Her black hair, still without a strand of gray,
was cropped fashionably short in the front and piled
high on her head in the back. She wore a gossamer-
thin silver overdress that hinted of the fine white
muslin beneath. Her irises were a light gray ringed
in black, and ebony lashes, so thick they seemed to
weigh down her lids, rimmed her eyes like a priceless frame.

"Liza, I'm so glad to meet you," the duchess said
in a pleasant alto.

"Thank you." Liza dipped a curtsy, bemused by
this woman who was so unnervingly like Alaistair.
Was she like him mentally and emotionally, as well?
Seeing the warm glow on her face and the softness
of her lips, she doubted it.

They moved together into the huge dining room. A starkly simple Hepplewhite mahogany table reposed in the center, leaving enough room for the twenty-four chairs around it. Silver plates, bowls, tureens and platters, all with the duke's coat of arms, were spread across two sideboards. A pair of crystal chandeliers illuminated the room. Liza felt like a pauper given a glimpse of a palace.

She looked up to see Lord Alaistair watching her, his eyes dark and inscrutable. She gave him a tight smile.

"I say," Lord Deverell said with a grin, "we aren't a pretentious bunch. It's just the house. Hard to live normally in a mausoleum."

He was so jovial that Liza couldn't help but smile back.

The Marquis of Langston prevented her having to answer. "You should have Alaistair take you on a tour after dinner. The portrait gallery runs the length of the house and can be of particular interest if viewed without extraneous people." He winked at Alaistair, an action that only increased Liza's discomfort.

"Boys," the duchess intervened, "this is Liza's first visit. Don't make her wish it to be her last."

Lord Deverell's grin remained unrepentant as he pulled out Liza's seat and whispered in her ear,

"Had I seen you first, Alaistair would be your brother-in-law."

Liza turned pink. Never in all her twenty-six years had she received such blatant admiration.

"Deverell," Alaistair drawled, his eyes at half-mast as he watched his brother and his wife, "leave Liza alone. She's not accustomed to your sort of flirtation."

Deverell gave Liza a roguish wink as he took his seat on her left. "Then no doubt you've been remiss in your attentions, big brother."

And so the dinner went, the brothers needling one another and the parents interjecting where necessary.

For Liza it was a mixed pleasure. Part of her enjoyed the teasing interaction of family members. All her life she'd longed for parents. But another part of her found it stressful. Lord Deverell's high spirits were at times reminiscent of Michael's, a comparison that brought painful memories.

"Liza," the duchess said, interrupting her troubled thoughts, "please join me in the drawing room. The boys will be quite a while with their port, I'm sure. They always are when the four of them get together."

"Now, my dear," the duke remonstrated, "you wrong us. You know there's nothing more we desire than to spend time in your company. And with Alaistair's beautiful young wife here, I'm confident he'll be just as eager to make this short.''

The duchess gave an unladylike snort as she rose and motioned for the butler to bring on the port. "We shall see," she said, a smile softening the words as she left the room.

Liza followed, wondering what she would say to the beautiful woman whose son had forced her into this marriage.

Seated on one of the numerous Hepplewhite chairs placed around the drawing room, Liza folded her hands in her lap. "Your Grace must keep very busy managing a home of these proportions."

The duchess smiled. "Please call me Mother—we are related now. Or Alicia, if you find it more comfortable. And yes, it took me a long time to adjust to this." She chuckled, her voice like the clear melodic ring of fine crystal. "I wasn't born to this opulence."

"You weren't?" Liza asked, fingering one of the black pearl eardrops.

The silver of the duchess's overdress shimmered in the candlelight as she shifted to a more comfortable position on the high-backed settee. Her black hair and creamy white skin made a striking contrast to the red satin upholstery.

"Oh, no. Don't misunderstand me. We were wealthy, but—" she waved a hand "—never like this. My father worked for the East India Company. The pearls you're wearing were a gift to him from a maharaja. I gave them to Alaistair in place of the Rundell family jewels, which will go to Jonathan. Deverell got emeralds for his future bride, another gift to my father."

"I see," Liza murmured, wondering where the conversation would turn now. Jewelry was a very limited topic in her opinion.

The duchess chuckled again. "But you don't, child. You don't have the vaguest idea of why I encouraged Rundell to keep the boys for port, a habit he doesn't normally indulge in when it's just family for dinner."

Apprehension tightened Liza's neck muscles. Here it came. Alaistair's mother was going to bring up Michael and the reason for this marriage, a topic she wasn't ready to discuss with anyone. "Your Grace—that is, Alicia..." She smiled apologetically. "I...Mother doesn't come easily. Mine died when I was eight."

Alicia jumped to her feet, concern pulling her dark brows together, and dragged a chair close to Liza's. Sitting down, she reached for Liza's hand. "Why, child, your hand is like ice. I'm sorry for bringing up sad memories. And don't bother about what to call me. Alicia is fine."

Her mother-in-law's warmth flowed over Liza, penetrating to the place in her heart where she had walled up the sorrow of losing her parents so long ago. It even managed to ease some of the ache caused by Michael's death. For a fleeting moment, she wished she could remain married to Lord Alaistair for his mother's sake alone.

"Alicia," she said, savoring the word and the emotional closeness it represented, "thank you. But that's an old hurt. To be honest, I was afraid you meant to speak of my brother."

The duchess patted Liza's hand. "No, child. I'm sorry it happened. Dreadfully. And yet it brought you and Alaistair together. I admit we were rather shocked at the unexpectedness of your marriage, though that is totally in keeping with my son's nature. But I can't be a hypocrite and deny my happiness over it. So perhaps something good will come of your brother's tragic demise." She paused and her eyes took on a pensive, faraway look. "I pray it will."

Liza longed to reassure this kind woman who had taken her in with open arms, but she couldn't do it. She had no hope for her marriage and wouldn't lie about it. The best she could do was remain silent.

The duchess drew herself up and smiled. Still holding Liza's hand, she said briskly, "And that's why I wanted to talk to you alone, and before your marriage to Alaistair has a chance to settle into a pattern. He's very much like his father, and I don't want the two of you to go through what we did."

Guilt stabbed at Liza. If she had any decency at all she would tell this woman there was no chance of the marriage settling into a rut. It wouldn't last that long.

"You see," Alicia said softly, forcing Liza to lean forward to hear, "my marriage hasn't always been happy. Rundell married me for money."

Liza sat back in surprise. "He needed money? He's the most powerful duke in England."

"Yes, and it takes plenty of blunt." She grinned. "Forgive me for using the word, but the boys do and it just seems so appropriate in this instance. For Rundell needed a fresh infusion. Oh, not that he wasn't wealthy then, but it never hurts to add more. And I was quite an heiress, the richest of the lot for the three Seasons I was out. Not that I had entrée everywhere, since Papa was in trade and untitled, but wealth opens a lot of doors."

Liza nodded in sympathetic understanding. "But not Almack's," she said, referring to the exclusive assembly rooms on King Street.

"No," Alicia agreed, smiling ruefully, "not Almack's. Although I'm not sure if that wasn't in my favor. You see, Rundell wanted a complaisant wife who'd be grateful for the favor of his name and title and demand nothing else."

"A marriage of convenience," Liza said quietly.

"Just so," the duchess said, unconsciously mimicking her middle son. "Rundell is a very handsome man. I was young, with stars in my eyes. I married for love ... and foolishly thought he had, too."

Compassion engulfed Liza for this woman who so bravely confessed her folly.

The duchess took a deep breath, her eyes solemn. "Rundell never professed love, you understand, it was just me. I quickly found out the way of our world. After I produced Jonathan, Rundell informed me that my duty was done, and if I were so inclined, I might take a cicisbeo. At first I didn't believe him. But a friend soon told me about Rundell's mistress, the one he'd been keeping since our marriage."

"The cad," Liza said, disliking her father-in-law and seeing where Lord Alaistair's personality came from.

The duchess patted Liza's hand. "It does sound awful. I try not to think of it often because it's no longer true. My only rival now is politics, and I can handle that very well by staying informed myself. Rundell turns to me for advice, not to another man, which is very unusual, I can tell you.''

"His Grace is a very...interesting man."

"And understanding."

"I don't think so," Liza said. "He sounds as if he expected his marriage to be for *his* convenience."

"It's the way of our world," Alicia replied gently.

"I know that," Liza said, her eyes flashing indignation, "but it hardly seems fair."

The duchess smiled. "I'm glad to hear you say so, because I feel such a marriage never brings true happiness. It didn't for me and it hasn't for any of my friends. No, only a love match can do that. Love is what makes people work to please each other and to stay together when things are hard." She paused to search Liza's face. She must have seen something that reassured her because she nodded slightly and continued. "And a marriage of love can evolve from one of convenience. I know, because mine has."

Liza sensed what was coming. Freeing her hands from the duchess's, she rose and paced to the fireplace to stare into the empty grate for a long moment. Resolution squared her shoulders as she turned back to the older woman.

"Your Grace, I don't think I'm what you believe me to be. Lord Alaistair and I have a marriage of convenience, and it can never be anything else. We don't love each other and neither one of us wants to try."

The duchess stood, her movements as graceful as her son's.

"Child," she said, "I know why Alaistair married you. I only wanted to tell you my story and hope that you will learn from it."

She stopped several feet from Liza and took down a Dresden shepherdess from the mantel. It was a dainty piece of work, but it was obvious that the figurine had been broken then glued back together, an oddity in a household that had the means to buy the whole factory. Alicia held it out to Liza, who took it gingerly, wondering what was coming next.

"Rundell broke that with his bare hands after Alaistair delivered me from my aborted attempt to run away with another man."

The soft words reverberated through Liza's head like an echo. "Another man?"

Alicia chuckled. "Yes. I keep the shepherdess to remind me that he cares even when he's engrossed in his politics or gone to sit in the House of Lords for days on end. I was miserable for many years, so tired of the masquerade of our marriage, living together with no real affection, that I looked around for someone to love me. And I found him.'' Her eyes took on a faraway look. ''That was five years ago, so it's not even a very old scandal.''

Liza's heartbeat quickened. Alaistair had married a woman with a scandal in her past, although Michael's suicide was nothing compared to what Alicia, Duchess of Rundell, had done. A woman of the ton might have lovers, but she *never* left her husband for one of them.

The duchess reached out her hand for the shepherdess, which Liza returned. Carefully Alicia returned it to the mantel.

''Alaistair was the one who caught us. He beat my lover with a horsewhip and left him for dead in the road.'' Her eyes glistened as though the memory were still painful. ''Nothing I did or said could make Alaistair go back to ensure he didn't die.'' Her lower lip trembled ever so slightly. ''He lived, for which I'm eternally grateful. And the incident so shocked Rundell that he talked to me about our marriage for the first time in twenty-seven years. Both of us determined to try and make it work. And we have. Love can grow when two people decide to work on it.''

Liza wanted to tell the duchess that she'd wasted her time in telling her the story, yet the tale tugged at her emotions. In spite of the errors of both people involved, a sad situation had been made better. It was a story of hope.

"Have you bored Liza to tears, Mother?" Alaistair inquired, preventing Liza from having to respond to the duchess.

Both doors to the drawing room were open and he stood between them, flanked by his two brothers, a dark figure between two fairer ones. He had the look of a fallen angel, and the sight of him casually teasing his mother, a slight smile parting his sensuous lips, created a longing within her that she preferred not to acknowledge.

Behind the three men, the Duke of Rundell raised his white brows in mock horror as he took in the picture of his wife and daughter-in-law beside the fireplace. His gaze shifted to the Dresden shepherdess and back to the women, lingering on his wife with a warmth that brought color to Liza's cheeks. It was obvious to her that the years had not doused the physical desire that flared between the two.

"I say," Lord Deverell said, advancing to Liza and taking her hand in a well-executed maneuver. Lifting it to his lips, he murmured wickedly, "Promise that when you tire of Saint, you'll come to me."

The blush that stained Liza's cheeks quickly drained away. His words were like a premonition of all the duchess had been trying to prevent. Nervously, Liza laughed, the sound catching in her throat and coming out as a cough.

"You clod," the marquis said, shoving his brother out of the way and offering her his handkerchief. "Pay him no mind. The fairies left out brains when they gifted him."

Taking the handkerchief, Liza used it to wipe her eyes. "I'm sure it was only a joke. My brother..." Her voice trailed off as the familiar ache spread through her chest. "My brother would say such outrageous things all the time."

Alaistair stepped between her and his brothers. "I think my bride has had enough of all of you for one night." He softened the words with a grin. "So, if you'll excuse us, we'll be on our way."

Caught unawares, but grateful to escape this unpredictable family, Liza made her goodbyes as quickly and graciously as possible.

"Liza," the duchess said, kissing her lightly on both cheeks, "please come again soon."

Liza returned the older woman's smile warmly. His mother's kindness and genuine affection would make it hard for her to leave Lord Alaistair. She had no wish to bring the scandal of an annulment or a runaway wife into the duchess's life.

But marriage to Alaistair was untenable, Liza told herself, watching him out of the corner of her eye as their coach made its way home. Even though he sat on the opposite seat, she felt as though she were suffocating from his nearness. Masculinity emanated from him in waves of heated desire that twisted her stomach.

And he wasn't even looking at her!

No, she decided, turning her attention to the smoking gaslights outside the carriage window, she must find a way to leave Alaistair St. Simon.

LATE THAT NIGHT, Liza woke with a start. She had been having the same nightmare, reliving the awful moment when she found Michael. And for the hundredth time, she was in Alaistair's arms, his warmth easing the chills that racked her. Pushing up on her elbows, she wiped the perspiration from her brow.

Squinting in the faint moonlight that came through an opening in the curtains like a silver sword, she saw by the clock that it was just past three. She'd been asleep only a couple of hours. Usually, she slept through the night and remembered the dream upon waking. What had disturbed her this time?

She threw back the covers and pulled on her robe and slippers to ward off the cold. Walking to the window, intending to look outside, she heard a sound. It was a muffled thud, as though someone or something had fallen against the floor. She couldn't tell exactly, but it seemed to come from Alaistair's room.

Drawing nearer to the adjoining wall, she heard the noise again. It did come from his room. Was he in trouble? Should she go to him? Her fingers gripped the door handle when she heard voices. Alaistair's and another man's. She couldn't understand what they were saying, but it kept her from turning the knob. Her hand dropped to her side.

Soon quiet reigned in the other room.

Puzzled, but unwilling to explore further when it meant entering her husband's bedchamber in the dead of night, Liza drew her robe tightly about her and went back to bed. She crawled in and pulled the covers to her chin.

Then it dawned on her. What a goose she was. Obviously Alaistair had gone out again after they'd returned home and was just now coming back—foxed. That explained the muffled thuds. It was Alaistair stumbling or falling.

The realization eased the knot in her stomach that she hadn't even known was there, and sleep began

to reclaim her. She needed all the rest she could get
to match wits with her husband. Tomorrow was another day in this marriage she was determined to
end.

CHAPTER EIGHT

LIZA HELD HER shoulders erect, trying to ignore the stares directed her way. A large portion of the Covent Garden Theatre's patrons might be Quality, but their manners were appalling. It was particularly difficult when one gentleman not ten feet away lifted his quizzing glass to peer at her. The distortion of the lens made his eye seem to bulge out, giving him the appearance of a lopsided Cyclops, and it was all Liza could do not to laugh. She felt some of her tension ease and was thankful Alaistair didn't sport that particular male fashion accessory.

Leaning over so that his breath wafted warmly against Liza's bare neck and shoulder, Alaistair whispered, "I can see Brauhm is enamored of you. He thinks he's a tulip of fashion and all the ladies are dying to meet him."

Liza's eyebrows rose. "He's nearly as bad as the ballet."

"There's Tris," Alaistair said, rising and waving to his friend. "He's with Deverell. Excuse me while I go talk to them."

Without waiting for her release, he left their box. Liza watched him make his way to his friends. Even in this bright, giddy crowd of the ton he stood out. Black became him as well as Madame Celeste said it did her. Perhaps better. It accentuated his midnight hair and the silver streaks that lent him distinction.

Several women rose from their seats and called out his name, waving their fans flirtatiously and smiling vacuously with their rouged lips. Liza felt a small prick of annoyance. She might not want Alaistair, but she didn't want to see other women falling all over him, either.

In the last week, she had started to learn just how prominent Alaistair was in Society. Cards arrived by the hour inviting him to functions, and this was only the Little Season, while Parliament was in session during the fall. Recently, her name had been included as word of their hasty marriage circulated.

This was their first public appearance and all eyes were on them, as though everyone were trying to see how Alaistair truly felt about her. So far, he'd been coolly responsive to her needs, not loverlike, but attentive.

She sat up straighter as a well-endowed, languidly moving woman stepped in front of Alaistair. The light from the chandeliers was reflected in the woman's rich chestnut hair and highlighted the low décolletage of her green gown. It was Marie Hardcastle.

"Ah, Lady Alaistair," came a low-pitched, familiar voice behind her. "Do you mind if I join you?"

Before she could say no to the Earl of Bent, he was in the box and sitting down in the seat Alaistair had vacated. Liza's hand dropped to her lap, where it formed a fist, the nails digging into her palm. She forced her muscles to relax. Bent could no longer harm her.

She met his amused look coldly. "It would please me greatly if you left," she said, not caring how rude she was to this libertine.

He leered at her, his cheeks flushed from imbibing too much punch. "Why, Lady Alaistair, I do believe we've met before." His eyes wandered lower to the deeply cut bosom of her evening gown, a gown Alaistair had insisted upon, even though she was still in mourning. "I never forget such remarkable features."

"Get out before I leave and everyone sees how unwelcome you are."

An ugly gleam entered Bent's eyes. "It will only hurt you. The on-dit of your, shall we say, sojourn under my roof are starting to make the rounds of the rumormongers."

The urge to slap his mocking face was so strong Liza raised her arm. His grin was the only thing that brought her back to reason. The man might be a snake, but to cause another scandal would be a big mistake. Being here at all, with Michael dead barely six months, was pushing the limits of acceptable behavior. Only the black she wore and Alaistair's arm band—and reputation—saved them from censure. To assault Bent physically would put them beyond the pale. She couldn't do that to her husband because it would have repercussions for his entire family.

She settled for words. "You are despicable! If that tale is circulating, it's because you've started it. No one else knows about it."

He smirked and leaned back in the chair. "Lord Alaistair knows."

Anger flared white-hot in her. "He wouldn't spread such rumors."

"He wouldn't?" Bent raised his quizzing glass to his eye and casually surveyed the throng. "Everyone is saying your marriage was a love match, or why else would he marry you when he could have any chit on the market? I wonder if that's true, particularly as he's lingering overlong with Marie, who's been entertaining him for several years now."

The sly words, meant to hurt, achieved their purpose. Liza glanced away from Bent to the two he spoke of. Alaistair was still talking to the woman, who had put her hand intimately on his arm and moved so her breasts brushed his jacket.

Liza told herself she didn't care. Looking away, she lifted her chin. "That's old news, Bent."

"So it is," he said, rising and executing an elegant leg. "So it is."

Liza watched him saunter out and make his way through the boxes. He bowed to someone she couldn't see at first. Then the man blocking her vision shifted and she saw the Duchess of Rundell. Her mother-in-law paled, then nodded briefly at Bent before turning back to her companion. Now Liza knew why the earl had harassed her: he enjoyed making Alicia suffer. What a toad.

Her gaze went back to Alaistair. He was no longer with Marie Hardcastle, but had joined Tristan Montford and Lord Deverell. The tightness in Liza's shoulders eased.

Slowly she began to fan herself, her eyes scanning the theater. No one was watching the stage; they were all in little groups, vying for one another's attention. She was the only one concentrating on the ballet when Alaistair returned.

Taking his seat, he murmured, "Tris and Deverell send their regards."

She gave him a cool smile and returned her attention to the mediocre dancing, which she wasn't enjoying. The young bucks in the gallery were hooting, some even throwing rotten tomatoes at the performers. It was the last straw.

"I'd like to go home, please." Not waiting for an answer, she rose and picked up her black satin cape.

Alaistair stood, took the cape from her and draped it over her shoulders. His fingers brushed her skin in the process, sending sparks shooting through her body. Alarmed by her response to his lightest touch, she forced herself not to flinch. He was the last man in the world she wanted to affect her like this.

They left the theater, ignoring the curious glances and stares directed their way. Outside, Liza took a deep breath of the night air, instantly regretting it as the metallic tang of soot settled on her tongue.

Their carriage pulled to the curb and Alaistair put his hand under her elbow, heating her with his warmth. She was about to step away from his disturbing touch, when a soft mewling caught her attention. She stopped and cocked her head to one side, concentrating on the direction the sound had come from. It was like the cry of a hurt animal.

Liza twisted around and rushed into the dark alley running along the side of the theater. The noise was louder there and Liza went to a heap of garbage piled against the wall. Two yellow orbs shone up at her in the scant light from the moon.

"It's all right," Liza crooned. "I won't hurt you. No, precious, I won't hurt you."

As her eyes adjusted to the darkness, she could make out the faint outline of a thin white body against the black pile of rubbish. It was a kitten, probably starved half to death.

The mewing intensified. Liza stooped down, holding her hand out and moving slowly. "Come to me, sweetheart," she murmured. The kitten didn't run away, which she took as a good sign. "Come, little one."

The tiny animal inched forward, its ears laid back. It took several steps more, then tentatively rubbed its head against her fingers. A surge of relief rushed through Liza. Gently, she petted the kitten, and when he arched under her caress, she knew he was hers. It wasn't long before she had the emaciated little animal cuddled against her heart.

"Here," came Alaistair's gruff voice from behind them, "you'd best wrap him in this. It may make it feel more secure." He handed her his jacket, which he'd folded into a nest.

Liza took it and placed the kitten in the center, where it burrowed into a tight ball. "Thank you," she said at the unexpected kindness.

Alaistair smiled, just as she'd once seen him smile at Tristan Montford. But the moment was gone before Liza could consider its implications.

"It's the cat who should thank me." He took her elbow and guided her out of the alley to the waiting coach. "I suppose you'll want the thing to sleep in your room, so when we get home I'll have Simpson fetch some old towels and a box."

"Thank you again," Liza said, settling onto the gray velvet squabs and securing the kitten on her lap.

Stroking the starved animal's ears, Liza wondered at Alaistair's thoughtfulness. Each act of kindness made it that much harder for her to continue hating him. It made her begin to wonder if Tristan Montford had been right when he'd said Alaistair had never intended to keep the vowel.

Reluctantly she glanced at her husband. Even in the cold, he appeared comfortable in just his shirtsleeves. He was so virile, and she was doing all she could not to respond to that potent masculinity.

She squeezed the kitten so hard he protested. "I'm sorry," she murmured.

No, Liza assured herself, these gestures of kindness were generated by a sense of duty, of obligation. She couldn't afford to think well of her husband, because that would be the first step on the road to loving him. And Alaistair St. Simon, by his words and deeds, had ensured that love was the one emotion that would never be a part of this marriage.

"YOUR REPUTATION precedes you, Lady Alaistair."

Liza struggled to keep the smile on her face as Sally, Countess of Jersey, eyed her from head to toe.

Standing beside his wife, Alaistair gave the countess a cool smile. "They don't call you Silence for nothing, do they, Sally?"

Lady Jersey had the grace to blush. "I may have talked a lot in Paris, Saint, but I was always entertaining."

"So is my wife," Alaistair said quietly, one black brow raised sardonically.

"If you will excuse me," Lady Jersey said with a brittle laugh.

Liza watched Almack's powerful patroness drift away through the throng crowding her drawing room and flowing over into the ballroom. "She doesn't mince words, does she?"

Alaistair shrugged and took Liza's arm. "Sally is a law unto herself, and so long as everyone else follows her lead she's generally content. At least she didn't give you the cut direct, so it's likely that no one else will."

Liza stopped in midstep. "Why would anyone do that? Surely not because of Michael?"

Alaistair's grip tightened as he pulled her along. "Michael wasn't the first young man to come to such an end. The ton understands that and accepts it. What's causing the stir tonight is word of your time under Bent's roof."

They came upon a small group of people, several of whom turned around to look at them. Liza recognized one of the women as Marie Hardcastle. A green silk evening gown clung to her voluptuous curves. She smiled at Alaistair, her green eyes flashing.

Liza's chest tightened and she felt an overwhelming urge to slap the woman's grinning face. But seconds later, the pang of jealousy was forgotten as Marie swept her gaze over Liza as though she weren't there, then, without a word, turned her back. It was the cut direct.

Several women in the small group tittered. The men craned their necks to see Liza's reaction, but none acknowledged her. Alaistair squeezed her fingers painfully until Liza had to cover his hand with hers and discreetly pry his grip loose. All the time, she felt hot with embarrassment.

"Bloody b—" Alaistair cut himself off.

Liza straightened her back. "It doesn't signify. Will you please get me something to drink? I find that running Society's gauntlet is thirsty work."

She wanted him away before her burning eyes actually shed tears. It was bad enough that the woman had cut her; what made it even worse was the knowledge that Marie Hardcastle was her husband's mistress.

Alaistair gave her a thorough look before he released her and blended into the crowd surrounding the punch bowl. Liza watched him go, keeping her head high and ignoring the curious glances directed her way. When he returned, she would ask to leave. The Polite World was too vicious for her liking.

While she waited, she found a seat off in a corner, a potted palm her only companion. Several times she glanced around the room, but whenever her gaze fell on someone who was also looking at her, the other person quickly turned away. The first time it deepened the pain of rejection caused by Marie Hardcastle. The third time, it merely hardened her resolve. The ton was made up of shallow people whom she refused to let intimidate her.

Determined not to be cowed, she glanced around once more. This time, however, her gaze alighted on Alaistair's mother, who looked very uncomfortable. Beside her, taking her arm and directing her out one of the French doors, his posture that of a supplicant, was Bent. Surprise made Liza drop the elaborate fan she'd been using. Why in the world would the Duchess of Rundell, a woman whose reputation had never fully recovered from her elopement, endanger her precarious standing in Society by slipping onto the balcony with the disreputable Earl of Bent?

Rising, Liza sauntered toward the doors, careful not to look at anyone. With luck, no one else had seen the duchess leaving.

She reached the balcony just in time to see Bent take the duchess's arm and pull her into the garden. Liza stood rooted to the ground, shock keeping her from rushing after them. Surely Alaistair's mother did not wish to go with Bent. Something had to be done.

BENT TIGHTENED his grip on Alicia's hand when she tried to free herself. He was determined not to let her go this time. She hadn't been happily married five years ago, and so he was sure she couldn't be now. He just had to convince her to run away with him.

He'd done it once before. "Please, Alicia, just this once, listen to me."

Alicia saw the pain in his bloodshot blue eyes and remembered them as they'd been five years ago, full of fire and energy. Heavy drinking and reckless living had aged him, and she knew that she was partly to blame. Her resistance melted away. No one had seen them leave, and Alaistair and Rundell were occupied.

"I will stay and speak with you," she acquiesced, "this once."

Triumph invigorated Bent. For the first time since their aborted elopement she was agreeing to speak with him in private. All this time he'd been unsure of her love for him, but now he knew she still loved him. Last week at the ballet and all the other times he'd approached her she had ignored him, but tonight he wouldn't let her go until she was melting in his arms, as eager to run away with him as she'd been once before.

Rounding a corner of boxwoods, he led her to a stone bench. He eased Alicia down onto it and sat next to her, so close that his thigh brushed hers. White lightning arced through his body, leaving him feeling excited and aroused.

The urge to touch her was overwhelming. Tentatively, not wanting to frighten her with the intensity of his emotions, he cupped the side of her face, feeling the satiny texture of her cheek. He rubbed his thumb along her flesh, marveling at the timeless beauty of her.

The half moon silvered her black hair and burnished the smooth perfection of her skin as he continued to stroke her. Her eyes were smoky pools, and his entire body ached with his need for her.

"God, I love you, Alicia," he said hoarsely, his throat tight with desire. "You can't know how I've dreamed of having you alone again." His hands slid down her arms and caught her fingers, bringing them up for his kiss. "I love you, dearest. Come away with me. We'll go to Paris. Anywhere."

She drew back, trying to free her fingers from his. "Steven, please, don't ask. I can't."

His grip on her tightened, not enough to bruise her or cause her pain. He'd rather cut out his heart than bring her discomfort, but he couldn't let her say things that weren't true.

"You don't mean that, Alicia. I know you don't."

She tried to stand, to get away, but he pulled her gently but firmly back down. "I do. We can't relive five years ago."

His puffy lips thinned. So, she was going to fight him because she was still ashamed of what they'd done. He knew that was the only reason she'd returned with her son. Otherwise she would never have left him.

Careful not to lose his temper and frighten her, he said, "You can come away with me again, just as you tried to do five years ago, just as you want to now. I can see it in your eyes. You still love me, and as God is my witness, I've never stopped loving you. I worship you."

Tears glistened in her eyes. She shook her head. "Please don't. Things are different now. I'm happy. Rundell and I have managed to forget our differences."

He let her go and covered his ears. He couldn't stand to listen to her say those things, those lies.

Appalled by his reaction, Alicia jumped up and staggered back, her eyes wide.

Bent gritted his teeth and stood, dropping his hands to his sides.

"I don't believe you," he said as calmly as he could, his hands bunching into fists with his effort not to grab her.

She took another step back until she was up against one of the tall boxwoods. "You must. It's the truth."

He could stand it no longer. He lunged at her, grabbing her arms and yanking her to him. "Don't torture me with these lies. You don't love him. You love me!''

Alicia struggled, her gown twisting around her legs and tripping her. She gasped as she fell against him, and his arms crushed her to his chest.

"I don't love you," she whispered. "I love my husband. He's...he's changed. My running away with you changed him.''

Bent shut out her words. She couldn't be happy. She couldn't love anyone but him. And if it hadn't been for her damnable son, she'd be living with him on the Continent now, not lying to him about her feelings for another man.

"I don't believe you. Rundell isn't fit to wipe your feet, let alone be your husband. You belong to me."

She freed her hands and pressed them against his chest in a desperate effort to push him away. "No, no, that's not true. Please, let me go. I don't want another scandal. I don't want to hurt Rundell.''

She didn't want to hurt that worthless bastard, yet she was hurting *him*. Bent felt as though his chest were ripping apart, and he struggled to get a breath. "To hell with Rundell.''

He squeezed her to him and rained kisses on the top of her head, her ear, her neck. Using one hand he forced her face up and took her lips with his. Fire roared through him, devouring everything but the feel of her mouth beneath his, her body pressed into his.

Alicia struggled against his superior strength. She tore her mouth away and gasped, "Stop. You can't do this. I . . . I don't want this."

His eyes filled with a fanatical light, and his florid complexion darkened. "Yes, you do. Remember when we made love? You wanted me so badly you whimpered for me to take you. That hasn't changed."

Tears coursed slowly down her flushed cheeks. "Don't shame me with those memories. I made a mistake."

Something in him snapped. He started to shake her. "Lies. All lies, do you hear me?"

"Damn you to hell, Bent!" Alaistair St. Simon's voice thundered as he grabbed Bent by the coat collar and yanked.

Bent's instinct was to hold tightly to Alicia. As long as she was in his arms, no one could take her from him. Her skirt and legs tangled with his and they tumbled to the ground in a bone-bruising heap.

Panting, Alicia struggled to free herself from Bent's grip. She managed to get to her knees. A hand reached down to her and she took it, using it as a lever to gain her footing. "Alaistair, please. Don't do anything rash. It's not—"

"It's not what it seems?" her son finished for her. "Bloody hell it isn't. If it hadn't been for Liza you'd be beneath Bent's body this very minute." He turned back to Bent. "I'll kill you this time."

Bent stared at the man who had condemned him to hell five years before, and the hatred he had nursed so long exploded in him. "I wish to hell you'd died at Salamanca."

"Name your seconds, coward," Alaistair cried.

Alicia shook off the hand holding her back and thrust herself between the two men. "Stop it. Please. Nothing happened."

Bent heard the agony in her voice. He reached for her, wanting to comfort her. A fist connected with his jaw, and lights sparked behind his eyes as he lost consciousness.

Liza watched Bent fall to the ground like a felled tree, horrified by the raw fury that galvanized Alaistair. She moved to make sure Bent was still alive.

"Leave him."

Alaistair's cold words brooked no denial. Liza stopped. Looking at Bent, she saw his chest rise and fall. At least he wasn't dead. She glanced at the duchess's tear-ravaged face. It would do no good to defy Alaistair and would only agitate his mother beyond her endurance.

Liza glared at her husband before taking the duchess's arm and guiding her away. Lady Alicia couldn't go back into the ballroom in her present condition. Everyone would know something had happened, and before they got out of the house, the scene in the garden would be on everyone's lips.

"Alaistair—" She stopped. "Call for your carriage while your mother and I wait here."

He gave her a nod of approval. Taking his mother's other arm, he said, "I've already sent for it. We'll circle around the side of the house where no one will see us. I'll send word back to my father and brothers."

CONCEALED BEHIND a topiary unicorn, Marie Hardcastle watched Alaistair leave with his mother and wife. The duchess's bowed shoulders still heaved with silent tears. Marie sneered. What a sniveling, spineless creature.

Her attention shifted to the man lying prone in the grass, his mouth slack, a repulsive specimen of manhood. She sighed dramatically and stepped out from behind the shrub. She'd learned long ago that one had to work with whatever material was available.

Kneeling fastidiously beside him, taking care to protect her gown from damage, she shook him until his eyes opened. "Bent, get a hold of yourself. There are certain matters we must discuss."

CHAPTER NINE

"WELL, TRIS," Alaistair said, squinting down the road, directly into the glare of the rising sun, "it appears that the bastard isn't going to show. I'm not surprised."

Tristan Montford watched his friend pace the clearing. "Saint, what would you have done if Bent *had* come. He named pistols as the weapon."

Alaistair stopped and shrugged. "I'd have used pistols. I challenged him. It's his choice and my honor."

"I suppose so," Tristan said, frowning into the distance. "Are things better, then?"

"Some." Alaistair's mouth curved up wryly. "At least I don't break out in a cold sweat when I know a gun is going to be fired. It's only when I'm not expecting it."

"Damn," Tristan muttered.

"Drop it," Alaistair said. It was bad enough living with the nightmares; he had no interest in a lengthy discussion of the subject. "How we got onto this boring topic, I'll never know."

Taking his cue, Tristan pushed away from the oak trunk he'd been lounging against. "Bent always was a coward. No honor, either. Couldn't expect the man to show for a duel."

Alaistair grinned. "It *was* asking too much. But damn the man, now I can't put him out of his misery."

"Or ensure that the duchess is not importuned by him again. The man is obsessed, Saint." Tristan shook his head, his fair hair burnished with the orange rays of the sun.

Alaistair frowned. "He is. I'm beginning to wonder where this will end. The man shouldn't have given my mother a second thought after she returned to Father. He didn't love her—it was all a game of pursuit and surrender. That's what his reputation has always been, even when his wife was alive."

Tristan shook his head slowly. "But somehow, I don't think Bent's playing fast and loose with her."

Alaistair strode to the tethered horses and swung into the saddle in one impatient, graceful movement. "You may be right. Perhaps I have misjudged him where Mother is concerned. Perhaps he did care for her more than I thought."

For a long time, they rode in silence.

"I say, Saint," Tristan said, casting his friend a mischievous look, "my man says you've a new resident in your house."

"News travels fast. Who, may I ask, is supposed to have joined us?"

Tristan chuckled. "A four-legged feline who's driving Rast to drink. Seems the fellow has taken a liking to your clean cravats."

"Ah, your Todham's been talking to Rast."

Tristan shrugged. "Can't blame 'em. The two were as much together in the Peninsula as we were."

"Probably more," Alaistair said dryly. "They didn't get to the battlefields. They stayed in camp the whole time."

"Well, whatever the cause, the two are thick as thieves. And Todham says Rast is threatening to give his notice because of the new kitten."

Alaistair laughed. "Rast may threaten, but I've seen the curmudgeon take several cravats that haven't been starched yet and set them on a chair by the window. Several hours later, the cat is comfortably situated in their midst."

Tristan shook his head. "Rast has a soft heart or he wouldn't have stayed this long. You tease him abominably."

Alaistair sobered, but a slight smile curved his lips as he thought of his beleaguered valet. "I am a trial to him, but I think he secretly enjoys it."

Shortly, they reached the outskirts of London. At Grosvenor Square, the two parted ways. Alaistair watched Tristan disappear before he turned his own horse in the opposite direction from his Town house. What better time to discuss with Marie the cut she gave Liza?

Alaistair rapped on Marie's door. The butler answered and allowed him in. It was long minutes before Marie appeared.

"Saint," she said, pausing dramatically in the doorway of the drawing room, her diaphanous gown flowing from a tiny bow between her breasts. Her chestnut hair fell in rumpled waves, as though she'd just left her bed, which was likely at this hour.

"Marie," he said, wondering whom she'd left upstairs.

"I knew you'd come back to me," she said triumphantly.

Before he could correct her, she was upon him, her arms wrapped around his neck, her mouth pressed to his. The strong smell of her perfume engulfed him, calling forth memories of Liza's lighter rose scent. He put Marie away from him.

She frowned up at him, hands on hips. "So, you aren't coming back."

Boredom entered his voice. "No, Marie. I've come to warn you off my wife. If you ever cut her again, I shall see to it that you're ostracized by the ton. And you may be assured that I'll be more successful than you were with my wife last Sunday."

"Humph!" She sauntered away, hips swaying. "Your amazon is already beyond the pale. Bent has said that he ruined her when she was his son's governess." A nasty laugh contorted her rouged face. "You'd do better to ensure that your heir isn't Bent's get."

Alaistair's stomach knotted in anger. He took a step forward before checking himself. "If I find that you've played any part in this, Marie, you'll regret it."

She backed away from the fury he made no effort to hide. "Get out."

"With pleasure." He brushed past her.

In the hall, he heard a man's querulous voice shouting for Marie. It was Wright. A sardonic smile twisted his lips. Leave it to Marie to keep one lover waiting while she met with another who held the promise of more wealth.

Once on the street again, Alaistair inhaled the crisp morning air, glad to be out of that cesspool.

He mounted his stallion and headed back the way he'd come. Turning onto Brook Street where his Town house was, he saw a light on in the second-story room that was Liza's bedchamber. Why was she up this early—or why had she stayed up this late?

She couldn't have known about his duel. He'd made sure to say nothing further about the incident in Sally Jersey's garden.

In his room, Alaistair rapidly shrugged off his jacket and untied and removed his cravat. Undoing the top two buttons of his shirt, he glanced toward the window. Sure enough, Baby, as Liza had named the stray, was curled up on a bed of white linen.

"Worthless cat," Alaistair said, moving toward the door between his and Liza's rooms.

Baby raised his head and opened his eyes. He gave Alaistair a very satisfied feline smile.

"Shameless, too."

The kitten, knowing a compliment when he heard it, meowed softly and laid his head down. Without another thought for the man, he went back to sleep.

Alaistair knocked on the adjoining door. When Liza bade him enter, he did so. She was curled up in a chair by the fireplace, a book on her lap. She wore a cream silk robe over her night shift, both garments purchased from Madame Celeste. Her bare feet were tucked beneath her. If his memory didn't fail him, and it rarely did, the chair she sat in was the same one he'd tossed aside on their wedding night.

"What book are you reading?" he asked, wondering if the book was the reason she was up so early.

"It's one of Walter Scott's Waverley novels." Her face had a worried expression, and the bright turquoise of her eyes had dimmed.

"What's the matter?" he asked, stopping a short distance from her.

She set the book on the nearby table, careful to save her place with an embroidered bookmark. "Did you duel with Bent?"

His eyes narrowed. "What do you know about it?"

She sighed, the fingers of her left hand twirling a loose curl. "You challenged him that night in Lady Jersey's garden. This morning I heard you moving about in your room before the sun was up. I couldn't think of any other reason for you to be about so early. You don't go to cockfights or seem interested in pugilism."

He jammed his fists into the pockets of his breeches. "In a marriage of convenience, a wife doesn't pry into her husband's affairs."

Her hand dropped into her lap and her chin rose. "I'm aware of that, my lord. But if you die, I'm a widow in the depressing situation of facing yet another year of mourning. I'd much rather get an annulment or a divorce. Either would be easier." In a quieter voice, she added, "Nor do I want your death on my conscience."

His eyes narrowed in dawning realization. Very quietly, he asked, "Why would I be on your conscience?"

"Because I'm the one who told you about Bent and your mother."

"You take too much credit," he said coldly. "I would have challenged Bent sooner or later. As it was, you enabled me to keep the bounder from harming my mother. That is something I'm trying to keep in mind right now, so that I don't lose my temper and tell you exactly what your place in this household is."

Affronted, she drew back into the tufted cushions of the chair. "How dare you? Is this how you treat someone who is only concerned for your safety?"

He glared at her. "'Twas not my safety you worried about, but your own remorse. You're wallowing in guilt because of your brother's suicide and allowing it to color everything you do and say. When are you going to realize you had nothing to do with Michael's death? He did what he had to do, given the person he was."

She rose, hands clenched at her sides, her mouth a thin coral line. "We've had this argument before. I don't want to repeat it or its consequences. Get out of my room!"

Alaistair stared at her, her words reminding him of the argument they'd had on their wedding night and how it had ended. As it had on that night, her hair hung in disarrayed curls down her back. Her breasts heaved with indignation, the nipples erect as though she were chilled . . . or aroused, and the urge to continue where they had left off caused his manhood to thicken.

He shook his head to clear it of the treacherous thoughts. He hadn't come here to seduce her, he'd come to see why her light was on. Now he knew, and it was time to leave—past time.

But his feet acted of their own will, propelled by urges he couldn't subvert. He advanced on her. Her eyes widened and her mouth fell open. A grim smile was his response.

"No," she said, putting out one hand as though she thought that would prevent him from coming closer. "There's no need for what you intend."

His smile widened. "I told you I expected an heir. Even from a marriage such as ours."

Liza darted around him to the door, which she flung open so that it banged against the wall. "Go. I've had enough of your talk of heirs. Our marriage won't produce one because we shall not be together long enough for that."

His jaw tensed, but he kept moving toward her. "Yes we shall. My room or yours, it's all the same."

"I'll scream," she threatened.

"Please do. Rast will be vastly entertained. He's always predicted that someday I'd meet a female who wouldn't fall into my arms. That woman being my wife will only make the jest the richer."

Frantic, knowing what he intended, she looked into his room. No escape. She turned back to him and saw that he was only feet away. Her face flooded with color. "You can't do this."

He could, and enjoy it. To pretend otherwise was to continue lying to himself.

He was close enough now to feel the heat of her body and smell the scent of roses clinging to her. Her robe was open, showing the transparent lawn of her nightdress. The rosy tips of her breasts were visible beneath the folds, intensifying his urge to bed her.

"Oh, yes I can. I've wanted to do this from the first time I saw you," he murmured, his fingers reaching out and trailing along her fine collarbone. "Your skin is as soft as silk."

Her eyes were like bright jewels, and the urge to touch her more intimately was greater than Alaistair could bear. He took the final step to close the distance between them.

Liza felt his body brush against hers and then an aching tightness rushed into her breasts. Through the material of her gown she could feel one mother-of-pearl button on his shirt press into her swollen flesh.

He was so close the wiry hairs of his torso touched her skin. She felt the rise and fall of his chest against hers and looked up into his heavy-lidded eyes, which glowed with a passion that would burn her to ashes.

The scent of sandalwood engulfed her, and she feared she would swoon.

Head spinning, she placed her palm against his chest, intending to push him away. The feel of fine linen was cool beneath her touch, but instead of pushing him away, her fingers curled into the shirt, holding him. Startled, she willed her muscles to relax and release him, but they only clung the tighter.

What was she doing? What was he doing to her?

Bewildered, she looked up at him. His face loomed over hers, lips parted, eyes smoldering coals. His mouth lowered to hers.

The feel of his lips on hers, his tongue dancing with hers, overwhelmed her senses. Everything blurred into a torrent of sensations as he seduced her with each stroke of his hand, each plunge of his tongue.

"That's it," he murmured, his fingers kneading her lower back before slipping down to cup her buttocks and lift her into him. He was tumescent and hot and hard against her abdomen.

"Oh!" A tiny gasp escaped her at the intimacy of the contact.

"I'm going to make love to you," he whispered.

With his teeth, he gently nibbled the lobe of her ear, then trailed his tongue lightly down the curve of her neck. The contrast of his warm moist lips and beard-roughened skin as he nuzzled her sensitized flesh turned her bones to liquid honey, and Liza feared her legs would give way and she would drag them to the floor.

Releasing his grip on her hips, he slipped his fingers beneath the neckline of her bodice and eased her gown down over her shoulders. Slowly, his hands slid the sleeves down her arms until the neckline bit into the swell of her breasts, sending hot darts of desire shooting through her.

Liza could stand to watch him no more. All fight left her, fleeing on the heels of common sense. Caught in the web of sensuality he wove around her, she leaned her head back against the wall, offering herself to him.

Even the touch of his mouth on her breast didn't jolt her out of this madness; instead it drew her in deeper. Through the fabric, his lips coaxed her nipples into taut buds, and Liza clawed at the wall behind her for purchase.

"What are you doing?" she gasped, lifting her breasts higher, wanting him to take off her shift so she could feel him without the barrier.

"Loving you," he said, his breath hot through the damp lawn. "Making you want me."

Tenderly, Alaistair loosened her shift and freed her breasts. They filled his hands as though they were made for him. Hunger darkened his eyes as he took in the sight of her surrendering to passion... passion he had created.

Her head lolled to one side, her magnificent hair streaming down around her. A tendril nestled in the valley between her breasts. He picked it up and kissed it before tucking it behind her shoulder and replacing the strand with his lips. The scent of roses engulfed him even as her body jerked upward in response, and she moaned softly in pleasure.

"Spread your legs," he whispered, raising his head and taking her lips as his own needs became more urgent. "Open for me."

Caught up in the mindless reaction of her body to his lovemaking, Liza did as he bade. He pushed his leg between hers and his right hand skimmed over her belly. Then his fingers brushed up her inner thighs and moved higher still. Liza felt a river of heat wherever he touched her and a raging hunger that she knew only he could satisfy.

"Meow!"

A white fur-ball careened into their entwined legs. Sharp claws raked at their flesh.

"Bloody hell."

Alaistair jerked his head from her breast and stared at her, and Liza could see her shock mirrored in the black pools of his eyes.

What was she doing? *Making love,* a small, mocking voice said. Her body stiffened at the realization.

She couldn't. Not with this man.

"Please . . . stop."

He continued to stare down at her, looking into her very soul. And in spite of what he saw, he released her.

"You want this as much as I do," he said. "But you're too cowardly to admit it. You're afraid that by making love to me you'll betray your brother."

She paled. Her fingers turned to ice and started shaking. "That's not true."

He stepped away, a sneer marring his handsome features. "You're lying."

Her body still throbbed where he'd caressed her. She took several gulping breaths to deaden the sensation. "It doesn't matter. I won't sleep with you. I won't give you an heir."

"This is merely a reprieve, not a pardon." He took several steps away, his hands held loosely at his sides. His eyes caught and held hers. "Don't delude yourself that you'll get out of this marriage. I won't let you destroy yourself or give my family another scandal to live down. I'll send you to the country before I let that happen."

"Bastard."

He made her a curt, mocking bow. "As you wish." Looking at the cat for the first time since it had separated them, he made another curt bow. "To a furry knight in shining armor." He gave Liza a sardonic look. "You saved the cat's life, and now he's saved your virtue. Enjoy it while you can."

He strode around her and into his own room, closing the heavy oak door silently.

Liza sank to the floor, staring at nothing. Oh Lord, what was she doing? She had almost given herself to him. She buried her head in her hands.

Baby butted at her fingers until she looked at him. Sitting regally, head held high, he watched the door for several minutes after Alaistair had left. With a meow, he began to clean himself meticulously. That done, he went over to the closed door and meowed again.

Liza shook her head in consternation and reluctant amusement, thankful for the kitten's intervention.

Swallowing hard, she said, "Now that you've saved me, you want to go back in and make amends. Probably you want to get back to that bed of crumpled cravats."

"Meow."

It was a demanding sound. Liza's mouth twitched as she did Baby's bidding. Cracking open the door enough for him to get through, she waited only until his tail disappeared before closing it again. "Good riddance," she whispered, not angry at the cat's defection but slightly hurt by it.

Alaistair heard the door opening and took a deep breath. He owed Liza an apology. No matter how tired he was or how much he desired her, he had no right to treat her as he had just done.

"Meow," Baby greeted him, twining between his legs.

Liza had only opened the door to let Baby back in. He told himself it was better this way. If he saw her again so soon after their interrupted lovemaking, he wasn't sure he could keep from finishing what they'd started. The urge to have her in his bed, responding to his caresses, was stronger than anything he'd ever felt before.

But he didn't intend to force her into his bed. He'd never taken a woman who wasn't eager to share in the physical pleasure with him. He'd be damned if he'd start with his own wife.

"Meow," Baby said again, louder and more demanding this time.

Alaistair stooped down to scratch the cat behind the ears. Baby began to purr contentedly.

Staring straight ahead, brows drawn together, Alaistair said to the cat, "I think it's time your mistress went to the country. For everyone's sake."

Ignoring a decision that had nothing to do with him, Baby butted up against Alaistair's fingers and encouraged his master to continue petting him.

THAT AFTERNOON Liza answered Alaistair's summons to the library with trepidation. The raw sensuality of the morning still lingered, and her body ached for some undefined fulfillment. Being alone with him would not be easy.

She hastily wiped her damp palm on the black muslin of her skirt before knocking. His answering "Come in" made it necessary for her to run her hands down her skirt again.

She walked in, closing the door carefully behind her. "You wanted to see me."

He rose and walked around the desk, leaning casually back against it, his booted feet crossed at the ankles. He was acting as though the morning encounter had never occurred—or had meant nothing to him.

Indignation at his seeming indifference to the passion he'd so easily unleashed in her filled Liza. "I haven't all day, Alaistair."

A lazy smile was her answer, accompanied by a thorough appraisal from smoldering eyes. "Neither have I. I'm sending you to my country estate, Ciudad Rodrigo. I expect you to be ready in two days."

"What?"

"Start packing. Nell will go with you, and Baby if you wish."

The cat, who was sleeping on a wadded cravat on the windowsill behind the desk, lifted his head and meowed. Liza glanced at him, then back at her husband. Alaistair's cravat was missing, his shirt open at the collar to show several wiry black hairs springing to freedom. Heat unfurled in her stomach. The country would be a safe haven from this unwelcome desire, but she didn't like being ordered to go.

"Why are you sending me?" At the dangerous narrowing of his eyes, she stood her ground. "I deserve to be given a reason for this abrupt banishment."

He moved like a hound after a fox. Before she could blink, his hands were on her shoulders, pressing her to him. His mouth crushed hers. It was a brutal, demanding kiss that made her head spin and her knees weaken. When she thought she might die from the pleasure, he lifted his head.

"That is the reason," he said, putting her from him, his breath ragged. "If you stay here, with only a door separating us, I'll have my heir before the summer's through."

Her face flamed. Her entire body flamed. The undefined ache in her loins became a hard knot of need. He was right.

"I'll be packed by tomorrow morning."

She didn't wait for his answer, didn't dare.

Alaistair watched her fly from the room, a grim, self-mocking smile twisting his lips.

CHAPTER TEN

I'LL HAVE MY HEIR before the summer's through.
Alaistair's words rang in Liza's mind as the coach
barreled down the road.

He was right, she knew. No matter how she
flogged herself with Michael's suicide, the fact remained: she responded to Alaistair St. Simon with
a passion she'd never known herself capable of.
He'd all but seduced her, and she'd reveled in his
ministrations, wanting more.

At that instant the carriage hit a hole in the dirt
road, bouncing Liza three feet into the air. Baby's
plaintive howl rent the air.

Liza picked the kitten up from his pile of cravats
and cradled him to her chest. "I know, sweetheart," she crooned, scratching his ears.

Baby responded with fitful purring. The cat
hadn't wanted to leave London and Alaistair. So
irate had the feline been that Alaistair had had to
pick Baby up and put him in the traveling basket
because he clawed anyone else who tried to do so.

For good measure, Rast had sent a bundle of fresh cravats.

Liza sighed and kept scratching the cat's ears. At least Baby kept her mind off her husband.

Peering out the window, Liza noted the gray storm clouds casting shadows over the rugged countryside. Heather-covered moors swept into the distance like a purple sea, and to the west rose the majestic crags of the Pennines.

They had spent the previous night in York, and she hoped to reach Alaistair's estate, Ciudad Rodrigo, in northern Yorkshire this afternoon.

They came to a crossroads. The coachman stopped and sent the groom to the open window.

"Beggin' yer pardon, milady," he said, pulling his forelock, "but we be stoppin' a while, if ye wish to walk about."

In the seat opposite Liza, Nell sighed with relief. "Me legs feel like rubber, milady, and me bottom is near bruised."

"I can certainly sympathize with that," Liza said, ducking her head and taking the hand the groom held out to assist her from the carriage.

Baby mewed so Liza lifted him out and set him on the ground to wander.

It was early November and London had been chilly, but here a cold, biting wind whistled over the

moors with no trees to provide shelter. The sun was
pale and watery, and fat rain clouds promised to
turn the dirt road they traversed into a river of mud
before much longer.

Liza wondered what crops were grown in this
forlorn countryside, though she knew Alaistair
wouldn't want her interfering in the business of
running his estate. Besides, he probably had an excellent steward.

All too soon it was time to reenter the coach. Liza
waved a cravat in the cat's face and Baby followed
eagerly. The rest of the journey was slow and
treacherous. Pellets of rain pummeled the carriage
like pistol shots, and the roads turned to quick-
sand, sucking at the wheels and hobbling the horses.

They were forced to spend the night at another
posting inn instead of the estate, but by the following day the roads had dried somewhat and the going was easier. Early afternoon saw them pulling off
the dirt road and onto a graveled one. Liza raised
the leather flap covering the window and peered
outside. They were on a well-maintained drive lined
on both sides with stately beeches.

Thirty minutes later, they rolled to a stop in front
of an imposing mansion at least ten times the size of
her beloved Thornyhold. They had arrived at
Alaistair's Ciudad Rodrigo.

Restless from six days spent cooped up in the coach, Liza leapt out the door before the groom could help her. Looking around with curiosity, she mounted the stone steps and opened the front door without knocking. She was mistress of this mansion and she would start as she intended to go on: casually and without pretension.

"Good afternoon, Miss Liza," an impertinently familiar voice said.

Liza wheeled around in time to see Timmens coming from a side room, his white hair still hanging in his eyes. He shuffled toward her.

"Timmens!" she exclaimed, delighted to see him. "What are you doing here?"

He cackled. "I went to his lordship and said I wanted a position where I'd still be in the family. Told him I'd been with the Johnstones all my life, and seeing as he was responsible for my being pensioned off, I felt it was only right that he give me a place." A smug smile lighted up his lined face. "He saw things my way." His grin widened, crinkling the skin around his rheumy eyes. "He sent me here. Said his old butler was needed someplace else."

Liza shook her head and told herself she shouldn't be surprised. Timmens had a mind of his own and wouldn't have hesitated to speak thus to Alaistair. She shouldn't even be surprised that he had obliged.

Her husband had shown himself capable of many kindnesses in the month she'd been with him. Even to her.

"If you'll follow me, Miss Liza," Timmens said, interrupting her thoughts, "I'll show you to your rooms."

He started up the stairs without seeing if she followed. She smiled wryly, thinking that nothing else could make her feel at home like Timmens's impertinence.

On the second floor, he paused to see if she was behind him. "Your room is right next to his lordship's. Down this hall." He lowered his voice. "You even have a water closet."

Liza wondered how she'd managed without him these last months. The answer came in Nell's labored breathing as she followed them up the stairs lugging Baby's basket. Nell gave her the same feeling of acceptance, not just as mistress but as a person, that Timmens had always provided. He was the one who'd told her to buck up and keep going after word of her parents' drowning reached them.

"Seems there's no lock to this room," Timmens continued, "but that shouldn't bother you, as his lordship isn't here and hasn't sent word he's coming." He shot her a shrewd glance.

Valued servant and friend he might be, but this was going too far. She met his look haughtily. "That's quite enough, Timmens."

"Humph!" He pushed open the door and allowed her to enter. "I'll be seeing to your baggage. And if you wish a bath, ring so that the water in the reservoir can be heated."

Before Liza could dismiss him, he was moving off down the hall toward the stairs.

"He do be a character," Nell said. "Lord Alaistair must have needed Upshot somethin' fierce somewhere else to have sent this man here as butler."

As much as Liza wanted to believe the worst of Alaistair, she knew better. He had sent Timmens here because the old man needed work. His position was Timmens's life's blood. She couldn't feel anything but gratitude toward her husband.

Alaistair's thoughtfulness created a warmth in her more potent than the sensual one he always evoked. It threatened to dissipate the ill will she tried so desperately to keep alive. It was becoming harder and harder to continue blaming Alaistair for Michael's suicide.

"Corblimey, milady." Nell's words intruded on Liza's disturbing thoughts. The young maid's eyes were as round as saucers as she unceremoniously dumped Baby and basket on the thickly carpeted floor. "This be a room fit for a queen."

Liza had to agree. Her room in London was a cubbyhole compared to this. A massive walnut tester bed dominated the center of the room, the gold and green curtains drawn back to reveal a mound of pillows. Baby, dragging a crumpled cravat, jumped onto the mattress and made himself at home. Liza couldn't help but smile at the cat's preoccupations: bed and cravats. Beside the bed was a dressing table with a three-piece mirror, with a matching wardrobe against the adjoining wall.

Through the door in the south wall was a sitting room. A settee and four chairs were grouped around several tables, with the fireplace a comfortable distance away. Beyond this room were Nell's quarters.

Next she tried the door on the north wall of her bedchamber. It opened to an equally large room decorated in browns and gold. Alaistair's room. Liza slammed the door shut and stood stock-still for several seconds, then drew in a deep breath to calm her jangling nerves. Just the thought of him occupying the room made her pulse pound. It was a good thing he was in London.

Embarrassed, Liza glanced around for Nell and was relieved to see the maid with her head and shoulders in the wardrobe, putting away clothing.

To take her mind off Alaistair, and to satisfy the curiosity Timmens had aroused, Liza opened the door on the east wall that must lead to the water closet.

She'd heard that a few wealthy people had built something like this, but she'd never thought to see one herself. It was impressive. A white porcelain bowl sat on the floor; hand-painted blue gentians decorated its rim. On top was a polished mahogany lid. A chain hung from another porcelain container set higher on the wall and a brass pipe connected the two.

Liza studied the contraption as she approached it. The chain must be for pulling. She yanked on it experimentally.

As she did so, she could hear water rushing through the pipe and into the closed porcelain bowl. Lifting the lid, she saw the last of the water going down an opening at the base. Understanding dawned.

"Corblimey," Nell breathed in reverential tones.

Liza glanced over her shoulder to where the maid stood hesitantly in the doorway. "And just look at the tub."

It stood proudly in the center of the small room, its brass body glistening in the light of a single candle set near its soap dish.

"Corblimey," Nell repeated.

"How decadent," Liza said, walking over for closer inspection.

She assessed the tub's size. It was long enough for her to lie down in and wide enough to hold three abreast. Her gaze darted around the room. Sure enough, there was a second door. She knew without looking where it led but opened it anyway. Alaistair's room, and there was no lock.

Well, Liza decided, closing the door, she'd enjoy this luxury to the fullest. Alaistair was in London. There would be no chance of him surprising her one night. At the thought, a sense of melancholy filled her.

She shook her head, trying to force it away. She didn't miss her husband. His presence created only turmoil in her life.

Resolutely, she returned to her room and told Nell to notify Timmens that she intended to try out the tub.

A WEEK LATER, Liza doubted if even the pleasure of a long hot bath in the golden tub could relax her. Clouds obscured the weak fall sun so that no light came through the library window behind her, casting the account books she'd been examining into shadow.

She pulled a brace of candles over and lit them. The one thing she didn't want to do was make a mistake reading the boldly written numbers. Calling someone a thief wasn't something to be done lightly.

For the third time in four hours, she went over the figures. They didn't add up. Again.

Closing the ledger, she pushed the leather wing chair she occupied away from the desk. She could send a letter to Alaistair and wait for his answer, but that might take days or perhaps weeks and meanwhile the steward would continue to embezzle money. Her only other choice was to fire the man right now. He was waiting outside the library door for her to summon him.

She pulled a strand of hair loose from her chignon and began to twirl it furiously. Alaistair would be furious with her, but she had the proof right here in black and white. If he spent more time here and less in London, he'd have caught this pilfering himself.

It had to be stopped now. After pulling her chair back up to the desk, she tucked the strand of hair behind her ear and rang for the steward to enter. She would have to risk Alaistair's ire.

John Petersham was of average build with brown hair and blue eyes. His features were pleasant, and he nearly always smiled. The previous day he'd shown her around the estate at her request. That was when she'd become suspicious. The books, which she'd gone over the night before, showed charges for repairs that she hadn't seen during the tour.

"Please have a seat," she said.

"How can I be of service, milady?" he asked, a relaxed smile curving his lips.

Liza sighed softly. He didn't seem like the type of man who would take money from his employer, but neither had her steward at Thornyhold.

"I've been going over the books."

His face took on a wary look, but his smile didn't waver. "Then you know this hasn't been a good year. The price for wool wasn't as high as I could have hoped, what with the war over and the army no longer needing so many uniforms. Then there were the repairs to several of the tenants' homes."

Liza nodded. She knew that the demand for supplies had slackened since Napoleon surrendered. "It's the repairs that bother me, Mr. Petersham."

Tension flattened the line of his lips. "They were necessary. I couldn't expect the men to do their best in the fields if their families weren't provided for properly."

His explanation was reasonable and consistent with a practice Liza had followed at Thornyhold.

"That's perfectly acceptable, but there are some entries for repairs that haven't been done yet, or if they have, I mistook the entry in the books for the wrong house."

Sweat broke out on his upper lip. "That must be the case, milady."

Liza forced herself to remain calm. Picking up the account book, she moved around the desk. "Then you won't mind coming with me right now and showing me where these repairs were done."

"I can't right now, milady. I've things to do if his lordship isn't to be disappointed in the way I run Ciudad Rodrigo."

She looked at him sadly. "You don't leave me any choice, Mr. Petersham. Unless you can show me these repairs, and I don't think you can, I must let you go."

He jumped up, his face red. "You can't do that. Lord Alaistair hired me. He's the only one who can get rid of me."

Liza's shoulders ached as she held herself regally erect, her eyes on a level with his. "Lord Alaistair is in London, and in his absence I am responsible for his estate. You've been stealing from my husband for the last six months. It must stop. Now."

His hands fisted but he made no move toward her. "The law says this property belongs to your husband, not you . . . milady."

Grimly she watched anger stiffen his body. "Then I shall be forced to send for the magistrate. I hadn't wanted to do that."

He swallowed so that his Adam's apple bobbed and his eyes spit fire. But he wheeled without another word and stalked from the room.

Liza breathed a sigh of relief. Taking away someone's livelihood was never easy, not even when the person's guilt was beyond question. But she had no choice. She couldn't let Petersham continue to siphon the estate's profits. Surely Alaistair would understand she had acted in his best interests.

"BLOODY HELL," Alaistair muttered a week later as he guided his stallion onto the gravel lane leading to Ciudad Rodrigo. "I'll have to hunt up Petersham and make amends."

Liza's message had arrived in London three days earlier and he'd stopped everything to ride posthaste. She'd no right to meddle in his affairs. That wasn't why he'd sent her to the country.

He rode to the stables and dismounted. The head groom rushed forward. "Lord Alaistair, we been expectin' ye."

Alaistair handed over the stallion to him and strode toward the front door. It was opened by Timmens.

"Good afternoon, your lordship," the butler greeted him. "I reckon you'll be wanting to see Miss Liza."

Alaistair glanced sharply at the servant. "Where is her ladyship?"

"In the library where it all happened," Timmens intoned, his expression bland. "And I might add...your lordship...Miss Liza managed Thornyhold from the time she was sixteen. Right nice inheritance it would have been, too."

Alaistair cast the butler another piercing look before storming past him into the library. At the doorway he stopped in his tracks. Sunlight streaming in from the window turned Liza's red hair into a fiery nimbus that took his breath away.

Then he noticed the open ledger on the desk before her, in which she was industriously writing.

"I see you've replaced my steward," he observed, entering the room.

Her head jerked up and a blob of black ink spread over the sheet. "Oh, Alaistair. You must have received my note."

He nodded and took the leather chair opposite her. Sprawling comfortably, he crossed his muddied boots at the ankles. "And have come directly to you without cleaning up first." His eyes met hers. "Just what exactly have you done and why?"

"Meow!" Alerted by Alaistair's voice, Baby rose from his cravats on the windowsill and leapt to the floor. "Meow," he demanded again, rising up on his rear legs and pressing his front paws against Alaistair's shins. At a nod, Baby jumped into his lap and made himself comfortable.

Liza smiled ruefully at the cat's undisguised pleasure in having his master home. However, the smile gave way to a frown as she met her husband's stern perusal without flinching. "Just what I said. I've let Petersham go for embezzling. I told you all of it in the letter."

He pressed his fingertips against one another and rested his chin on them, watching her. He'd forgotten just how vibrant her coloring was. The black dress she still insisted on wearing was a dramatic foil for her magnolia skin, and her eyes were a bright, turbulent turquoise.

"How did you know he was stealing? The man's worked for me since I inherited this estate."

Liza's chin lifted. "If you doubt my word, I can show you."

Not waiting for his reply, she got up and moved around the desk. In the process, she rang a small silver bell. Timmens answered her summons so promptly that Alaistair suspected him of listening at the door.

"Yes, Miss Liza?"

Her lips tightened, but she said calmly, "Please have the gig brought around immediately. His lordship and I wish to tour the estate."

"At once, Miss Liza." As he left the room he gave Alaistair an "I told you so" look from beneath his beetle brows.

"Bloody impertinent servant," Alaistair said quietly.

Liza looked at him, agreement softening the hard glitter of her eyes. "I was surprised that you hired him."

His mouth turned up wryly. "He didn't give me much choice."

She appeared skeptical. "Somehow, I doubt that."

With a shrug, he set Baby back on the cravats and followed her outside where the carriage waited. As he helped her in, he told the driver, "I'll take it. Go on back to the stables."

"I never intended you to drive, only to come along," Liza said. "You must be exhausted. It couldn't have taken you more than two days to get here."

"One and a half."

"Perhaps we should wait till tomorrow when you're rested."

His hands tightened on the reins. "That won't be necessary."

Her shoulders stiffened. In clipped tones she told him where to go first. Thirty minutes later, Alaistair reined the horse to a stop in front of a stone fence she'd had repaired.

Alaistair stared at the fence, which was used to keep the sheep in their grazing area. "There's no way to tell if you just had it repaired or if it was repaired several months ago."

Liza gripped the side of the gig with her right hand until her arm ached from the tension. She kept her voice level with effort. "I didn't feel I could wait to see whether you'd come immediately. There was extensive damage and the sheep were wandering off. I know from looking at your ledgers that wool and mutton form a large part of your revenues."

"Where's the next place?"

Unable to look at him for fear she would lose the fragile control she held on her temper, she gave him directions. A short time later they came to a stop in front of a cottage.

He scowled. He didn't need to get out of the gig. Even from the path he could see that the thatch needed repair.

"Is this one supposed to be fixed?"

"Yes. The books show it was repaired a fortnight ago. When I mentioned it to Petersham, he told me I didn't know what to look for." She drew herself up so that the back of the carriage seat didn't touch her spine. "I know what to look for. I've had to re-thatch many a roof at Thornyhold."

And so the afternoon went. There were five stops in all, three of the sites repaired already.

Alaistair scowled as he looked at the last place in the gathering dusk. "You haven't shown me any evidence that's conclusive. It's your word against Petersham's."

The implication hung heavily between them. He didn't trust her.

Turning so that her shoulder was to Alaistair, Liza looked off into the distance. She wouldn't deign to argue with him.

Petersham had been cunning. He hadn't embezzled a large amount of money, which made his skimming harder to detect.

Night was drawing near and clouds were moving in. The breeze had picked up, and though the chill wind stung her cheeks, it was nothing compared to her stinging pride.

They traveled back to the stable in silence. When they arrived, Liza jumped down before the groom could help her. Anger coursed through her. She strode toward the house, determined to escape Alaistair St. Simon as quickly as possible.

From behind her, she heard him talking briefly to the groom about the care of the horse. Then his footsteps crunched on the gravel path.

"Liza," came his deep voice, "I intend to find Petersham and speak with him before making a decision."

It was the last straw, the dreadful culmination of a horrible two weeks. She whirled around, hands on hips. "Do that. He's obviously more loyal to you than I."

Not waiting for the scathing reply she knew was sure to come, she turned and stalked to the house. If he didn't believe her, he didn't. What could she expect from this sham of a marriage?

Viciously, she swiped at a drop of moisture on her cheek. It must be starting to rain, she told herself. That was all.

CHAPTER ELEVEN

LIZA LAY STARING at the ceiling for an eternity as the sounds of the house died away. She felt strangely bereft with Baby sleeping in Alaistair's room this night. Since he had arrived earlier in the day, the kitten had dogged his steps.

She tossed in bed, unable to get comfortable as her thoughts churned endlessly. Her husband had as good as called her a liar earlier, and she still seethed with hurt pride.

Sitting up, she pummeled her feather pillow into a soft mound. She lay back on it, only to sit up again and pound it some more. No matter what she did, she couldn't relax.

And to think she'd been glad to see him. It irritated her even more to remember how her heart had begun to race and her fingers to shake when he had startled her in the library. She must be insane.

Thud!

Liza jumped. It sounded as though something had hit the floor, something heavy, in the adjoining room.

"No! Oh God, not again." It was Alaistair, his muffled voice laced with pain as it penetrated the massive door separating their rooms. "Damnation to hell! I won't have it." Now anger filled his voice, replacing the despair of seconds earlier.

She'd only heard that tone once before; the time he'd challenged Bent to a duel. Something was terribly wrong. Liza put on her slippers and pulled her robe around her shoulders.

The light from a full moon shone into her room through the open drapes and she had no need of a candle. Quickly, she went to the door and opened it. There was no light at all in Alaistair's room.

Standing silently in the doorway, she waited for her eyes to adjust to the darkness. A flicker of orange flame caught her attention. Rast was entering through the door that connected his room to Alaistair's.

He raised his single candle high enough to illuminate both of them. Dressed in his nightshirt, with a cap pulled down to his brows, he wore a worried frown.

"He's having one of his nightmares," he said softly, jerking his head in the direction of the large four-poster bed. "They come on him sudden when he's not up to snuff. It was a tiring journey from London, and then the goings-on this afternoon..."

Liza nodded, unable to speak. She'd never seen Alaistair like this. The memory of his scathing words that afternoon faded.

"I told you not to let it happen again," Alaistair said, his voice icy. "I'll have you shot."

"He's remembering Salamanca," Rast told Liza. "We had a sergeant who kept sneaking off to see a little senorita. The problem was he always did it when it was his watch. Not the thing to do. Put the rest of us in danger." He paused and rubbed his eyes with his free hand. "His lordship warned him. Then one night he did it and we were attacked. Men died. Lord Alaistair had the sergeant shot."

"I see." Liza's stomach churned.

In the candlelight, Rast's eyes were like two dark holes. "I doubt you do. That was only one of many incidents. His lordship was in the thick of things during the whole Peninsular War. It was bloody hell." His voice lowered to a barely audible whisper. "Lord Alaistair can't forget."

She didn't know how to respond, how to express the pain and horror she felt. So she asked, "Are you here to comfort him?"

Seeming to pull himself together, Rast said, "Yes, your ladyship. If you'll excuse us."

He lifted the candle once more and made his way toward the bed. Alaistair tossed back and forth in the pool of light, the bed creaking beneath him.

Just minutes before Liza had been unable to sleep because of the anger she felt toward this man. Now she watched as he was tormented by powerful memories freed from the constraints of conscious thought. His suffering created in her a wave of strong emotion she could not explain. All she could do was act.

Moving beside Rast, she reached to take the candle from him. He let it go easily, surprise arching his brows beneath the nightcap that covered his sparse hair.

"I...I'll stay with Lord Alaistair," she said, heat rising in her cheeks. Rast knew she'd never spent the night with his master.

A grateful smile softened the servant's lined face. "You'll be able to help him more than I can."

She set the candle on the bedside table, not taking the time to ponder the valet's words.

As she sat on the edge of the bed, she was only dimly aware of the door closing. How could she comfort Alaistair? Despite the animosity she felt toward him, she wanted to ease his agony somehow.

She could hold him the way she'd held Michael when he was younger and had skinned a knee or elbow. To her surprise, the memory of her brother didn't bring its customary pain, but that was something she didn't have time to ponder right now.

Leaning forward, she wrapped her arms around Alaistair's shoulders and held on as he tried to buck away from her. A heady blend of sandalwood and musk engulfed her.

He twisted and thrashed, but her determination hardened and she clung to him like a leech. In a desperate bid not to be flung from the bed, she wrapped her legs tightly around his.

He stilled. Sweat drenched him and soaked through her night shift. The sheets they lay on were wet and his skin was slick where her legs clung to him.

With a start, she realized he was naked. She began to shiver, the chills racking her body a direct contrast to the scorching heat where his skin pressed boldly into hers. He was fully aroused.

Dear Lord, how had she gotten herself into this mess? She had acted out of kindness. Nothing more.

Liza gulped. "Alaistair," she whispered, hoping he would awaken in a calmer state so she could get away.

He shifted within the circle of her legs and pleasure darted through her.

"Alaistair," she said more loudly. If he didn't come to his senses soon, he would have her on this bed and she— A sob caught in her throat. She would enjoy every second of it. His touch was doing strange things to her body, things she'd tried desperately not to remember these last weeks without him.

His shaft rubbed the tender flesh between her thighs, creating a tight sensation in her abdomen. It was like the times he'd kissed her and caressed her bare breasts, only more intense.

Her nails dug into his shoulders. "Alaistair, wake up. It's only a dream. A nightmare." She gasped as his hips thrust against hers. "Oh Lord, wake up."

His eyes were still squeezed shut and the muscles in his shoulders were tight cords, but his legs eased their thrashing motion.

Relief flooded Liza. He was relaxing. Soon she could leave. He wasn't awake, but surely the horror of the nightmare was past or he would continue to fight her.

She eased herself away from the disturbing proximity of his loins, intending to slip out of the bed while he lay quiescent. But she couldn't resist the urge to brush the damp hair back from his forehead. Sweeping her fingers through the thick black mass, she noted the glint of silver her ministrations exposed. He was young to have so much gray.

He stirred at her caress. She must go. She feared what would follow if he awakened and found her this way.

Tentatively, not wanting to wake him now that he was calm, she tried to pull one leg away. Her thigh skimmed his muscular flank and she was just about to lift her leg off his when his hand clamped down just above her knee, pinioning her.

Startled, she looked back at his face. His eyes were open, the pupils dilated in the dim light. And he was gazing at her with stark hunger.

"Liza," he murmured, his hold on her easing slightly.

"Alaistair," she managed.

"Why are you here?" He frowned in puzzlement. "Why am I lying between your legs?"

She was glad the light was behind her so he couldn't see her expression. She didn't want him to know the blood was rushing through her and her face was flushed with the desire to finish what they'd unwittingly started.

"You were having a nightmare. I heard you." She took a deep breath to make herself slow down. "Rast said it happens often."

"Sometimes."

His hand slid up the outside of her leg, the rough calluses on his palms tickling, making Liza catch her breath. Unlike most gentlemen, he didn't wear gloves when he rode.

He kept his eyes on hers as his fingers moved up her thigh, taking the night shift with them, the candlelight accentuating the sensual curve of his mouth as he smiled.

"I...I think I ought to go," Liza said. She reached for his wrist to stop his hand's progress. "You're better now."

"Not yet." He kept moving his hand in spite of her efforts to halt him. "I might have a relapse."

By now his warm palm had reached the underside of her breast—a breast taut and tingling with anticipation.

"If you keep this up, you very well might," she said, trying not to tremble. "You need to sleep and recover."

His mouth widened in a wolfish grin. "I'll sleep much better when we're through."

He cupped her breast, kneading it with his palm while his thumb strummed the tight peak of her nipple. Sparks shot through Liza, igniting a fire in the pit of her womb. She squirmed, not sure whether she wanted to get closer to that disturbing hardness he made no effort to check or to escape before she did something she would later regret.

"Let me go."

"I will," he promised, eyes aglow. "Later."

His mouth caught hers and her head began to spin. But instead of trying to push his hand away from her aching breast, she clung to him. Her lips opened and he delved inside. It was just as she remembered. A welcoming response welled up inside her as she shifted slightly to meet the thrust of his tongue. A rumble of satisfaction sounded deep in his throat, sending shivers vibrating through her.

Her leg still rode his outer hip, exposing her heated core. She didn't care. All that mattered was his mouth on hers and his fingers stroking her breast.

Just as she began to play tag with his tongue, he withdrew. Liza opened her eyes as chagrin lanced through her.

"Alaistair?" she whispered in a voice husky with passion.

"I know," he murmured, inching down the bed so that her leg rested on his ribs and his face snuggled in her bosom. "I feel it, too."

It was impossible, but his words created a hot rush of exultation. He couldn't want her as badly as she wanted him. Liza threaded her hands through his hair and hung on for dear life.

Through the sheer fabric of her nightgown he drew one nipple into the heated moistness of his mouth. Liza felt as though that nipple were directly connected to a spot between her thighs. A liquid warmth filled her legs and her head lolled back, her eyes drifting shut.

"That's it," he whispered against her lush breasts. "Enjoy this. Forget everything but this..."

The words drifted over Liza in a sensual haze. *Forget everything*. It sounded wonderful. What he was doing was wonderful.

She cradled his head closer, wishing she knew what to do to increase this pleasure.

"Alaistair," she said softly, not sure how to say it, not sure she should. "Touch me...lower."

He stopped everything as her words penetrated his awareness. "What did you say?"

Liza, swathed in sensations of his making, said without consideration, "Touch me...touch me where it aches."

Desire rushed through him like wildfire. Taking
her breast back into his mouth, he slid his hand
along the outer curve of her thigh and down to her
knee, where it rested on his ribs. She was open for
him.

His fingers skimmed her inner thigh, up to the
fiery bush at the apex of her legs. This was what he
wanted from her, had wanted from the moment he
saw her. She was offering herself to him, and he'd
be damned if he'd refuse.

Her hips undulated so that his fingers brushed
against her moist flesh. Already aroused, Alaistair's shaft ached with a hunger that demanded ap-
peasement. With his thumb, he circled the pearl at
her core, reveling in her damp warmth.

"You're like fine honey," he murmured, drawing her nipple deep into his mouth.

Small moans of pleasure bubbled up in Liza as
her entire being focus on the growing ache between
her thighs.

Rising above her, Alaistair saw the blush of
arousal tinge her silken skin. Her cheeks were
flushed and her hair spread over the white sheets like
flames. A fierce need to possess her consumed him.

Inserting a finger into her molten core, he
watched her features become taut with passion.
When he withdrew, she edged her hips forward with

a little cry of frustration as she sought his touch again. He smiled. She was his. For this moment.

His thumb began to knead the small pearl of flesh in an age-old rhythm, and it was only with a colossal effort of will that he kept from thrusting himself into her hot, tight depths and striving for his own oblivion.

Liza's body convulsed, her fingers digging into Alaistair's flesh. A low moan rose from her softly parted lips as he brought her to the sought-after consummation.

When her climax subsided, Liza lay there, eyes closed, her body limp. Never in her twenty-six years had she experienced such earth-shattering sensations as Alaistair had just created in her.

Her mouth felt hot and swollen, her eyelids felt weighted down. Somehow, she managed to look at him.

He was between her legs, his face level with her chest. His eyes were black with desire and his mouth was full and curved with sensual knowledge.

Without him saying a word, Liza knew what was next. The mental lethargy left her. She was still physically exhausted, but her mind was alert once more.

"I'm glad you liked that," he said, pushing himself up so his face was above hers.

The languor that had filled her limbs evaporated at the thrust of his swollen shaft against her nether lips. He intended to insert himself inside her. He intended to consummate their marriage.

Her eyes widened with panic. If they continued as he intended, she'd never get an annulment. And wives couldn't initiate a divorce. She'd be irrevocably tied to the man responsible for Michael's death. It was too much too soon. She wasn't ready to commit herself to him.

"You can't do this," she said, desperation making her voice sharp. She tried to wriggle away from him but he held her firmly. "I don't want to make love with you."

His eyes narrowed dangerously. "You just did."

"No. No, I didn't. Not really. You haven't taken me. I can still get an annulment."

His fingers tightened on her thigh. "So that's what this is all about."

"I..." Her face felt hot and her legs were beginning to tremble in the aftermath of passion. "I don't want to go further."

"You're a tease," he sneered. "You've gotten your pleasure, so you're finished. A whore in lady's clothing."

Fierce anger swamped Liza. "How dare you!"

She swung at him but he caught her wrist and held it motionless.

"I dare a lot," he said, pinning her arm to the bed. "Spread your legs for me."

It was an order. His weight pressed her down into the mattress, his mouth inches from hers. She thrashed beneath him, trying to dislodge him. It did no good, only allowed him to slip forward between her thighs so that his turgid shaft pressed against her.

"Oh!" she gasped, realizing where he was positioned.

"Stop fighting me, Liza," he said, his voice husky. "You can't prevent me from finishing what you started."

She stared up at him, seeing the truth of his words in the depths of his dark eyes. He wanted her and he was going to have her.

"I hate you," she said through lips swollen from his kisses.

"That's nothing new," he murmured, lowering his mouth to her neck.

She arched away from him but only succeeded in giving him easier access to her flesh. He trailed his tongue along the corded ridge of her neck and pleasure shot through her. She hated him even more for making her feel this way.

"Stop," she pleaded, knowing that soon she wouldn't want him to.

He ignored her. Through hooded eyes he watched her as he rose to his knees between her legs. Releasing her wrist, he slid his hands down her arms, over her aching breasts to her hips. Gripping her bottom, he positioned her for his penetration.

As Liza watched him, desire sharpened his features. His lips drew back from his teeth and his head bowed. Then he thrust forward, impaling her.

"Oh my God," she gasped as pain made her try to draw away from him.

His gaze flicked to her face and she saw that his eyes were completely dilated, his skin sheened with sweat.

"It will only hurt for a second," he said, his words slurred by passion as he began to thrust into her with the same rhythm he'd used earlier.

He was right, Liza realized as a familiar tension began to build once more in her loins. Heat flowed from where he possessed her to every part of her body.

He drove himself deeper and deeper into her until Liza felt her hips respond with a matching rhythm. Her world began to spiral out of control as her body responded to him with a will of its own.

Liza dug her fingers into the mattress as she met him thrust for thrust, her moans turning to gasps as her body surged with release.

Alaistair heard her cries and gave up trying to control himself. His back arched, and with a shout of triumph he drove into her one last time.

Liza lay beneath him, her breathing slowly returning to normal. Sweat slicked her skin and the musk of lovemaking filled her nostrils.

Bent on his own pleasure, he'd taken her completely, refusing to stop even when she'd pleaded with him. And to her shame, she'd been unable to keep herself from responding.

"How could you?" she demanded, pushing at his shoulders to free herself. "You took me against my will."

He rolled away from her and onto his back, one arm flung over his eyes. "Go away, Liza," he drawled. "I'm in no mood to listen to your diatribe."

Liza jumped from the bed, yanking her gown down over her hips. Fury made her breathing ragged. She wanted to hit him, she wanted to throw the candlestick at him.

Bitterly she said. "You made love to me only thinking of yourself. Now I can never get an annulment. I can never be free from you."

His only reply was a yawn. Liza stared down at him where he lay on the rumpled sheet, his broad shoulders tapering into lean hips, his manhood still erect in the nest of black curls at the junction of his thighs. He was a wild animal with no shame at his nakedness. He was magnificent.

"Damn you," she said, choking back tears of pain and frustration, fighting the desire for him that pulled at her even now. "You've ruined me."

CHAPTER TWELVE

LIZA ENTERED the foyer, glad of the warmth after several hours on horseback. Although her riding habit was of heavy black wool, it had not kept the damp cold from penetrating to her bones. She grimaced. She shouldn't have ridden in this weather but she'd needed the exertion.

After returning to her room last night, she'd been unable to sleep. Memories of Alaistair's lovemaking had echoed in her body and haunted her thoughts. She hadn't slept until the early morning hours when it was time for the servants to be up and about, and she felt tired and irritable.

"Ahem." Timmens's rusty voice intruded.

Liza started, not having heard his approach. "Yes, Timmens?"

"I almost forgot to tell you that his lordship requests your presence in the library at your convenience." His bent shoulders straightened as much as they were able and his eyes dared her to comment.

Liza shook her head in exasperation but there was no point in rebuking him. "How long ago was that?"

His face impassive, he replied, "I believe it was earlier this morning. I told Lord Alaistair that you were not up and that you would go for your morning ride first."

Liza couldn't keep from chuckling. That was typical of Timmens, and it was perfectly in keeping with her mood. "Thank you, Timmens. You couldn't have done better."

"Humph!" A flush tinged his weathered cheeks. "He's got that Petersham in with him right now. If you want my opinion, the man's no better than he should be."

Liza's smile faded and her palms grew moist. She should have realized immediately that her husband's summons would have something to do with the fired steward. Alaistair had made it abundantly clear last night that his only use for her was in his bed, certainly not in the management of his estate.

Anger flared anew. Now he wanted to humiliate her in front of Petersham. She drew herself up to her full, imposing height. Let him try.

"And if you take my advice, Miss Liza," Timmens said, "you will stand your ground about those repairs. Any of the servants will vouch for you. They know you are honest and fair. Petersham is not well liked. The gamekeeper tells me there were several incidents where he thought Petersham was not doing what he should to keep the estate up, but he had no way to prove his suspicions.''

Liza shook her head in admiration. ''Thank you.''

Using her anger as a shield against the embarrassment she felt at seeing her husband after what had occurred last night, Liza marched to the library door. She rapped imperiously on the thick oak.

Timmens, who had hurried up behind her, shouldered her aside. Glancing at him, she saw that he intended to announce her. He was right. She straightened her shoulders and waited.

When Alaistair acknowledged the knock, Timmens threw open the door and said in stentorian tones, ''Lady Stone.''

Liza sailed past him, her face coolly composed. It took all her determination not to stumble when she saw her husband.

He looked every inch the country gentleman and devastatingly handsome into the bargain. His loosely fitting blue jacket emphasized the broadness of his shoulders, and at the open neck of his fine lawn shirt, tiny black hairs curled enticingly. The memory of those same hairs tangled around her fingers brought a threatening blush and Liza took a deep breath, willing her mind elsewhere.

She forced her attention to his face. His eyes were expressionless, but his tone was sardonic. "Thank you for gracing us with your presence."

His biting sarcasm hardened her resolve to keep him from shaming her in front of his former steward, whom she sensed in one of the two chairs pulled up to Alaistair's desk. "I have other matters to attend to Lord Alaistair, so if you would get to the point of this meeting . . ."

It was an impertinence and she would not have spoken in that way in front of a retainer if she had not been so incensed with his treatment of her. As it was, she unconsciously took a step back at the blaze of fury in Alaistair's eyes.

"Might I remind you that it was you who let my steward go without first consulting with me?"

Liza swallowed. He appeared relaxed, but she knew from the thinning of his lips and the slight narrowing of his eyes that this was not the case. The perception caught her off guard. When had she grown to know him well enough to note those subtle, betraying characteristics?

"Please sit down," Alaistair said into the silence that had fallen.

Liza did so, glancing at Petersham first. He sat respectfully, his posture erect and his hands clasped in his lap. His light brown hair was brushed neatly away from his face, and his brown eyes were earnest. He was a consummate actor, Liza decided in disgust.

"As you know, Petersham," Alaistair said, seating himself behind his desk, "my wife has accused you of embezzlement. Do you have anything to say for yourself?"

The man leaned forward, his fingers creasing the brim of the wool felt hat he held. "I'm not guilty, m'lord. I've been with you five years, and I've never done anything to be ashamed of." He turned to Liza, his face darkening. "Then she came, and suddenly I'm treated like a criminal."

Liza's hackles rose at his insolence. "I'd wager that had I been able to find the books for the last five years instead of just the current one—which I had to force you to give to me—I would have found further evidence of your tampering."

"I have the other books," Alaistair said quietly, "and there's nothing in them that can be disputed."

Liza glared at him. He wasn't going to support her, no matter what. Bitterness welled up in her. "I can see that you've already made your decision. So be it.'' She rose to leave.

"Sit down, Liza," Alaistair said, his voice brooking no argument. "I said there was no evidence. I didn't say I believe Petersham is innocent.'' He leaned back in his chair and steepled his fingers. He directed his next words at Petersham. "In fact, I tend to think you did everything my wife accused you of.''

Confusion overrode relief as Liza stared at her husband. What was he doing? Petersham had become agitated, his earlier appearance of earnest honesty replaced by a hunted look.

"M'lord," Petersham said, his voice rising. "I thought you believed me innocent. That's why you sent for me, to give me back my position.''

Liza almost felt sorry for the man, he was so pitiable. But he'd taken money that should have gone to repairs on the estate, some of it for the houses the tenants lived in. She hardened her resolve.

Alaistair rose abruptly and went to the door. Opening it, he said, "I'm glad you were on time, Horsely. Please come in.''

Liza recognized the name of the gamekeeper. Apparently Timmens wasn't the only person who'd been asking questions. She began to wonder what Alaistair was up to.

Horsely, a short, stout man with gray hair and brown eyes, entered the room. "Thank 'ee, m'lord."

Returning to his seat behind the desk, Alaistair said, "I've been looking through the ledgers and talking with the servants, Petersham. It seems that, to a man, they think you capable of stealing."

Petersham's face turned gray and when he spoke, his words were tinged with acid. "They all resent me being steward and in charge while you were away. They think that just because my da was a tenant here that I'm not good enough to be your steward. They're envious."

"Beggin' your pardon," the gamekeeper protested, "but the shoe be on the other foot. You thought jest 'cause you ran the estate you was as good as his lordship here. Everyone knows you've been gamblin' at the Cock's Feather more 'n you should."

Liza recognized the Cock's Feather as the tavern in the nearby village. "Did you take the money because of gambling debts?" she asked, unable to stop herself. How many lives had gambling ruined?

Petersham turned to her with a sneer. "What do you know about gambling debts and the pressure to wager more 'n what you earn? You're a rich man's daughter who's known nothin' but luxury.'' The fury he felt laced his speech.

Before her eyes, she watched the man's composure disappear. "Alaistair—" she took a deep breath "—don't punish him further.'' Liza knew if she saw another man ruined because of gambling, she would lose her sanity. "Please.''

Alaistair watched her dispassionately before turning his attention to Petersham. "Did you embezzle money from the estate?''

Defeated, head hanging, he nodded.

The gamekeeper stepped forward and grabbed Petersham's shoulder in a rough grip. "I'll see he gets to Squire for punishment.''

Never once looking at Liza, Alaistair said quietly, "No, Horsely. He's been punished enough by losing his job and the shame he'll reap when he doesn't pay his debts. I won't make it worse by taking him to the magistrate.'' He rose and rounded the desk. "My wife did the right thing when she dismissed him. I won't do differently.'' He stopped in front of Petersham, and his voice would have reduced a less brazen man to a whining coward. "But if I ever hear that you've maligned my wife again, I'll see that you're brought to justice.''

Two steps more and Alaistair was beside Liza's chair, his hand extended to her. "Come along, Liza. This is no place for you."

When they were in the hallway and she was sure no one could hear them, she turned on him. Scowling, she asked, "Did you always suspect him—even yesterday?"

"No." He stared at her, his eyes dark. "But I'm not a fool, and I trust my servants. I began asking questions. It was only a matter of time before I learned of his excessive gambling and the escalating deterioration of the estate. Putting two and two together, I decided that Petersham hadn't always been dishonest but that he was in over his head financially." He shrugged. "Embezzlement was the next logical step. It was the only way he could find the funds to pay his debts."

Liza's hands fisted in the folds of her skirts. "Gambling is like a disease. It has taken yet another weak soul as its victim." She took a deep, soothing breath. "But if you already suspected him, why did you bring him here?"

He gave her a condescending glance. "Because the man was innocent until he confessed his guilt. While you were right about improvements being paid for that were in fact never done, your own repairs covered up most of the evidence. I wanted him to confess." He paused and his black brows drew together. "I also wanted to impress upon him the danger of continuing to slander you."

Liza's eyes widened. He hadn't called her in to belittle her in front of Petersham, but to show her Petersham's admitted guilt. And he'd tried to protect her name.

Before she could respond, he turned and strode away from her. It was as simple as that. He'd done what he intended to do and now he was walking away. Her nails dug into the palms of her hands as she stood stiffly and tried to control the urge to run after him. But what did she want from him anyway, she asked herself, the question only adding to her frustration.

"Excuse me, Miss Liza," Timmens said. "Lord Alaistair brought this letter for you from London."

Liza jumped, not having heard him enter. Spinning around to face him, she said, "Excuse me?"

Timmens clicked his tongue disapprovingly. "I have a letter for you from London. His lordship brought it with him."

Instead of handing it to her on a silver tray, he held it out in a gloved hand. Liza considered correcting him, but one look at his rheumy eyes told her it was impossible. Timmens knew better, he was just being Timmens.

With a sigh of exasperation, she took the letter
and examined the script. It wasn't Sarah, for she
knew her friend's hand well. This writing was boldly
black, yet delicately executed. Lavender wafted
from the sealing wax. Looking closely, Liza recognized the Duke of Rundell's coat of arms.

She smiled. Excitement made her fingers clumsy
as she ripped the letter open, hoping it was from the
duchess. It would be a bright spot in a day that
promised precious few of them. She'd enjoyed what
little time she'd spent with her mother-in-law and
found that she missed her.

Alicia, Duchess of Rundell, wrote a cozy letter
filled with tiny details of life that widened Liza's
smile. When she was through, Liza felt as though
she had had a conversation with Alaistair's mother.

There was no mention of Bent in the letter and no
allusion to the incident in Lady Jersey's garden.
There never had been. But Liza couldn't help the
shiver that chased down her spine at the memory.
Bent could have very easily ruined the duchess.

While Alaistair's mother wasn't totally ostracized from Society because of her elopement, she
also wasn't welcomed in the highest drawing rooms.
Lady Jersey was an exception that Liza had learned
was because Sally Jersey and Alicia had become
friends their first Season, before either was mar-

ried. It was a bond that had never been broken. Lady Jersey might be notoriously high in the instep, but she was also equally loyal.

Still, Liza wondered why Alicia had ever gone into the garden with Bent. But it was pointless of her to worry over something that did not concern her. All that should matter to her was that Bent was out of her life.

THE EARL OF BENT started on his second bottle of wine as he waited for Marie Hardcastle to explain her plan for destroying Alaistair St. Simon. Swaddled in a dark cape, she had appeared on his doorstep five minutes earlier. He'd had to shoo his current doxy upstairs.

"Hurry up, Marie," he said, taking a gulp directly from the bottle and wiping the subsequent dribble from his chin with his sleeve. "I don't have all night."

Disgust curled her crimson lips. "I wish to heaven there was someone I could go to besides you, Bent. You have the manners of a pig."

He leered at her, leaning forward so that his wine-soaked breath overwhelmed her. "I have the manners of a nobleman. And besides—" he sat back, having made his point "—no one else in the ton sympathizes with your plight. The ladies want to take your place with Lord Alaistair and the men want to replace him in your bed."

Come directly from a ball, Marie still had her fan attached to her wrist. She flicked it open and tried to fan away the fumes of his stinking breath. "Enough, Bent. As you've said, you're the only one I can turn to. No one else has been in love with the Duchess of Rundell for the last five years, been beaten with a horsewhip by Saint and then refused to meet him in a duel of honor."

Bent's already reddened face became scarlet. "Beware lest you go too far, Marie. I may want revenge on the man, but that's something I can do with or without your help."

She caught her scathing reply before it left her lips. He had a point. "You know he has sent his new wife to the country."

He took another swig of wine. "That's old news."

Her mouth tightened, emphasizing the tiny lines beginning to form at the corners. "Well, he left for Ciudad Rodrigo four days ago. I think he plans on making a go of this marriage."

Bent belched. "He doesn't want his wife running away with another man. Won't tolerate infidelity. You know that, don't you, m'dear?"

Marie glared at him, but her voice was sickly sweet. "I thought you were cleverer than this, Bent.

It's disappointing that you don't see the means for revenge in this that I do."

Her insult bounced off his wine-induced euphoria. "Sticks and stones may—"

"Oh, stop it." Standing, she hissed, "I can see that you're not the right person after all."

Before she could reach the foyer, he had her wrist in a painful grip. "Don't underestimate me." He dragged her back into the drawing room and shut the door. Leaning against the wall to keep himself erect, he said, "You want to make it impossible for him to fall in love with his wife. You want to discredit and shame the new Lady Alaistair."

She nodded, her green eyes glowing. "Exactly. Perhaps I *was* wrong about you."

He pushed her away and took another gulp of his wine. "You're a vindictive bitch, Marie, with a vicious mind." The last word was slurred as the wine began to affect his speech. "But I believe we can arrange a rendezvous between Lady Alaistair and a man of unsavory reputation, a man with nothing to lose by debauching her."

LIZA GLARED at Alaistair, who rode not more than ten feet away from her. The slight breeze ruffled his hair and the frigid air put color in his high cheekbones. His long fingers skillfully guided the stallion over a tumble of stones that was once a creek bed.

It had been two days since their lovemaking and her skin still burned at the memory. She quickly glanced away so that he wouldn't see her flush. He acted as though his body had never possessed hers. He'd never said a word about what they'd done, and neither had she.

It was one day since the confrontation with Petersham. Alaistair was just as reticent about that as he was about their lovemaking. But this was the second time he had accompanied her on the estate rounds.

They turned left, leaving the path on the open moor and entering a thicket of pine trees. Sunlight penetrated in dabbles of gold that glinted off the bed of dried needles crunching under their horses' hooves. Occasionally, the chirp of a bird broke the silence.

Liza knew that unless she said something they would continue the journey to the next tenant's cottage without a word. That was what had happened the previous time. But today she felt rebellious.

"Will you be returning to London soon?" she asked, hoping his answer would be yes and at the same time perversely hoping it would be no. She told herself she didn't care.

He glanced at her, his eyes shadowed. "When things are put to rights here." One black brow rose. "Are you so eager to see the last of me?"

"Yes." She had lain in bed the previous night wondering if he was going to come to her and vowed to fight him if he did. Dawn had broken before she fell into a restless sleep.

Yet even now, part of her wished he would stop the horses, pull her onto the carpet of pine needles and recreate the wonder of their lovemaking. He had awakened a woman's desire in her that begged for fulfillment. It was only her determination not to succumb to him—a determination that was becoming harder to sustain with each restless night—that kept her from offering herself to him.

Bang!

A shot rang through the forest. Liza's mare reared up, forcing her to grip the pommel with her leg and lean into the animal's neck to keep from sliding off.

"It's probably a poacher," she said, trying to soothe her mount. The shot had come from somewhere in the distance.

A second later, she was torn from the saddle and tossed to the ground. Alaistair held her down while he crouched above her, his eyes scanning the surrounding area.

"Wha—?"

His hand clamped on her mouth and he shook his head to indicate she wasn't to speak. Liza stared at him, wondering if he'd gone mad.

When he was satisfied no one was about, he dragged her behind a large tree trunk. "Stay here," he ordered.

Thoroughly confused and beginning to be a little frightened, Liza dug her fingers into his forearm. "What are you doing?" she whispered.

"Do as you're told," he said harshly.

His eyes were dangerous slits, and his pulse beat rapidly in the vein at his temple. Liza began to shake.

Alaistair gave her one last look and hoped like hell she'd stay put. Crouching down to present the smallest possible target, he crept through the undergrowth in the direction from which the shot had come.

Sweat coated his whole body. He was dimly aware that his reaction was excessive, but he couldn't help himself.

It was Salamanca all over again.

Liza watched Alaistair slink through the trees. What was he doing? Why was he acting as though someone were trying to kill them?

Her inclination was to follow him. Barring that, she felt someone should fetch the horses. Right now they were grazing on tufts of grass sprouting in one of the sunny areas, but there was no telling when they would decide to wander off. It was a long way back to Ciudad Rodrigo.

But Alaistair had said to stay put. She would wait a few minutes and see what he was planning to do.

She didn't have long to wait.

He gathered the horses' reins as he strode back to her. His chin was cut where a branch had caught him and his hair was in total disarray, curling around his forehead and jaw. Sweat glistened at the base of his throat and his shirt clung to his skin.

"Did you find anything?" she asked, standing up and brushing off her riding skirt.

"Some footprints."

His eyes were cold and haunted and tension radiated from him. He looked like a wild animal ready to pounce on its prey. A shiver skipped down her back.

"Do you think someone shot at us?" Her fingers felt like ice as she took her mare's reins from him.

He shrugged, his eyes hooded. "Possibly. It wouldn't surprise me to find out Petersham did it. He has a grudge to settle, and killing one or both of us would certainly be a way to do it."

She shuddered. "Perhaps we should return to Ciudad Rodrigo."

"I'm not such a weakling as that, and if it was Petersham, he won't try again today. Here, use my hands," he ordered when she started to lead her mare to a fallen tree trunk so she could mount.

In an effort to ease some of the tension, Liza forced herself to grin. "I'll only use you for a mounting block if you promise not to throw me over the saddle and onto the opposite side."

Her words seemed to jolt him, and for the first time since the shot he focused on her, some of the strain easing from his features.

"My apologies, Liza. I didn't mean to upset you." He spoke the words calmly, but he didn't return her smile. "Unexpected gunshots send me back in time."

The word Salamanca was unspoken, but she knew that was what he referred to. "It's all right."

Placing her foot in his clasped hands, she allowed him to hoist her up. By the time she was properly situated, he was ready. They turned the horses in the direction they'd been traveling before the shot.

Liza glanced up at him, trying to gauge his emotions. He appeared calm but not totally relaxed. In spite of their past confrontations, she found herself wanting to help him. "Would you like to talk about it?" she ventured. "Sometimes it helps."

He looked at her, his eyes silver bright. "How would you know?"

It was a cold, cynical question and Liza felt her anger rising at his attitude toward her. But she didn't want to quarrel with him now.

She took a deep breath. "I know because when my parents died I thought the world had ended. Michael and I were alone in the world with no close relatives, no grandparents, aunts or uncles. For days I spoke to no one, not even Michael. The vicar and his wife did their best to comfort us, but it wasn't enough."

Her lips curved in the hint of a smile. "Then one day Timmens took me aside. First he lectured me about my duties as the new mistress. I was only eight at the time and most of what he said was meaningless, but that's Timmens. Then he took me onto his knees and told me to let the pain out. To talk about it. He said that nothing else would ease the loss like sharing it with another person who cared. It was what I needed. It was the beginning of my healing."

Neither of them spoke for long minutes as their horses followed the path through the pines without guidance. Overhead a flock of rooks took flight, alarmed at the human intrusion.

Alaistair reached for her reins and pulled both horses to a stop. "Thank you. It wasn't easy for you to tell me those things."

She smiled wistfully into his eyes. What she saw was the hunger she was beginning to expect whenever he looked at her, but this time there was more. There was a gentleness that had never been there before. And she knew the gentleness was for her and for what she'd shared with him. It created a strange, unsettled sensation in the pit of her stomach.

"It's never easy to reveal a hurt to another person." She paused to take a deep breath, her fingers tightening on the reins. "Particularly someone you've been blaming for your loss."

His fingers grazed her chin, and she blinked at the pleasure his touch brought.

"You're a remarkable woman."

Before she could reply, he leaned forward and kissed her. It wasn't a demanding or invasive kiss. Instead it spoke of concern. Yet underlying it was a hint of desire held firmly in check.

It was over too soon. Liza put out one hand to steady herself. Her palm rested on Alaistair's chest, just above his heart, which beat strong and hard.

She gave him a tentative smile. He returned it before pulling his horse away.

"We'd best be on our way, lest I forget myself and drag you to the ground. I don't want a repetition of two nights ago."

Liza frowned at his back. His bluntness hurt, but she shouldn't have expected anything else from him. She didn't want anything else from him. She didn't.

CHAPTER THIRTEEN

THAT NIGHT AFTER DINNER, Alaistair took the bottle of port Timmens brought and asked for a second glass.

"Beggin' your pardon, m'lord," Timmens said, "but it doesn't bode well when a gentleman intends to drink his port from two glasses."

"Just so," Alaistair replied. "But rest easy, Timmens, one of the glasses is for her ladyship."

Timmens cast Liza a glance. "Miss Liza prefers sherry. I'll bring a decanter of that with the second glass."

"Thank you, Timmens," Alaistair said dryly.

Liza smothered a laugh in her napkin. "He can be trying at times."

His eyes met hers. "But he can also bring comfort."

She nodded. "I tell myself that every time he's impertinent."

"Which is often," Alaistair said for her.

Sharing this moment with Alaistair felt incredibly intimate, and Liza had to suppress an impulse to rise from her seat and go to him. She wanted to push the ebony hair off his brow and run her fingers through the thick waves. She wanted . . .

Luckily, Timmens returned at the moment.

Setting a tray with a decanter of sherry and a second glass on the table, he asked, "Will there be anything else, m'lord?"

"No, thank you," Alaistair said, rising and putting the port and his glass on the tray. Picking it up, he asked, "Liza, will you join me in the library? I'd like to continue our discussion of this afternoon."

Feeling relief mixed with apprehension, Liza followed him. When he hadn't confided in her that afternoon, she'd decided he didn't intend to. Now it seemed that he would and she was not sure if she wanted it. How would she feel if he shared his fears with her? Would she be able to maintain the emotional barrier she'd erected when he'd made it impossible for her to annul their marriage? Or would she succumb to the passion she tried to deny that would make the coming night another sleepless one?

Taking a seat far away from the biscuit table where Alaistair had set the tray, Liza watched him pour her a glass of sherry. Their fingers grazed as he gave it to her, and she drew back slightly at the heat his touch generated. When she glanced up to see if he'd noticed, his eyes were black.

A wry smile twisted his lips. "I didn't ask you in here to seduce you." He picked up a decanter filled with golden brown liquid.

"What's that?"

He turned to her, his lips twisting in self-mockery. "Whiskey. I find that port isn't strong enough tonight." He poured a large measure into the glass. "Would you like to try some?"

Liza studied her amber sherry, then took a sip of it. It moved warmly down her throat. Perhaps this was a night to explore. "Yes, please."

He poured a smaller amount into a second tumbler and gave it to her, his glass in his other hand. "Sip it. It will burn going down."

Again his fingers brushed hers, sending fire sparking along the dry tinder of her nerves. Her gaze fastened on him and boldly met his dark appraisal. She was strong enough to resist the allure he held for her, she told herself.

He looked away and chose a seat far enough from her that she would not be able to touch him without getting up. A soft sigh of relief escaped her. It was better this way.

She took a sip of her whiskey—and gasped for breath. It burnt her tongue and blazed a trail to her stomach.

He smiled. "It takes time to get used to."

She nodded, still unable to speak.

Swirling the liquid in his glass, he added, "It also gives false courage. Many's the time I saw men drunk on this go bravely into battle. Sometimes they survived. Sometimes they didn't." His mouth twisted bitterly and his eyes were bleak. Liza's heart went out to him.

"War is hell," he muttered, "and once you're in it, there's only one way out until it's over."

Hell. Now she understood. "That's how you knew what I was going through with Michael. Because of Salamanca—the war—and what it did to you."

His angular cheeks were burnished by the fire. "And I lived to tell the story."

In one last gulp, he drained his glass. Liza took another sip of hers, wanting the false sense of comfort the whiskey provided.

"Is that what your nightmares are about?" she asked.

He shrugged. "I think so. Rast says I talk about the battles, but when I awaken I can't remember."

"You forget them because they are so horrible."

Setting his empty glass down on a table, he rose and went to the fireplace. He propped one booted foot on the grate and stared into the dancing flames. "Do you think so? Then why don't I forget the actual battles?"

"I...I don't know," she said, joining him. "Perhaps you can tolerate the memories when you're awake and can turn your thoughts elsewhere, but in your dreams you have no control. When you sleep, your mind takes you where it wishes and all you can do is endure."

He turned his brooding gaze on her. "Perhaps."

"It's the only explanation I can think of." Her straight auburn brows drew together as she thought some more about it. "Perhaps if I awaken you immediately when I hear you having a nightmare, you'll be able to remember it and talk about it. Maybe that will help you get over this." She looked hopefully at him. "What do you think?"

He smiled down at her, some of the darkness leaving his eyes. "I think you're a remarkable woman."

She flushed. Suddenly, the fire was uncomfortably hot. She reached up for a stray lock of hair to twist. "Thank you. But anyone would try to help."

"I doubt it." He caught her hand.

Strength and security flowed from him. He was so masculine and yet, at this moment, so vulnerable.

Unable to resist the temptation any longer, she rose and lightly pushed the strand of hair from his forehead. It was like touching silk. She wanted to bury her fingers in his hair.

His eyes took on a hooded look, the lashes a heavy shadow.

"Liza," he murmured, "don't do such things unless you're willing to suffer the consequences."

Her face flamed and she yanked her hand back. "I'm sorry. I didn't think."

He smiled. "That's encouraging."

The implication in his words made her eyes widen. Was he saying he wanted more from her than a marriage of convenience? She must be mistaken.

Before she could stumble through an answer, he asked, "What about you, Liza? Do you ever have nightmares? God knows you've been through enough to warrant them."

His question took her by surprise, and she answered without thinking. "Sometimes," she said, her voice soft. "Sometimes they haunt my nights, but I always remember them. They're always about Michael."

For Liza, the magic of the moment was broken. She must never forget what he had done.

She twisted away and went back to her seat. Sinking into the leather cushions, she picked up her glass and took another sip of whiskey. She found that it helped to calm the churning in her stomach.

"I've started you remembering again." He pushed away from the fireplace and poured himself another glass of whiskey. "It seems this is a night for memories and pain."

He downed the liquor in one long gulp.

"If the memory of the war is so distasteful, why did you choose a Spanish name for your estate—a name that must bring back memories every time you hear it?"

He poured himself another drink. "Punishment? At the time, I told myself it was so that I'd never forget the horrors of war, the pain and death and broken dreams. And it's done that." He gulped the whiskey.

Liza watched him, beginning to understand the devils that drove him. But she'd had enough revelations for one day. She didn't think she could endure much more of this baring of souls, this closeness that was slowly chipping away at her resolve never to harbor warm emotions toward him.

Rising from her seat, she said quietly, "It's time for me to retire. So, if you'll excuse me..."

He went to the door and opened it for her. Liza picked up her half-full glass and went past him into the hall.

"Thank you." She started in the direction of the stairs, hoping there would be a candle on the table at the foot of them. The servants had gone to bed and the hall was pitch-black.

A light flickered behind her. It was Alaistair, carrying a candle. He came beside her and took her arm with his free hand.

Tremors moved through her, leaving her disturbed and restless. It was an effort not to lean into him; her body was weaker than her will.

Still holding tightly to the glass of whiskey, she let him lead her up the stairs and down the hall to her room. He opened the door and stood aside so that she could get by him. Her shoulder brushed his chest in passing.

Here, with her room before them, the bed dominating the scene, she was intensely aware of him. His breathing was deep and even, and the scent of whiskey wafted to her nostrils.

Would he taste like whiskey? Would his kiss spin her mind and burn her throat the way whiskey did?

Without realizing she did so, she turned her face up to his. His eyes glittered in the candle flame as he lit the wall sconce by her door, then he snuffed the candle he'd carried and set it on the floor.

He groaned as he stood back up. His head lowered to hers. "I can't deny you twice in one night."

His mouth took hers with a fierce possessiveness that sapped her strength. The glass of whiskey fell unheeded from her hand. Her fingers curled around the open collar of his shirt, the wiry texture of the hair there tickling her skin and inviting her questing fingers inside to explore the hard muscles of his chest. His skin was smooth except where the swirling hair textured it. She delved deeper, searching.

"Liza," Alaistair gasped as her fingers found his nipples and skimmed around the ruched edges.

Amazement made her smile against his lips. A simple touch, and his breath quickened and his heart pounded. What would happen if she explored him more thoroughly? It was an exciting and dangerous idea.

His tongue laved her lips, seeking admittance, which she gladly granted. Slowly at first, then increasing in speed, it delved inside her mouth. His hips emulated the motion of his tongue, and Liza's hands stopped stroking him and clung to him instead as her knees weakened even more.

His arms circled her waist and slid down her hips to cup her buttocks and lift her to his swollen flesh.

The press of him, hard and full against her aching stomach, made her mind reel.

Once more, the abyss of his lovemaking was swallowing her. All her fine resolve disappeared in the spiraling vortex of emotions he evoked.

"Milady, be that ye?"

Nell's sleepy voice from beyond Liza's room caused them to draw apart. Alaistair set her away from him, keeping his hands firmly on her shoulders. His mouth was full and sensual. The sight of it set Liza's heart beating like the wings of a bird.

"Come to my room," he whispered, his voice a deep rasp, as he drew her to the doorway to his adjoining room.

Temptation beckoned to her. She knew the magic he could conjure in her body, but she also knew the pain he could inflict so well. Pulling back, she said through kiss-swollen lips, "I don't think so."

His eyes mocked her, the slumberous look of seconds before gone. "Coward. You're afraid of what I make you feel. You're only a girl in a woman's body."

Her temper flared. She drew herself up so that her head reached the bottom of his chin. "And you're a coldhearted libertine who thinks of no one but himself. Well, I'm not so weak as to succumb to your skills yet again."

"Milady?" came Nell's voice once more.

Knowing that if she stayed their fight would escalate, Liza gathered up her skirts and fled into her room. She closed the door, then leaned back against the solid mahogany. The fury of seconds before dissipated. His parting words had been a verbal slap, but she couldn't hate him for them. To her shame, everything he'd said was true. She feared the strong emotions he made her feel. They were dangerous.

"Milady?" Nell's worried voice broke through her troubled thoughts.

Liza forced a smile. "Go to bed, Nell. Everything is fine."

The maid nodded before disappearing into the small room where her trundle bed was. Liza was grateful for the girl's compliance. She needed to be alone. She had to think.

Alaistair was a troubled man, but he was a fair man. And he wanted her. He didn't love her and she didn't love him, but the desire between them was like a living thing, throbbing with intensity.

And she'd promised to go to him if his nightmare returned. She was not stupid. With that promise, she had committed herself to make love to him again.

The thought was both exciting and frightening.

LIZA WAS LATE for breakfast the next morning, having lain awake most of the night listening for

Alaistair. Nothing happened, however, except that she got very little sleep. Barely awake she stumbled into the morning room and went straight to the sideboard, where she poured herself a cup of coffee.

"No hot chocolate this morning?" Timmens asked, entering from the serving area.

She glanced at him. "No, I need something stronger."

"Not sleeping well?" came Alaistair's deep voice, making her jump and spill the coffee onto the carpet.

"Damnation," she muttered, driven beyond endurance. Twisting around, she looked at him with ill-concealed exasperation.

He sat at the head of the table, just finishing his breakfast. It was obvious he hadn't been bothered last night and that he'd been up for some time. Liza's ire rose.

"Testy?" he queried.

"No," she answered haughtily, "merely preoccupied."

He gave her a knowing look, his gaze wandering slowly over her person. "Worried about Petersham?"

The question took her by surprise, and from the taunting gleam in her husband's eyes, he had intended it to. Composing her features, she asked coolly, "Should I be?"

"Not anymore." He rose and pulled a chair out for her, his face hard. "Horsely caught him yesterday, and he confessed to shooting at us. He's on his way to a ship bound for North America."

Liza took the seat he offered, glad that the grim smile on his face wasn't directed at her. "I suppose you could have been harder on him."

"I could have had him hanged."

There was nothing to say to that. Liza swallowed hard, knowing he spoke the truth. She took a drink of the strong coffee to give herself something to do.

"Timmens," he said in an aside, "her ladyship will need some fresh toast and a piece of ham. And while you're in the kitchen, have Cook prepare a picnic luncheon."

Liza took another sip and another, the hot liquid reviving her. "Are you going somewhere special?"

His smile was enigmatic, easing the harsh lines of his face. "*We* are."

Liza raised her eyebrows. "We are?"

He moved to stand behind her chair. "After you eat."

Liza fought the tingle of awareness caused by his nearness. She spread marmalade on a piece of toast and took a bite.

Alaistair bent over her. "You look as if you didn't sleep at all." With his index finger, he gently touched the delicate skin beneath her eyes. "You could have been the loser in a prizefight with these dark circles."

His concern was unexpected and unnerving. Liza took another bite of toast and made a production of chewing it, as though eating were the only thing that mattered to her. There was no need for him to know just how much he affected her.

When she didn't answer, he said, "Were you regretting your decision last night? Is that why you didn't sleep?"

It was an outrageous question. She stared at him in cold disapproval, and her mouth went dry at the undisguised hunger she saw there.

"Aren't you going to answer me?" he asked softly.

He was toying with her, she knew, but it didn't keep her hands from shaking so that she had to put down the piece of toast lest he see the effect he had on her. "No. I'm not going to play into your game by answering."

He returned to his seat, the tension disappearing from him as he grinned. "I didn't think so, but I had to try." Before she could rebuke him, he ordered, "Finish eating so we can be on our way."

Liza cleared her throat to tell him no.

"Ahem." Timmens appeared in the doorway. "Your picnic lunch is ready, m'lord. Do you want it packed in a basket?"

As though he knew exactly what she'd been getting ready to say, Alaistair grinned at her before turning to the butler. "Excellent timing, Timmens."

Timmens drew himself up regally. "I pride myself on my punctuality, m'lord."

"I'm sure you do," Alaistair murmured. Louder, he said, "Please pack the food into saddlebags along with a blanket and a flask of wine."

"Yes, sir." Timmens bowed, his glance going from Alaistair to Liza.

"Everything is fine," Liza hastened to assure her old retainer.

"Doesn't appear that way to me, Miss Liza," Timmens said, having the last word as he left the room.

Liza shook her head apologetically. "He's always said exactly what he thinks. I don't think we can change that."

"I wouldn't want to. He's a singular fellow and he's only concerned about you. You can't condemn loyalty."

Liza shot her husband a questioning look. She should have known he would appreciate loyalty. After all, he had Rast.

"Meow!" Baby's greeting preceded his jump into Alaistair's lap by seconds. Kneading his master's thighs through his buckskin breeches, the cat sought a comfortable position. When he was settled, Baby's purr reverberated throughout the room.

"I think he likes you," Liza said, trying not to grin.

"A very discerning animal," Alaistair replied with a grimace. "But I wish he'd stop sticking his claws into my clothing. Rast is beside himself. It's one thing to give the beast extra cravats, but quite another to replace leather breeches."

Liza laughed in spite of her earlier irritation, causing Baby to give her an aggrieved look. "My apologies, Baby. I wasn't making fun of you, just appreciating the ease of your assimilation into a noble household. You must have come from a long line of well-bred felines."

"Undoubtedly." Alaistair carefully removed the cat's claws from his breeches and stood. "Your mistress and I have things to do today, old boy." So saying, he resettled Baby on the empty chair and gave Liza his hand. "I'll meet you at the stables in thirty minutes."

Her earlier sense of ill-usage returned. "Where are we going? I thought I'd been over all of Ciudad Rodrigo. And you can't just tell me we're going on a picnic on a moment's notice."

"I can't?" He paused in the doorway. "Does this mean you aren't coming?"

Liza frowned. Instead of apologizing for his presumption, or asking her politely, he turned the tables on her. Carefully considering her words, she murmured, "Well, I suppose your offer of an outing is the best I'll receive today."

He laughed outright at her. "Don't be late. Patience is a quality I have little of these days. I want to show you the moors."

WHEN THEY REINED in their mounts several hours later, Liza's eyes widened at the desolate beauty spread out before her. The Pennines formed a backdrop of stark shadows and brilliant peaks. At their base, a lake spread out, so still it appeared to be a gray mirror, frost rimming its edge.

"It's magnificent," Liza said, sliding down from her saddle and pulling her cape tight against the cold breeze.

Alaistair joined her, so close his shoulder brushed hers. "It's called Semerwater." His eyes held mischievous glints. "And today it's so clear and calm that if we try hard enough we may be able to see the city on its floor."

"A city?" She smiled up at him, noting the fun in his eyes. "You're bamming me, of course."

He took her hand, his flesh warm through the glove she wore, and led her through the rushes to the edge. "I'm perfectly serious. Legend has it that a gilded city lies beneath its waves, put there long ago by a curse."

Liza shivered with delight. "Like a fairy story. Tell me about it."

He smiled down at her before assuming a serious demeanor. "'Tis a sad tale of greed and revenge."

She couldn't help laughing; he looked so morose and it was all a sham. "Tell me anyway."

Still holding her hand, he began. "Long ago there was a rich town here, exactly where Semerwater lies, but it was a greedy town. One day a poor man with supernatural powers came to the city. He tried in vain to find food or shelter at one of the wealthy houses, but no one would give him either. Finally, in a poor shack on one of the surrounding hillsides, he was given both. In revenge, the man cursed the city with these words—'Semerwater rise, Semerwater sink, And swallow all the town save this little house, Where they gave me food and drink.' Immediately, a great flood engulfed the wicked city and it's never been seen since.''

A hush fell over them when he had finished. Liza peered into the waters, knowing there was no city but caught up in the tale anyway.

''The moral of the story,'' Alaistair said lightly, ''is never to turn a beggar from your door.''

''At Thornyhold we never turned anyone away who was cold or hungry.''

He released her hand and went back to the horses, where he unloaded the bags of food and spread the blanket under a large elm tree. She followed him.

Rummaging in the bags, he pulled out thick, juicy meat pasties, a wedge of aged cheddar cheese and two delicious-smelling apples. Next was a flask of wine, but no glasses.

He grimaced. ''Rast must have packed this luncheon. He never did remember glasses in the Peninsula.''

''We'll drink straight from the bottle,'' Liza said, enjoying the novelty of eating out-of-doors, intrigued by this change in the man she'd married. This was the first time she'd seen him lighthearted and, against her better judgment, she was enjoying it. ''There's no one here to deplore our manners but the birds and our horses.''

''So be it.''

He handed her a dripping pastry, the aroma of beef floating up to Liza's nostrils. She took a big bite, the juice dribbling down her chin. "Oh dear," she muttered, looking for a napkin.

"Let me." Alaistair's husky voice drew her attention to him.

For a heart-stopping moment, she thought he meant to lick the juice from her chin, so intense were his eyes. Just as she leaned back, afraid of her reaction if he did, he lifted a napkin to her face and wiped the gravy away with it.

"Thank you," she managed to reply calmly in spite of the riotous beating of her pulse.

"Cook makes the best pasties in Yorkshire, but they're messy," he said, his voice only slightly less husky than before.

Liza sat frozen. The gesture was so intimate, as though they'd been married and caring for each other for years. The thought was disturbing.

Her empty stomach complained loudly, dissolving the tension.

"You'd best satisfy yourself," he said, taking a huge bite of his own pasty. "For I intend to finish whatever you don't."

The moment was gone, and Liza told herself to be grateful that it was over before anything else happened.

The wind whipped the trees and chilled their flesh before they finished their repast. Liza packed the empty wine flask and napkins while Alaistair folded the blanket.

"Fall isn't the best time for a picnic in north Yorkshire," he said, squinting his eyes as he looked into the wind. "But you've got to take what life offers, when it offers."

Liza understood. With his hair tumbling down over his brow and his face relaxed, he appeared infinitely approachable. She'd never seen him like this before. It created a twinge in the vicinity of her heart, then a lurch, boding ill for her serenity.

"'Tis time to go," he said, glancing up at the sky. "A storm's brewing. We'd best be on our way."

Liza looked up. The pale sun was hidden by scuttling gray clouds.

"And even then, we'll probably not make it," she predicted.

She was right. After fifteen minutes of hard riding, the first splash of rain hit them. From then on it was a race to see if they could outdistance the body of the storm, a race they lost. By the time they cantered into the stable yard, both were soaked to the skin and Liza's teeth chattered uncontrollably.

Two stable boys splashed through the mud to take the steaming horses. Liza jumped down without help, not willing to keep her mare out in the beastly weather any longer than absolutely necessary.

"See that you rub them until they're dry," Alaistair directed. "And give them extra oats. Then get yourselves to a fire and dry out. Cook will have some warm milk and scones."

"Yes, sir," both boys chorused, grins splitting their faces.

Liza's smile at the boys was cut short as Alaistair grabbed her wrist and yanked her toward the house. They ran through puddles up to their ankles and rain that coated their faces, not stopping until they were in the foyer, dripping pools of water onto the cream marble floor.

"Oh dear," Timmens intoned, seemingly appearing from nowhere, "Mrs. Neddles will be fit to be tied over this. She just had these tiles polished this morning."

Alaistair slicked his hair back from his face. "Mrs. Neddles is no stranger to storms, Timmens."

The butler eyed him doubtfully. "If you say so, m'lord."

"I do," Alaistair stated before turning his back on the butler to look at Liza. He stood stock-still.

Liza's riding bonnet was a soggy mess, its single ostrich feather drooping about her ear. But that wasn't what held him spellbound. Her rain-drenched clothing clung to her like the finest silk, her nipples hard pebbles pressed against the wool of her jacket.

His mind conjured up pictures of her the night she'd come to save him from the nightmare. He could almost feel the sleek satin of her skin beneath his fingers.

A dull ache started in his loins and spread through his body in seconds. He wanted her.

"Miss Liza," Timmens said, stepping between her and Alaistair, "you'd best be getting upstairs to a hot bath before you catch your death of cold." He shot a sideways look at his employer. "Or worse."

Alaistair bit back a sharp retort. "Correct as always, Timmens."

Liza gave them both a puzzled glance before shaking her head and hurrying up the stairs. Alaistair watched her, his eyes shadowed.

"She deserves better than a marriage of convenience," Timmens said quietly.

Anger flared in Alaistair, but he quickly tamped it down. "What we want and what we deserve are often far removed, Timmens," he replied, before starting up the stairs himself.

CHAPTER FOURTEEN

HOURS LATER, Liza woke with a start.

The room was dark, the fire having died long ago. Lightning lit the windows, even through the draperies. Thunder crashed overhead. The storm that had drenched them that afternoon was continuing unabated. If anything, it was worse.

Propping herself on her elbows, she decided it must have been the thunder that woke her. It rumbled through the house, the furniture vibrating with its force.

A resounding crack rattled the windows, then was followed by deathly silence. Not even the sound of the rain hitting the panes alleviated the stillness that seeped coldly into Liza's bones.

Then she heard it.

Sitting straight up, she strained to hear.

"No, I said!"

Alaistair's voice rose above the resuming thunder, as though he strove to make himself heard in spite of it. Liza knew better. It wasn't the storm he was trying to overcome, it was cannon fire and the screams of wounded men.

"God damn it! I told you not to go."

His words beat away the sounds of the storm. Liza knew he was tossing in his bed, his arms flailing, his body covered with sweat. He needed her.

Her hands stilled as she moved to throw the covers back. If she went to him, she would end up making love to him. But she had promised him.

Her eyes stared into the darkness to another time. Eighteen years ago she'd promised her dead mother that she would take care of her brother, and she had failed. She couldn't break her promise to Alaistair. She wouldn't allow her anxiety about his lovemaking to keep her from going to his aid.

Moving rapidly, she crossed to the door separating their rooms. As before, Rast stood just inside the bedroom, a candle illuminating his concerned countenance. Liza nodded to him as she made her way to the bed and her husband. Rast slipped away, taking the candle with him, but a glow from the fire's embers illuminated the room.

In the dim light Alaistair was a writhing black mound. Moans rose from deep in his throat as he relived past horrors that continued to be part of his present.

"Alaistair," Liza whispered, knowing she had to awaken him and preferring to do it out of his bed. "Alaistair," she repeated louder when her first effort failed.

"Come back!" His shout echoed in the silent room.

A chill shivered through Liza. She reached out to him, intending to shake him, but he flung his arm out, catching her in the chest and sending her reeling against the nightstand.

Startled, she gripped the edge of the stand to keep her balance. This was worse than the previous time.

Approaching the bed again, she made out his silhouette in the darkness. He was twisting and gyrating just as he had the other time, and she knew he'd be drenched in sweat.

Taking a deep breath, she slipped onto the bed. His heated flesh was like a searing brand against her restraining arms, and though his nakedness came as no surprise, still she felt herself hesitate.

Dismissing the momentary weakness, she pressed her body firmly into his in an effort to calm him. "Alaistair, it's me... Liza. Wake up."

He bucked against her, nearly sending her sprawling. Knowing that she had to wake him, and do so while he was still in the throes of the dream,

Liza let him go. Leaning away, she brought her arm up and slapped his face hard.

He jerked, his body stiffening.

"Alaistair," she said loudly, knowing Rast wouldn't interfere if he heard her.

Alaistair's eyes opened, unfocused at first, then slowly showing awareness. "Liza?"

Tentatively, she reached out to him, not sure if he was fully conscious or whether he'd swing out at her again. When he remained still, she gently brushed the damp hair back from his forehead.

"You were having a nightmare. I think the thunder brought it on." She spoke softly, not wanting to break his train of thought. He had to remember.

He rolled onto his back, one arm covering his eyes, the other lying at his side, fingers clenched. "Yes."

"Do you remember it?" She prayed that he did and would share it with her. She could think of no other way to stop his torment. Lying on her side, raised up on one elbow, she waited.

He took a deep breath. "Some. More than I like."

His chest rose and fell with each deep breath he took. She wanted to comfort him, to touch him, but was afraid it would ruin everything.

"Will you tell me?"

He groaned in despair. "God knows I don't want to."

"You must. It's the only way." She didn't know if that was true, she only hoped it would help.

Slowly, each word punctuated by pain, he began. "I think it's the same dream I always have, but I can't be sure. It starts with my telling the sergeant he can't leave camp anymore. The next thing I know, he's being shot on my orders." He stopped and rubbed his temples. "That part really happened."

Liza longed to ease his agony but dared not do anything. It pained her that all she could do was listen and encourage him to relive his personal hell once more.

"After that, it becomes even worse." He laughed bitterly. "We're in the midst of battle. Men are falling all around me. Their screams are like knives in my gut. Cannon shot is drowned out by their cries of pain. Blood darkens the ground. The stench of death is unbearable."

Liza's stomach roiled. He was describing hell on earth and there was nothing she could do to comfort him.

Alaistair's breathing slowed. "Then he steps in front of me. Just like that." He paused, and his voice became deathly calm. "He steps in front of me. I hear a cannon go off...he's blown into tiny pieces. It was supposed to be me.''

Liza felt her blood run cold and she sought desperately for the right words. "It wasn't your fault," she said lamely.

"It was supposed to be me. He died for me. He was blown to bits instead of me."

The agony in his voice, the stiff way he lay beside her, tore at Liza. "It wasn't your fault, Alaistair! You didn't make him step in front of you. You couldn't have stopped him."

He turned on her, suddenly fierce. "Yes, I could have."

Her first inclination was to flee from the fury and raw pain in his voice, but she forced herself to hold her ground. She had to, for his sake. "How could you have prevented him?"

He groaned, rolling onto his back again. "I don't know. Not exactly. I just could have."

He was living the same hell she lived, whenever she thought of Michael's death. Firmly, she said, "You couldn't have kept him from stepping in front of you unless you knew he was going to do it. Did you know?" For long minutes he didn't answer. More loudly, she demanded, "Did you know?"

He sighed. "No." His voice was dull. "How could I know? I didn't even know who he was."

"Then you couldn't have prevented his death. You must stop blaming yourself for something you had no control over. You've got to let the guilt go."

He laughed softly, derisively. "'Tis easier said than done."

"Yes." She knew it only too well. "Yes, it is."

"So hard," he murmured. Turning back to her, he said, "Thank you for coming tonight."

"I wish I could do more. It seems so inadequate."

His eyes were dark circles she could not read in his shadowed face. She felt his fingers gently brush her cheek.

"You've done more for me tonight than I ever expected from another person, Liza. Talking about it helped. It's as though a crushing weight has become bearable, and for that I thank you."

Her heart went out to him. He was so proud and yet so vulnerable. "I couldn't let you continue to suffer without trying to do something. I'm glad it's helped. I only hope that you stop suffering from these memories."

"But even if I don't," he whispered, "your being here is something I'll never forget."

Instinctively, she moved closer to him, savoring the warmth of his naked body. She was beginning to feel things that she wasn't prepared for, yet wasn't willing to deny. Heaven help her.

"I'll do this again, if need be," she vowed.

"Thank you." He spoke quietly, and his breath caressed her neck.

"I . . . I'd better return to my bed," she mumbled, trying to break his spell over her. There were so many things she had to think over.

He sighed. "No." The hand that had so recently stroked her cheek clasped her shoulder. "Please, stay with me. For a little while. I promise not to do anything."

She echoed his sigh, wondering if she truly could stay with him. But she didn't have the strength to deny him. Not after what he'd just been through.

"For a while," she acquiesced.

He drew her down into the bed and nestled against her spoon fashion. Liza was acutely aware of his flesh burning through her thin nightdress.

Butterflies jostled in her stomach and breathing was difficult, nearly impossible. She wasn't sure how long she could tolerate this.

In the end, he fell asleep, his arm a tight band around her waist and the steady rise and fall of his chest a calming influence on her tense body. Before the sun rose, Liza managed to extricate herself from his embrace and make her way back to her own bed.

Staring into the darkness, she felt the cold emptiness that had consumed her since Michael's death begin to fill with warmth. Knowing the depths of Alaistair's suffering, she found it impossible to continue blaming him for Michael's death. She had to accept that Alaistair had truly meant to return the vowel that day, as he said. A man who had experienced such pain himself could never have willingly inflicted similar suffering on an innocent like Michael.

And she had to forgive herself. She couldn't have kept Michael from killing himself any more than Alaistair could have stopped that man from stepping in front of him. People were responsible for their own actions.

Tears seeped from Liza's eyes and she made no effort to check them. She had to face the reality that she'd done her best—just as Alaistair had done his best. Perhaps it hadn't been enough, but it was the most she was capable of at the time. She had tried.

Now she had to let it go. She had to find peace within herself . . . for herself and for Alaistair. It wouldn't be easy, she knew.

Her tears continued to fall as dawn tinted the room pink.

THE FOLLOWING DAYS were hell for Liza. Her nerves were strung at a dangerously high pitch.

Having come to terms with herself over Alaistair's part in Michael's suicide, she had to accept the growing awareness that she enjoyed being with her husband—wanted to be with him as much as possible.

Her day brightened when she heard Alaistair's voice or footsteps. She couldn't keep from smiling at him first thing in the morning while they ate breakfast. Every night, he joined her in her dreams. Every night, she longed for the door between their bedchambers to open and for him to walk into her room and take her into his arms.

She knew love wasn't in his plans. She didn't want it to be part of hers, either, but didn't know how to stop it. If she loved him, she knew she would end up being hurt.

With a sigh, she forced herself to concentrate on the estate books, spread before her on the library desk. Alaistair had hired a new steward, and though the man seemed competent, Liza had taken it upon herself to monitor the estate's accounts. She didn't want a repeat of Petersham's dishonesty.

Outside the weather was growing cold. Winter would soon be upon them.

"Liza." Alaistair's deep voice startled her. "I thought I'd find you here. We should discuss a few matters before I leave."

She looked up, watching him warily as he came toward her, Baby at his heels. "You're leaving?"

"For London. I must see my man of business." He took a seat opposite the desk and Baby jumped into his lap and settled down.

She nodded, her breath coming a little easier now. "When do you leave?"

"Tomorrow. That's why I want to talk to you today."

Liza stared at him, only dimly aware of Baby's purring and the snap of a log as it split in the fireplace. Weak sunlight came through the window behind her but wasn't enough to take away the chill that had settled in her bones at Alaistair's announcement. Perhaps she was coming down with a cold, she told herself.

Carefully, she closed the account book and forced her eyes to meet his. "What do you wish to discuss?"

"Us."

The single word fell between them with a thud. Liza saw Alaistair's jaw harden and his eyes take on the familiar gunmetal sheen. Neither change boded well for what was to come.

She began to twirl a strand of loose hair. "What is there to say? Will you stay there permanently while I reside here? That arrangement would be perfect for a marriage of convenience.''

The words tumbled from her, making little sense, but he'd taken her by surprise. He never interrupted her when she was doing the books. *He hadn't mentioned leaving.*

His fingers stilled in their scratching of Baby's head. ''I don't know how long I'll be gone. However long it takes. As for a marriage of convenience, that's what brings me here.''

She licked her dry lips. Suddenly, she didn't want a marriage of convenience. She didn't want him to go. *She loved him.*

The shock of that realization made her close her eyes against the sight of him lounging across from her, against the sight of his handsome, autocratic face.

''I want to make it clear to you before I leave that when I return, our marriage will be a marriage in more than name only. We've made love once before, and I intend to continue doing so.''

His words hit her like a bolt of lightning, searing her nerves with the images of passion that sprang to her mind. Perversely, she fought her reaction. Marriage to a man who didn't love her would be hell. She didn't want to follow in the footsteps of Alaistair's mother. She wanted his love from the beginning.

She glared at him. "You mean you want a marriage of *your* convenience. And what if I don't wish to share your bed?"

"Oh, you'll share my bed. You enjoyed our lovemaking as much as I did." He spoke with deadly calm. "And I can remind you of that anytime I choose to do so."

She glared at him, fighting her body's treacherous response to his suggestive words. It made her voice sharp and her words sharper.

"First you ruin my brother through gambling, then you force me to marry you against my will, and lastly you force me to make love with you. Well, I refuse to share your bed—now or in the future."

He blanched. In one swift motion, he was up and upon her. Fingers biting into her shoulders, he yanked her to her feet.

Baby meowed indignantly from the floor, where he'd managed to land right side up. No one paid him any mind.

"Damn you! I'm bloody tired of this game you play."

He shook her so that the pins holding her chignon loosened. With his fingers he pulled them out and her hair cascaded in flaming waves down her back. Angry though she was, Liza found herself longing for him to end this fight by kissing her, kissing her until she lost all possibility of rational thought.

"You can't spend the rest of your life blaming me for something your brother did. I won't let you." His eyes bored into her. "I want you. I want you in my bed every night, your thighs wrapped around me, your mouth swollen from my kisses. I don't want the ghost of your brother lying between us."

A sob escaped her lips. It was both heaven and hell to hear him say these things. If only he loved her, she could tell him she no longer held him responsible for Michael's death.

Agonized, she stared at him mutely.

His grip eased and one hand stroked up her arm and around her nape to hold her securely. "Liza, I've wanted you from the instant I first saw you. Before we ever found Michael. I've never stopped wanting you."

She gulped, her hands clenched at her sides. She shut her eyes against the hunger in his, the same hunger that knotted her stomach and closed her throat.

Her words came haltingly, saying not what she should say but what she had to say. "What about love?"

His jaw tensed. "You desire me. That's enough. I'm not asking for love."

The blood drained from her face and her eyes widened in shocked pain. "You ask a great deal," she managed to whisper through stiff lips.

"Nothing you aren't capable of giving."

She turned her face away, unable to look at him. She wanted more than physical passion in her marriage.

"Bloody hell! Look at me," he ordered, his fingers biting into her flesh.

He took her chin and forced her face toward him. His mouth covered hers, fiercely, demanding a response.

His arms wrapped around her and urgency surged from his body to hers, making her pulse pound in her temples. She responded to him, couldn't stop herself. She was too weak. A sob escaped from her and was swallowed up by his mouth, but he heard.

"Damnation," he growled, drawing back. The sight of her anguished face blunted his ardor. He released her and stepped away. "I never meant to hurt you, Liza. Nothing I've done in the past and nothing I intend to do in the future is aimed at making you suffer. I owe you too much. But when I return from London you'll sleep in my bed."

At his words she stumbled backward and would have fallen if the desk hadn't been behind her. Dazed, she watched him leave, closing the door silently behind him.

For long minutes she continued to stare at the closed door. He wanted her, owed her. But he didn't want her love.

It was too much.

She sank onto the floor, her black skirts spreading like a pool around her. Baby pressed himself against her side, demanding attention. Absentmindedly, she petted the cat.

What was to become of her? If she ran from him, he would hunt her down. If she stayed with him, he would break her heart. What choice did she have?

CHAPTER FIFTEEN

ALAISTAIR SAT in the library of his London Town house, fingers steepled as he listened to Winkly's report.

"Bent ain't done nothin' out of the ord'nary—for 'im, that is." Winkly's nose wrinkled as though a stench filled the room. "Been to sev'ral goin's-on of the Quality. Been often to 'is favorite brothel. Man must spend a fortune there."

"Where?"

Alaistair rose and poured each of them a tumbler of whiskey. He handed Winkly his, then took a gulp of his own. It exploded in his stomach, reminding him of the evening he'd introduced Liza to the heady delights of good Scottish whiskey.

"Oi say, guv, did you 'ear me?" Winkly eyed his employer. "Ain't like you not to pay attention."

No, it wasn't. Alaistair set his glass down and returned to his desk empty-handed. If seemed that in the past weeks almost everything he did reminded him of Liza. Now he couldn't even enjoy a drink without thinking of her.

"Continue, Winkly. I'm all yours."

"Ain't much more to tell. Like I was sayin', Bent don' do nothin' he didn't do before. 'Cept maybe frequent that fancy 'ouse more."

Alaistair frowned. Most men of Society had a mistress in one form or another. Some kept a woman under their protection. Others relieved themselves with serving girls, and many more went to brothels. The method usually depended on the gentleman's means. Bent should be able to keep a mistress in style.

"Check into the brothel. See if he goes to one woman all the time or if he spreads his wealth."

"Right-o, guv'nor." Winkly downed the last of his whiskey, and crammed his crumpled wool felt hat onto his head. "Bloody cold," he said on his way out the door.

Alaistair leaned back in the chair, the weak sunlight filtering through the French door at his back. Bent had always been lecherous, even when his wife was alive, but until now most of his long-term liaisons had been with opera dancers or other highfliers. The news that he was frequenting a house of prostitution niggled. Something wasn't right.

THE EARL OF BENT rapped on the nondescript door set back from the rain-soaked pavement of Pall Mall. When the door wasn't immediately opened, he knocked harder, using the silver handle of his walking cane. Just inches from his back, water fell in a rivulet from the drainage pipe. A cold wind filled the doorway and penetrated his wool greatcoat.

"Open this bloody door," he bellowed.

A round circle of light appeared in the small pane of glass in the paneled door. It was blotted out and the door cracked inwards, a bulky shape darkening the opening.

"State yer purpose," a voice asked.

"What the hell do you think my purpose in a thieving dive like this would be?" Bent's fleshy face quivered with irritation. No matter how many times he frequented this brothel, the guard always asked the same question. "I want to fornicate with one of your girls. Now open up or I'll take my business elsewhere."

There was a shuffling of feet on the other side, followed by some murmuring, and then the door was opened wide. Julius, the guard, stood in the warm glow of several candles. His thinning gray hair swept back from a large round face with heavy jowls. A serviceable jacket and breeches clothed his ample six-foot frame.

"Lord Bent," he said ingratiatingly, bowing and waving the newcomer in. "We was wonderin' if you was tired of us." He guffawed. "Or if we'd done summat to give you a disgust."

Bent thrust past the man, glad to be inside where the wind wouldn't knife through his clothing. Taking off his coat, he handed it to Julius. "Have this dry and pressed when I leave."

Julius took the coat and shook it so that water splattered everywhere, several drops hitting Bent in the face. "Er, beggin' your lordship's pardon," he said with a sly grin.

Bent raised his cane to hit the man but thought better of it. "Insolent cur."

Twisting from side to side, Bent tried to see into the dim recesses of the smoke-filled rooms off the foyer. The sounds of a pianoforte and women laughing quickened his pulse. "Is Millie about?"

Julius's grin widened. "Per'aps."

Bent turned his attention back to the guard. "How much?"

"Golden Boy."

"You're worse than a pimp," Bent grumbled as he fished the money out of his pocket. "And I suppose Millie will be charging double, as well."

Julius shrugged his massive shoulders. "Follow me, your earlship." It was the pet name they had given Bent here.

Bent knew he was being insulted, but the need to see Millie was too great.

They rounded a corner and entered a smaller room where several women were sitting about on ebony lacquered chairs, all the rage in London several seasons before but now out of fashion. They were attired in half-unlaced chemises and stockings with the garters showing seductively beneath their slips.

On a settee by the well-tended fireplace lounged a woman whose black hair sparkled like jet in the light cast from the fire. Her skin glowed snow-white against the deep blue-red of her velvet evening gown, and her lush breasts spilled over its bodice. She wore her hair piled atop her head so that her large, almond-shaped eyes were accentuated. If Bent tried hard enough, he could fool himself into thinking they were gray, not hazel.

"Millie," Bent said, making his way toward the courtesan.

She turned languidly to watch him. "Why, duckie," she cooed, stretching out an ungloved hand to him. "Oi thought you'd left me fer good, oi did."

Her untutored cockney accent grated on his nerves, but he pushed his irritation aside. Her face and figure were perfection. There was only one other woman more beautiful and he couldn't have her. Millie would have to do.

He frowned as he took her hand and raised it for a kiss. "Be the lady for me, Millie."

Her black brows rose. "You want me to speak like a lady," she said. "That'll cost extrie y'know."

He pulled her to her feet and murmured into her ear, "It helps me. You know it excites me."

She sighed and nodded. "I reckon that's somethin' to consider." As he squeezed her fingers, she relented. "Oh, all right, m'lord. I'll be your lady for the night." She rolled her eyes. "Thank the good Lord I was raised in a swell's house."

Arm in arm, they mounted the stairs to Millie's room. It was large enough for a massive bed, a chest of drawers, a chair and mismatched wardrobe. The chair, like the bed, was there for the comfort of the client. Bent sat down in it.

"Undress for me, Millie. Very slowly." His eyes held an avid look and his lips were pursed.

Millie watched him, carefully judging his state of arousal as she began to take off each piece of clothing. When he sat on the edge of the chair, his breeches bulging, she paused.

"What's this lady like, duckie? The one you always want me to pretend to be." She was truly curious. Bent had been coming to her for five years and in all that time his fantasy had never changed.

The glazed look left his eyes and the taut line of his jaw sagged. "Damn you," he whispered, his voice ragged. "She's not for the likes of you to talk about."

Millie's mouth thinned and her nails dug into her palms. Otherwise she showed nothing of the anger his words provoked. "Oi see."

"Damn whore," Bent swore as she reverted back to her own speech. "Earn your bloody money."

"Right," she said, sauntering over to the chair where he still sat and dropping to her knees. Adroitly, she undid the flap in his breeches and reached inside. She pulled out his now flaccid member, swallowing a betraying giggle.

"Go on, suck me," he ordered her. "You know you want to."

It was a game they played and Millie knew her part so well she could do it asleep. "Yes, Steven, I want to drain you dry. I want to pleasure you more than anything else in the world. I love you."

So saying, she took him into her mouth until he was full and heavy. She did as she had done so many times before until his body jerked and his fingers tangled in her hair so tightly it was painful.

"Oh God, Alicia," he groaned. "I love you so much." His hips pumped one last time and he collapsed back into the chair. Only then did he let Millie up. She sat in his lap and placed her head on his shoulder, as was part of this ritual. "Say you love me, too," he demanded, kissing her.

"I love you, Steven," Millie whispered against his lips. "I love you more than you'll ever know."

He stroked her hair as his tears fell onto her cheeks.

DOWNSTAIRS, Winkly handed three Golden Boys to Julius for the information about Bent. Lord Alaistair wouldn't like this.

Winkly was right.

"Damn it to bloody hell," Alaistair stormed when Winkly told him about Millie.

"Doorman said the whore reminds Bent of some grand lady 'e's besotted with." Winkly shook his head. "'Ate to say it, guv, but sounds like 'er grace, whot with 'er black 'air and 'im callin' 'er Alicia. That's yer mother's name, ain't it?"

"Bloody bastard." Alaistair slammed his fist into the desk. "Watch the duchess, Winkly. There's no telling what's in Bent's perverted mind."

"Right-o, guv." Winkly hesitated, cap in hand. "Gonna warn 'er?"

Thoughtfully, Alaistair shook his head. "There's no sense in worrying her or my father. She's suffered enough at that animal's hands. Chances are Bent won't do anything. But I want you around, just in case." He'd learned the hard way in the war that it paid to take precautions, even when you didn't expect anything.

"Be on me way, then," Winkly said. "Oi'll let you know straight away if anythin' comes up."

Alaistair nodded.

Sitting back down in the chair behind his desk, he absentmindedly picked up a quill and fiddled with it. This changed his plans. Liza would have to come back to London on her own instead of his fetching her. Tristan said the gossip started by Bent during the Season had almost dissipated, what with people leaving for Paris in droves now that the Continent was open again. Liza's stay in Bent's household was no longer grist for the gossip mills.

Just the thought of how Bent had tried to ruin his wife added fuel to his fury. He should have finished Bent off five years ago. If he had, none of this would be happening now.

A sharp snap drew his eyes downward. The quill was split in two.

Grimacing at his lack of control, Alaistair tossed the pieces onto the desk and rose. He'd send a groom to Ciudad Rodrigo with directions to bring Liza back immediately.

A lazy smile curved his lips. Once she was here, their marriage would begin in earnest.

"MEOW!" Baby fussed from his position at the coach window. "Meow!"

Liza indulgently petted the feline behind the ears. Baby had been impossible from the moment they entered the carriage three days earlier. With the arrival of snow in Yorkshire, they'd been lucky that all of the roads were passable.

Looking out the window, Liza marveled at the hubbub of London. It was after five and the sun had set, yet vendors still hawked their wares on every corner. Lanterns shone in shop windows and people milled in the street despite the cold fog coming in from the Thames.

"It do be chilly," Nell said from the other seat. "Nothin' like Yorkshire, though."

Liza handed Nell a blanket, which the maid promptly wrapped herself in. "It'll be warm when we get home."

The words slipped from her mouth so naturally that it was several minutes before Liza realized exactly what she'd said. *Home.* She was calling Alaistair's Town house home. It hadn't felt like home several months before. Then, it had felt like a prison. What made it home now?

Alaistair.

The carriage rumbled to a stop on the cobbles. Picking Baby up before he could bound out, Liza stepped down.

The front door opened to a golden glow that promised warmth from the cold evening air. Stepping with alacrity, Liza entered, glad to be out of the tossing coach. Her eyes darted around the foyer, seeking the man whom she refused to admit even to herself that she longed to see. He was nowhere around. Her shoulders slumped momentarily before she drew herself up. Of course he wouldn't come to greet her.

"Milady..." Simpson, Alaistair's butler, appeared. "If you'll follow me, his lordship has ordered tea to be served in the library immediately upon your arrival." He bowed formally.

Liza smiled at him, already missing Timmens's irreverent manner. "Thank you."

"And Cook has dinner for your maid."

"Go and get yourself warm, Nell," Liza said, amused by the girl's apple red cheeks and bashful glances at the imposing Simpson.

Before following the butler, Liza put Baby on the floor. The cat would make himself at home as soon as he found Alaistair or some of Alaistair's cravats. Instead of making for the stairs, Baby, tail standing straight up except for a top curl, pranced down the hall in the direction of the library.

Anticipation quickened Liza's step. If Baby was going that way, then Alaistair must be there. The knowledge both excited and frightened her. She wanted to see her husband, but she hadn't forgotten his parting words.

Liza entered the darkened room. The only light came from a crackling fire, but she didn't need to see Alaistair to know he was there. Her skin tingled and a hard knot twisted her stomach.

Baby was a white blur as he scampered across the room and with a graceful bound landed in his master's lap. Only then did Liza discern her husband sitting in the shadows.

Without rising he said, "I trust your journey was as comfortable as could be expected." One hand was busy scratching Baby's ears while the cat's purr reverberated through the room.

Liza grinned wryly. "You certainly have a way with animals that I lack. He fussed the entire time you were gone and was most ungentlemanly on the trip here."

A soft chuckle was Alaistair's answer. "Sit down near the fire, Liza. You must be tired and cold. Help yourself to tea and food."

Doing as he bid, Liza let the exhaustion she'd been holding at bay sweep over her. She felt safe here and, for the first time since he'd left Ciudad Rodrigo, truly at ease.

She watched him through her lowered lashes as she sipped hot tea and nibbled on a scone piled high with clotted cream and strawberry preserves. His jaw was tense in spite of the slight smile tugging at the corners of his mouth as Baby burrowed into his lap. The flames of the fire cast dark shadows across his cheeks and highlighted the silver at his temples. Even at his leisure, power emanated from him, but his eyes were heavy-lidded and he looked tired. Her heart went out to him.

"Have you been sleeping well?" she asked, thinking that his nightmares must be plaguing him.

"Some nights are better than others. I expect to do better now that you're here."

The implication was unmistakable. Liza's heart started to pound. "I meant, are your nightmares keeping you awake?"

He continued to scratch Baby's ears, his eyes holding hers captive with their intensity. "No more than usual. But now I awaken and can put them aside. It's an improvement."

"I see." She downed the last of her tea and finished the scone. This was a topic of conversation that would only lead her to trouble.

Abruptly, he rose, setting Baby onto the chair. In two long strides he was beside Liza, one hand touching her hair. "You look tired." He met her apprehensive gaze. "I won't carry out my threat tonight. You need a good night's sleep if those dark circles under your eyes are any indication."

She gulped, trying desperately to ignore the heat permeating her body at his touch. "So do you," she retorted, determined to meet him directly.

He made her a mock bow. "As usual, you're right. Shall we retire—to separate beds? You may sleep soundly tonight."

Relief mingled with disappointment as Liza rose to follow him out the door. They hadn't gone two steps before Baby's plaintive "meow" called Alaistair back. Cat in his arms, he followed Liza. At her door, they parted ways, Baby going with Alaistair.

Once inside her room, Liza began to undress, glad that Nell wasn't finished with her repast. This meeting with her husband had unsettled her more than she'd thought. Unfinished business always left her feeling on edge and at loose ends, and the prospect of sharing Alaistair's bed was definitely unfinished business.

Still restless, Liza donned her nightdress and waited for Nell. When the girl finally came to her, Liza sent her to bed, and went wearily to her own.

Nevertheless, sleep eluded her. Her mind spun with troubled thoughts. Alaistair would give her one reprieve, but that was all. She'd seen it in his eyes as he bade her good-night.

Liza squeezed her eyes shut in a futile attempt to erase his picture from her memory. He would have her... and she wanted him to.

Not even the memory of Michael's death and Alaistair's part in it could cool the heat in her belly or dry the moisture in her loins. She would never forget her brother, nor how Alaistair had gambled with him, but no longer could she hide behind that excuse. She wanted her husband, for she—fool that she was—was no wiser than the duchess had been. She could only pray that her marriage wouldn't travel the same road.

The fire had burned down to embers before she finally dozed off.

CHAPTER SIXTEEN

THE NEXT DAY Liza rose early and ordered the coach to be brought around. It was not quite light when she climbed aboard and gave the driver directions. Clammy fog hung over London, seeping through her wool cape and making her hair cling in damp tendrils to her face. Shivering, she curled up in her seat to endure the drive.

When the coachman stopped, she let herself out. He stood stiffly, a look of disapproval on his long face.

"I wish to go alone," she said, picking up her skirts to keep them from getting soaked by the wet grass.

Fog drifted around the tombstones like smoke, obscuring and revealing without rhyme or reason. Trees, their limbs bare and brittle, cast shadows in the pale light that was beginning to appear. Liza held her lantern higher, even though she could have walked this path blindfolded.

When she reached Michael's grave, she was chilled to the bone, her teeth chattering. London in November was damp and cold.

Carefully setting the lantern on the hard ground, she knelt beside it. "Michael, it's me. I've come to... to talk to you." She had to believe that somehow he could hear her. "I want to let you go, Michael."

She took a deep breath, gazing into the shifting fog, thinking about her reasons for being here. "I love you, Michael, and I'd do anything to have you back... but... but I must get on with my life now. I learned that from Alaistair."

The cool air made her eyes sting. She hadn't brought a handkerchief. "I want you to know I'm in love with him." She smiled through her sorrow. "I never expected to be, but it's happened. I fought it. I fought it tooth and nail, but I cannot deny my love for him. And his suffering has helped to heal me. He has lived through horrors that have scarred him just as your death scarred me. But he continues on. I can do no less."

She took a deep, shuddering breath. "Please forgive me for loving him and understand that I didn't want to. It just happened."

She fell silent. The chilly air swirled around her kneeling figure. Cold seeped from the ground into her knees and into her body, yet warmth was there too. The warmth that came from finally accepting that her love for Alaistair and her love for her brother could coexist without bitter recriminations.

Stiffness had settled into her limbs when Alaistair found her.

He squatted beside her. "I thought I'd find you here." His voice was quiet, in keeping with their surroundings.

It felt right for him to be with her. His hair was wind-tossed, the ebony locks tumbling onto his forehead so that she automatically reached to push them back. Beneath her fingers, his skin burned with life. He folded her hand in his large one, giving her his warmth.

Gently, she smiled. "You know me."

He returned her smile, his teeth strong and white. "I know this part of you."

She looked away, a sigh purging her of the final pain. "He's been dead almost six months."

"And you're finally ready to let him go."

"Yes," she whispered. "I've learned from you that I can't continue to berate myself or you for what happened. Michael would have done something like that sooner or later." She shivered. "He liked to gamble. He thought it was exciting."

His fingers tightened on hers. "I'm sorry. This isn't easy."

She glanced back at him. "No, it isn't. Just as your talking to me wasn't easy. But it helps."

He nodded. "Yes, it helps."

She took a deep breath. "I'm ready to go now."

When she tried to stand, her legs protested, buckling under her. Alaistair's arms shot around her.

"You're half-frozen," he growled, picking her up. "How long were you here before I came."

"I don't know. A while."

The abrupt change in position made her head swim, and she wrapped her arms around his neck. It felt right. It felt good. It didn't matter that he didn't love her. He cared, or he wouldn't have followed her here. That would do for now.

THAT NIGHT, Liza studied herself dispassionately in the mirror while Nell tidied up behind her. Madame Celeste hadn't wanted to make this dress. It wasn't black. She was now officially in half mourning, and lavender became her.

The door to Alaistair's room opened. "You may go, Nell."

His baritone voice burned through her like whiskey. Liza turned to face him.

He was dressed in a black coat and pantaloons. His cravat was tied in what she'd learned to recognize as the Saint's Simplicity. He was immaculate, and very, very masculine.

She smiled at him, his presence making her giddy. "Why do they call you Saint?"

He grinned as his gaze roved leisurely over her. "Because of my saintly qualities."

"Or lack thereof?"

His grin turned boyish. "Possibly." He sobered. "But I didn't come here to discuss my sterling qualities. I came to give you these."

He held out the blue velvet box containing the black pearls. This time, Liza accepted them willingly. She was reconciled to her marriage, even beginning to find happiness in it. And with time, she might even gain his love.

"Thank you. These will complement my dress."

His eyes darkened and he caught her fingers as she reached for the pearls. "I have something else."

His look was so intense, that the tingles moving through her intensified. "Thank you, but these are lovely enough. You don't have to give me more."

"I want to."

From the pocket of his jacket, he withdrew a ring box. Flipping it open, he held it out to her. Inside were two rings, a simple gold band and another with a large canary diamond surrounded by black seed pearls. They matched the necklace and earrings.

Not knowing what they meant, she could only stare helplessly at him. "Thank you."

His eyes burned into her. "They're a wedding band and an engagement ring. It's time you had them."

"They're beautiful. But you didn't have to."

He caught her hand and slipped the band on her ring finger, following it with the engagement ring. They fit perfectly.

Bringing her fingers to his lips, he said, "I wanted to."

Desire smoldered in the depth of his eyes, igniting emotions in Liza that she had tried desperately to keep banked. To want him for a lover, even to love him, was one thing. To desire him above life itself could mean losing herself to him completely.

"We'll be late if we don't hurry," she mumbled, trying to ease the tension stretching between them.

Instead of releasing her as she'd half hoped, he drew her toward him. "Prinny can wait, and you don't have the necklace and earrings on yet."

Heat radiated from his body to hers, joining with the warmth already spiraling inside her. "The Prince Regent wait?" She laughed nervously and tried to free her fingers on the pretext of donning the jewelry. "I can't put them on if you don't let go."

His eyes gleamed with mischief. "I'll put them on you."

"Oh, well, if you insist."

He released her hand only to grip her bare shoulders and turn her around so that her back brushed against his chest. His fingers skimmed her nape, setting the hairs on end as he fastened the necklace. Heat bolted down her spine. She squeezed her eyes shut and willed her legs not to quiver. Then his mouth pressed against her shoulder, his tongue moist and rough on her skin. She gasped and leaned back into him.

"I want you," he whispered into her ear.

She licked her lips. "I...I know."

He laughed, a rich rumble that sent vibrations from his chest through her body. Slowly, enticingly, his hands slid down her arms and around her ribs to cup her swollen breasts through the thin fabric of her gown. Her nipples hardened.

He nuzzled her neck. "Remember what I promised?"

"Oh, yes," she gasped as gooseflesh rippled across her skin.

He massaged her breasts and stroked her nipples through the lavender muslin. Tremors of pleasure radiated from his ministrations. Liza thought she had died and gone to paradise.

"And this time, there's no white cat to save you."

She barely registered his words, her senses consumed by physical delights. "No?"

"No," he murmured, tracing the rim of her ear with his tongue. "Baby's with Rast, ironing cravats."

"How nice," Liza murmured, turning her head so he could nip her earlobe. "I never knew ears were so sensitive."

He laughed. "They're only one small part of you. Imagine how much more there is to experience."

She was flooded with the memory of her time in his bed, the intense excitement he'd roused in her. Her knees buckled but he caught her.

With one finger, he slowly outlined the edge of her bodice, leaving fire in his wake.

This had to cease or they'd never leave. "We must go," Liza managed to say, not wanting him to stop but . . .

"Prinny won't miss us," he murmured, trailing his lips down the back of her neck and slipping one hand inside her chemise.

She felt seared to the bone. "He won't?"

"No, he won't."

The rough calluses on his palms abraded her tender flesh, and the effect was tantalizing. "Are you sure?"

"Very."

With his free hand he began to undo the hooks of her bodice, his lips following the resultant opening with moist insistence. Every muscle in Liza's body tightened in anticipation.

The gown fell to her waist and Alaistair started on her stays. Her chemise and petticoat followed until she stood naked except for her pale silk stockings, held in place with lavender garters. The black pearls were cool against her neck. She felt wildly decadent.

He turned her around and his eyes moved lazily over her, bringing a blush to every inch of her flesh. Liza met his gaze openly.

"Now your hair," he said, his voice a husky drawl.

He removed the pins, his fingers combing through the tresses so they flared around her like leaping flames. One finger trailed down her left breast, over her nipple and down her ribs. At her waist, it slipped inward to trace the indentation and slight mound of her belly. He took a step toward her as his fingers tangled in the copper triangle between her legs, and he lowered his mouth to hers.

Liza swayed into him, her fingers clutching the lapels of his coat as his lips penetrated hers. She gasped and his tongue surged deeper into her welcoming mouth. The world ceased to exist for her.

When he lifted his lips from hers, Alaistair watched as her eyes opened, their turquoise clarity impaling him. "You're so beautiful," he murmured, "and you're all mine."

The ache that had been simmering in him increased. His loins would meld with hers until neither of them knew where one ended and the other began. He would possess her completely, body and soul.

"There's no stopping this time," he warned her, his desire urging him to tumble her to the floor and join her body to his. But he fought for control, wanting to prolong their pleasure.

Her eyes met his without flinching. "No turning back, ever again."

Exultation rushed through him. Lifting her in his arms, he strode to the chair by the roaring fire so that the flames would keep her warm. Carefully, he deposited her on the blue-and-gold damask.

Her russet curls fanned over the chair's back, blending with the gold thread of the embroidery. Her eyes were startling turquoise pools in the pale cream of her face, her mouth a coral slash of sensuality. Alaistair's loins tightened painfully.

Kneeling in front of her so his face was on a level with hers, he urged her to part her legs for him. "Let me in, Liza," he said, running his palms along her silken flank. "Let me make love to you."

Liza watched the reflection of her ardor in the dilated pupils of Alaistair's eyes. Blood rushed to that part of her body he'd awakened once before.

She nodded ever so slightly.

Alaistair shrugged out of his coat and took off his cravat. She eased the silk shirt from his body, marveling at the sleek muscles as his shoulders and arms flexed beneath her fingers.

He stopped her as her hands reached his breeches. "Not yet. I don't think I can wait if you continue to touch me, and I want you to enjoy this, too."

Liza experienced a surge of power at the knowledge that she affected him as greatly as he did her. "You're the expert," she teased, her finger twirling in the sweep of wiry black hairs that narrowed at his breeches.

He groaned. "You learn quickly." Catching her hand, he lifted it to his lips.

She sucked in her breath when his tongue touched her palm. Excitement shot along her nerves.

Slowly, tantalizingly, he lowered his head to hers, his eyes holding her captive. When his mouth took hers, it was all Liza could do not to melt from the delicious sensation.

It was a hungry kiss, driven by passions neither fully understood. His tongue danced with hers, his teeth nipped her lips. She clung to his shoulders, the skin beneath her fingers sheened with sweat.

"Oh!" she gasped when his hands slipped to her hips and pulled her forward in the chair so that his loins were cradled between her thighs.

"Wrap your legs around me," he murmured, drawing away from her long enough to speak.

Warmth suffused her at the blunt command for greater intimacy, but she did his bidding. Her thighs rode his hips, her ankles crossed over his buttocks. The feel of his silk breeches heightened her desire, and she nibbled his lips, then sucked his tongue into her mouth.

"That's it," he said when she released it again, his voice a hoarse whisper. "Play with me."

At his words, tremors started in her belly and radiated outward. She knew the pleasure she was giving him, knew the pleasure he would give her, and she wanted it.

His tongue trailed down the side of her neck and over her collarbone, sending shivers of delight coursing through her.

As his lips found first one lush breast and then the other, her soft moans filled the firelit room. His hands massaged along her ribs to her abdomen, where he rubbed the tense muscles just above her auburn thatch.

Eagerness made Liza wriggle her hips beneath his exploring fingers. She knew what came next, and she wanted it . . . had always wanted it from him.

His hand slipped lower to cup the russet-covered mound at the apex of her thighs. He lifted his head, his eyes narrowing as he watched her response.

She lay sprawled in the chair, her head resting on its back, her hips poised at the edge of the seat. Strands of flame-bright hair trailed between her upturned breasts, beckoning him. With one hand, he caught a lock and twirled it around his neck, binding her to him.

But it wasn't enough. It would never be enough until he was buried so deeply in her that they were one.

Her legs were silken weights around his hips that urged him onward. The urge to possess her was too great.

His eyes never leaving hers, he inserted one finger in her moist warmth and felt his own arousal harden as she moved to accommodate him.

"That's it," he encouraged, "let me in."

Liza felt him inside her and wanted more. Lifting heavy lids, she gazed at him.

"Love me," she demanded softly.

Inflamed by her order, Alaistair lowered his face to her loins and with bold strokes licked the delicate bud buried in the silken threads.

Gasps of pleasure shook Liza and her muscles spasmed.

"That's it," Alaistair murmured, his breath hot against her quivering flesh. "Hold me."

Her entire body tensed as he withdrew his fingers, only to reinsert them, his tongue never ceasing. Liza was aware of nothing but Alaistair and what he was doing to her.

Her hands slipped from his shoulders to the chair, clutching the cushioned seat as his loving sent her deeper into the abyss of pleasure. Her hips moved with the rhythm of his hand.

When she thought she could take no more, he withdrew. Stunned, she forced her eyes open.

"I can't wait any longer," he groaned.

With shaking fingers, he undid his breeches and pushed them over his hips. Liza's eyes widened. His manhood was full and stiff, jutting proudly from its ebony bed.

She licked suddenly dry lips. Of its own volition her hand reached for him, her fingers wrapping around his throbbing flesh. He was soft as velvet, yet strong as iron.

Alaistair groaned and squeezed his eyes shut as he fought to control himself against the surging pleasure of her caress. "Enough," he managed to say through gritted teeth.

Gently, he removed her fingers and placed them on his chest. Seizing her hips, he positioned her on the chair and thrust his turgid shaft into her welcoming warmth.

Liza moaned as he filled her, and the rocking of her hips urged him deeper.

"Oh God," he groaned. "If you keep that up, this will be over before we have a chance to enjoy it."

His mouth closed over hers and he began to thrust rhythmically into her, his fingers stroking her engorged flesh. Liza knew she was going mad as the pressure mounted inside her.

"Please," she begged, dragging her mouth from his, "please do something. I can't stand this."

A satisfied smile pulled his lips upward. "Soon," he promised.

Sweat broke out on his brow. Liza felt it on his buttocks where she gripped him, trying desperately to make him complete what he'd begun. He surged into her, again and again.

She clung to him, her nails scoring his back and buttocks, her legs gripping his hips. A cry of pleasure escaped her parted lips as the tension in her body exploded with release.

Alaistair's shout of ecstasy joined hers as he spilled his seed into her.

Dazed, Liza opened her eyes a few minutes later and gazed down at Alaistair's head resting on her bosom. She stroked her fingers through the satin softness of his tumbled hair, smoothing it from his brow. He looked so vulnerable.

"I..." *I love you.* The words welled up inside her, a feeble expression of the emotions he elicited in her. She bit her lips to keep from saying them. "I...I enjoyed that greatly."

Rising, he grinned roguishly at her. "And I."

Liza sensed that it was over for now, and not wanting to be any more susceptible to him than she already was, she took the hand he offered to pull her up. He kissed her lightly on the lips.

"It's past time to dress for Carlton House," she said breathlessly, striving for the cool detachment he seemed to have donned.

He nodded, his eyes hooded once more. "Perhaps you'd prefer not to go."

Though her body tingled with a certain tenderness in the aftermath of their impassioned lovemaking, she in no way wanted to stay here alone with him. Not after what she'd almost confessed to him.

"No, we'd best attend."

With an enigmatic look, he picked up his clothing and returned to his room. Liza watched him go, wondering where this all would end.

CHAPTER SEVENTEEN

LIZA STOOD in the Chinese drawing room of Carlton House, struck motionless with awe. "How vulgar," she finally said in an undertone.

Alaistair smiled at her. "Don't let Prinny hear you. He thinks these bright colors and opulent furnishings are all the crack. You'd immediately be banished and there would go all chances of my establishing you in Society."

She grimaced at him. "If Society is so trivial, I don't want to belong."

He took her arm and guided her toward the dining room. "You're obviously in need of a tonic so that you can begin to appreciate the gaiety and debauchery awaiting you."

"Saint," a contralto voice interrupted. "Is your darling wife ailing?" Marie Hardcastle swayed up to them, stopping several feet away, her décolletage artfully exposed by the light coming from a wall sconce over her shoulder. She appraised Liza critically, her gaze lingering on the black pearls at her ears and throat. A distorted smile twisted Marie's crimson lips. "How sad. It must be a fever giving her that hectic color."

The woman's venom fueled Liza's outrage, and she glanced quickly at her husband to see how he would react. A dangerous gleam flickered in his dark eyes.

Coldly, he said, "You always did have a tongue too clever for your own good, Marie."

The woman paled, but quickly recovered. Tossing her chestnut curls, she laughed brittlely. "And you were always one to champion the underdog, Saint. I see that part of you hasn't changed."

Liza had had enough of the woman's insults. "And a bitch in heat remains so until satisfied. I see, Madam, that you continue to suffer from that condition."

Marie's painted lips fell open.

"Best close your mouth, Marie," Alaistair advised. "Someone might take it for an invitation."

Liza, chin high, put her hand on his proffered arm and they turned away from Marie. "I'm sorry if I've caused trouble for you," she said, "but I've never been one to accept treatment of that sort for long."

"Bravo for you," Alaistair murmured, bending close so that his breath fanned her bare neck.

Liza's flush deepened as the sensations he'd awakened in her earlier rushed over her. With the memories came the realization of just why Marie Hardcastle was so venomous. Jealousy followed, and with it a coolness in her manner.

"I believe I see your mother waving to you," she said.

One black brow rose. "Is something the matter?"

Liza considered him. There was so much between them that they'd managed to overcome, it didn't seem right to let this new development separate them.

"Marie Hardcastle."

"Ah, you've heard."

"At least you don't try to pretend it isn't happening." She was grateful that he at least respected her intelligence enough not to lie to her.

His arm beneath her hand flexed. "Carlton House isn't the place for a discussion like this. Can it wait long enough for us to pay our respects to my mother?"

"It can wait forever," she snapped.

Alaistair's mouth thinned as he escorted her to his parents. "Good evening, Mother. Father."

Alicia, Duchess of Rundell, smiled at her son then clasped Liza's hands warmly in her own. "I'm so glad you're back, my dear."

There was a wealth of meaning in the words and in the look the duchess gave Liza. Some of Liza's hurt over Alaistair's mistress dissipated. She smiled at her mother-in-law. "So am I."

The duke, his mouth quirking up at one corner, said, "I heard that you were well occupied at Ciudad Rodrigo."

Liza saw the humor illuminating her father-in-law's handsome features and suddenly understood why the duchess had kept loving her husband despite his infidelities.

"I managed to keep busy," she replied with a deprecating grin.

Alaistair, his voice grim, said, "I see Prinny coming this way. If you'll excuse us, I don't think either of us is up to His Highness's exuberance, or as the case may be, his depression."

With that, he steered Liza in the opposite direction. She had time enough to say, "Please come to tea," to her in-laws before they were immersed in the crowd on their way to the door.

He ordered their coach brought around, even as a steady stream of newcomers arrived to take their place. Privacy was something the Prince Regent cared little for.

Frost haloed the lamps of several waiting carriages, and their coach soon appeared behind them. Liza, not willing to remain there any longer than necessary, stepped out toward it. Alaistair followed her lead.

Inside, he covered her with a blanket before taking a seat on the opposite side. Liza was grateful to him for that. He could be a considerate man.

Leaning back, arms crossed over his chest, he said, "You're wrong."

He didn't need to explain what he was talking about. The interlude with his parents had done nothing to erase the memory of Marie Hardcastle.

"I'd like to be. I'd like to think she's so vindictive because I *am* wrong." She couldn't keep the question from her voice.

"I ended my liaison with her the night we found your brother. That's why she's made it her business to help Bent sully your reputation."

Relief engulfed Liza. And something more: a happiness she hadn't thought possible blossomed in her heart. If Alaistair didn't have a mistress, then there was a chance for her to win his love.

"Hell hath no fury..." she murmured in an attempt at levity to help slow her suddenly rapid heartbeat.

"...like a woman scorned," he finished for her. "Or a man, for that matter."

Her curiosity piqued, she asked, "A man?"

His eyes glowed in the light from the carriage's interior lantern. "A slip of the tongue."

Liza knew there was more to it than that, but she also knew that he wasn't prepared to discuss it. Turning away, she lifted the leather curtain hanging over the window and stared out. A light rain had started to fall, and by morning ice would glaze the cobbled streets. The mansions they passed here in the west end of London were ablaze with candles. Carriages came and went with regularity. Parliament was in session and the Little Season still in full swing.

"Do you think you will be successful in making me part of Society this time?" she asked, more for conversation than real concern. Her success in Society was of utter indifference to her. Any desire she had to fit in arose only from her husband's prominent role in it.

"I'm not without influence in the ton. And Tris says everyone has forgotten about your brief stay under Bent's roof." He grinned sardonically. "Too many exciting things are happening, what with Wellington taking Castlereagh's place at the Congress of Vienna and Europe once more safe for Englishmen and their eager wives.''

And so they passed the remainder of their journey. As she accepted Alaistair's hand out of the coach, Liza wasn't sure whether she was relieved that nothing more had come of their time together or disappointed. She loved her husband. And, God help her, she desired him.

Hours later, tucked into bed with a heated brick at her feet and an eiderdown pulled up to her chin, she hoped he would come to her. Her nerves still tingled with the physical pleasures of marriage and thoughts of their lovemaking played havoc with her senses.

She tossed from side to side, fretting, then plumped up her pillows and straightened the bedclothes binding her limbs.

Perhaps she should go to him. After all, he might not realize she wanted him. She'd fought him and the attraction between them from the beginning, and he could very well think that what had happened earlier came about only because he had overwhelmed her. He might want her but not want to force her twice in one night.

It was a persuasive argument.

Quickly, before she lost her courage, Liza slipped from bed and sped across the room, not stopping for robe or slippers. Opening the door, she paused, the floor cold beneath her bare feet.

Alaistair's bedchamber was dark and chilly, the red glow of the embers illuminating a small portion of the room. On a chair, curled in white cravats that matched his fur, lay Baby. His yellow eyes glittered as he watched her.

He emitted a curious "Meow?" but when she didn't come to him, he gave up and put his head back down on his folded paws.

Even with the kitten's tacit acceptance, Liza found her courage deserting her. No sound came from the shadow-shrouded bed, not even that made by a body shifting in sleep. She tiptoed closer so that if her courage completely deserted her, she would be able to leave without Alaistair even knowing she'd come.

"I hoped you would come."

"Oh!" Liza jumped and her heart began to pound.

Spinning around, she strained to see him in the dark. Just when she was about to give up and move toward his voice, he stepped forward, away from the window. The meager light of the embers glinted off the silver-threaded dragons of his robe. Beneath it, he was naked. Liza gulped, regretting her foolishness in coming to him.

Without another word, he approached her. His eyes caught and held hers, and in their depths she saw hunger and desire and something she refused to name for fear she was mistaken.

As his mouth descended on hers, a storm of passion raged through her, and all her reservations scattered in its wake.

MUCH LATER, as she lay in his arms, Liza woke with a start. Alaistair's chest was covered in sweat and his muscles were rigid.

"Alaistair?" she whispered, rising on one arm and looking down at him. His features were tense with concentration.

Then she heard the thunder. It had woken him and he'd immediately thought he was back in Salamanca. She laid a hand tentatively on his arm.

"It's all right," he said through clenched teeth. "I have it under control this time."

"Are you sure?"

The semblance of a smile curved his lips. "I didn't toss you to the floor, did I?"

"No..."

"A month ago I would have."

"True." She hoped and prayed he really was improving.

A clap of thunder shook the room. Liza jumped and Alaistair stiffened.

"It's all right," Alaistair said again, his voice low.

She looked down at him. "Are you sure?"

He pulled her back onto his chest. "I've been awake for a while now. It didn't take me back to the war this time. Just gave me a bloody awful start."

With a sigh of relief, she rested on him. "I suppose that's something to be thankful for."

"I owe you a great deal," he murmured, stroking her hair. "When I first woke, my heart started pounding and sweat broke out on my back, but I was able to shake off the horrors. Unlike before."

"Thank God," she said fervently.

"Thank *you*," he said, his mouth seeking hers.

Liza wrapped her arms around him and sank into the oblivion of desire that only he could create in her.

THE NEXT MORNING, Liza woke feeling relaxed and sated. Stretching, she literally purred.

"Meow?"

Baby never slept with her. Her eyes flew open. Memory flooded back. She'd spent the night in Alaistair's bed. Twisting around, she searched for him, but he was gone. Even his side of the bed was cold.

Warmth tinged her cheeks as she remembered how he'd said goodbye. At the time, she hadn't realized he was preparing to get up or she would have gone back to her room.

A noise from Rast's room caught her attention. The last thing she wanted was for the valet to catch her here. He might surmise what she and Alaistair were doing, but she wasn't ready to see the certain knowledge reflected in his eyes.

She jumped from the bed and sped to her room. The door safely closed behind her, she leaned against it and steadied her breathing.

"Corblimey," Nell said, dropping the clothing she was carrying. "That is, I be meanin', milady..." Her eyes round as saucers, she stooped and picked up the scattered dresses and chemises. "I was meanin' to clean these an' all."

Liza couldn't suppress her smile at the maid's surprise. "Now they must need it."

"Corblimey, you and his lordship... It do be all right and tight." She grinned from ear to ear. "I told 'em it'd be just dandy. I knew it."

Nell's exuberance was delightful, even if premature. Alaistair didn't love her. Not yet.

"Don't let me keep you from your chores, Nell," she said, dismissing the girl. "I won't be needing you to dress."

"Yes, milady." Nell scampered from the room, her cheeks even redder than her mistress's.

When Liza reached the breakfast room, she was in dire need of a cup of coffee. Alaistair had kept her awake most of the night with his lovemaking, and as much as she had enjoyed it, it made getting through the day difficult. Still, a small, secret smile of pleasure lingered on her lips.

"Liza," said the object of her thoughts, "please come to the library when you're through."

Anxiety bit into her with sharp teeth. Was he going to send her to the country again? Well, she would refuse to go this time. She had too much at stake here.

After preparing a cup of hot coffee with cream, she made her way to the library, her feet dragging. When she reached the door, she paused as memories of the night before warmed her blood. Heat swept over her like wildfire.

How could she face him after the things he'd done to her last night, and with her cooperation? She took several deep breaths to calm her racing pulse, then knocked.

"Come in."

Alaistair's deep voice sent pleasure surging through her. It was all Liza could do to walk into the room and close the door behind her. She was thankful she hadn't waited for the butler to announce her. This response to Alaistair was too overpowering for her to hide, and she didn't want the entire staff to realize the effect her husband had on her.

Clearing her throat, she asked, "You wanted to see me?"

He gave her a quizzical look. "You could have finished your coffee first. Much as I want to be with you, I don't want to deprive you of nourishment." He grinned. "I have too many uses for you to tolerate your wasting away on me."

A blush crept over her, staining her cheeks. But she'd learned long ago that it did no good to retreat from his advances. "I've no intention of letting myself sicken when I've so much to look forward to, my lord."

His eyes brightened in a way she now knew so well.

"In that case, come here."

He pushed away from his desk and beckoned for her to sit on his lap. Momentarily taken aback by his boldness, she gaped.

His grin widened. "I'd promise not to eat you, but I'm not sure I can keep such a vow."

Her flush deepened, but her feet moved of their own accord until she stood in front of him. It was only a matter of seconds before he pulled her down on to the ridged muscles of his thighs. With only thin muslin skirts and buckskin breeches between them, his arousal was blatantly evident between her legs.

"Alaistair," she gasped, "you're insatiable."

"With you I am. But this isn't why I wanted to see you, and if we don't stop, I'll never get to the matter...and it is important."

He set her away from him and crossed the room to what appeared to be a painting draped in oilcloth. "I had this brought up, thinking you'd prefer to have it where you can see it every day."

Gooseflesh broke out on Liza's arms. It could only be one thing—the portrait of her family. She was beside him before he finished speaking.

"Alaistair...but how?" Bewildered, she looked to him for an explanation even as her eyes misted. "I thought this was sold with the other things. I...I never dreamed I'd see it again."

He put his arm around her and drew her to his side. Gently, he caught one tear on the tip of his finger. "I didn't surprise you to make you cry."

"My tears are tears of joy," she mumbled, searching for a handkerchief in her pocket. When he handed her his, she took it gratefully. "Those are my parents." She pointed to her mother and then her father. "That's Michael, in Mother's arms, and that's me." She hiccuped.

"You have a look of your mother."

Liza smiled softly. "And Michael took after Father's side." Impulsively, she flung her arms around Alaistair's neck. "Thank you. You can't know how much this means to me."

He held her tightly, stroking her hair with one hand. "I'm glad you like it. I hope you'll like visiting Thornyhold for New Year's Eve just as much."

"Thornyhold?" Liza thought her happiness would know no end.

Smiling, he traced her lips with one finger. "When your solicitor put your property on the block, I bought it."

"But why? Everything was sold to pay Michael's vowel to you."

"I know. But I never intended to redeem the vowel, not even when you refused to take it back. So, the only thing I could do was buy Thornyhold, the portrait and everything else you auctioned and then keep them for you."

She could barely believe her ears, yet it was something she knew he would do. Love for him welled up in her and would no longer be denied.

"I love you," she whispered.

His eyes blazed. "What did you say?" he asked, his voice harsh.

Liza swallowed. "I love you."

The words were barely out of her mouth before it was crushed beneath his. Arms around one another, legs entwined, they sank to the floor.

"No marriage of convenience for us," Alaistair murmured as he fitted himself to her perfectly.

THE EARL OF BENT watched Alaistair St. Simon fill his wife's plate with Carlisle's lobster patties and peas. They were disgustingly engrossed in each other. Lord Alaistair hadn't even glanced at another woman since arriving.

A cruel smile curved Bent's lips, hiding his blue eyes in the puffy folds of his skin. It appeared Lord Alaistair was becoming enamored of his wife.

His gaze swiveled back to where Marie Hardcastle stood, her fine complexion blotched with rage. She'd never learn.

To his right, he sensed Alicia. Shifting, he saw his love on the arm of her husband. Sick despair clawed at his gut. He had to turn away in order not to cast up the very fine salmon patties Carlisle was serving.

Fresh air would help.

Outside, he gestured for his carriage but was stopped from entering it by a hand on his arm. It was Marie, her red mouth sullen in the sooty haze of a gas lamp.

"Did you see them?" she asked, her voice acrimonious.

"Who?" he inquired with feigned disinterest.

"You know who, you disgusting excuse for a man," she hissed, her breath white in the cold air.

He stepped back, removing her fingers from his coat. "Tsk, tsk, Marie, you should watch your temper. No man wants to bed a shrew...or has Lord Alaistair already told you that?"

It was a direct hit. The blood drained from her face and her eyes narrowed to green flames.

"Bastard. You should talk. I saw you drooling over your beloved Alicia." She lowered her voice. "It's no different from the way Wright slobbers over me. Utterly distasteful. You're probably no better in bed than Wright is, either. Quick as a rutting rabbit. No wonder she returned to Rundell." She kept her malignant gaze on him. "Now there's a man I've heard knows how to pleasure a woman."

In spite of the fury that made his fingers shake, Bent managed to keep his voice level. "Like his son? Or has it been so long you've forgotten?"

She sneered at him. "I didn't seek you out to exchange insults."

"You appeared to do exactly that," he retorted, beginning to weary of her waspish tongue. A woman was good for only one thing in his mind—except for Alicia, of course.

"Get into your coach," she ordered, following him. "You may take me home. Wright will just have to wander around Carlisle's house like the lost, untrained puppy he is. We have to talk."

Settling himself on the thick velvet squabs of his seat, Bent waited her out. She was going to ask him when he planned to enact their plot for revenge. He'd let her suffer a while.

"Did you see what she had on?" she asked, her voice bitter.

"I wasn't as close as you."

"Of course you weren't. The duchess wasn't with her son," she said hatefully. "He's given her the pearls."

Bent knew the jewels she was talking about. Alicia had given Lord Alaistair the set of priceless black pearls after her son had aborted their flight five years ago. Everyone in the ton knew of their worth and magnificence. Rumor had it that she gave them to him for saving her from a dreadful mistake, and a fate worse than death. Bent's jaw locked.

"She *is* his wife, or have you forgotten?"

"I'll never forget. Just as you've never forgotten that Alicia is married to Rundell and chooses to stay with him, even though you continue to profess your love for her." She paused for emphasis. "Or *have* you forgotten?"

As coolly as he was able, Bent said, "You're a slut, Marie, and no amount of polish will ever gloss that over. That's why Saint left you and married that woman. She may be an amazon and poor as a church mouse, but she's Quality and it shows."

The carriage light cast shadows on Marie's face, making her appear every year of her age and more. "Is this your *polite* way of saying you no longer want to ruin her?"

He forced himself to be calm. "I have a score to settle, and she's the only true means of revenge I have."

"Just so," Marie replied.

"But you must give me time, Marie. Abduction and rape require careful planning."

"And who should know better than you," she responded. "But time is running short. If you wait much longer, she'll be heavy with Saint's child." Her mouth twisted cruelly. "I want her to carry yours. Think of the irony. You can't have the mother, so you give the son your child."

Her laughter rose maniacally in the closed confines of the carriage.

Bent grinned. "Poetic justice?" he quipped, beginning to like the idea. He could imagine he was begetting a child with Alicia.

"But you'll have to hurry," Marie warned. "I know the look in Saint's eyes tonight. He's bedding his wife as much and as long as he can. Soon his seed will take root and yours will be rejected."

"But not soon enough," Bent said, licking his lips.

CHAPTER EIGHTEEN

IT WAS BITTERLY COLD, a hint of snow in the air as Alaistair kissed Liza goodbye. "I wish you'd wait for me," he said, frowning down at her. "I won't be more than thirty minutes."

She smiled at him. If only he loved her, everything would be perfect. "No, love," she said, stroking his beard-roughened cheek. "I want to take fresh flowers to Michael's grave."

"As you wish." He released her. "But take the groom with you when you leave the carriage."

She raised her auburn brows. "Why? I never have before."

He sighed with exasperation. "I know. But..." He turned from her and paced the library floor. "I feel something is not right. It reminds me of the foreboding I used to get before a battle."

"Ah," she said, understanding his anxiety at last. "Nothing will happen." Calmly and distinctly, she added, "This isn't Salamanca."

His countenance lightened. "You're right." He strode back to her and took her in his arms. "What would I do without you?"

"Carry on," she said lightly, ignoring the little voice that wished he would say he loved her.

His lips sought hers and her sadness disappeared as her knees weakened and the blood rushed to her head.

When he released her, Alaistair gave her a little nudge and said ruefully, "You'd better go or I won't be able to stop what we've started."

Liza flushed, the world slowly righting itself. "Yes . . . yes, I'd better."

She took a deep breath, her hand sneaking up to catch a loose tendril of hair at her temple. He caught her fingers and kissed them one by one.

"Liza—" his voice was solemn and tender "—do I make you so nervous that you must do that?"

She frowned. "How do you know I do that when I'm nervous?"

A chuckle rumbled deep in his chest. "You do it every time something is happening that you don't like or find distasteful." He smiled. "Or when something is happening to you over which you have no control."

Her blush deepened. "You're very perceptive."

"Sometimes."

Liza studied his countenance, the sharp angles of his jaw, his dark eyes, and realized that if she only knew how to read his emotions, she would see more in his face than mere desire. But what it would be, she wasn't sure. Perhaps it was better not to know.

"Well, I'd best go. I have an appointment with Madame Celeste for another fitting this afternoon."

Alaistair watched her leave the room before turning to his desk. He expected Winkly at any moment and was glad Liza would not be here to meet the Bow Street Runner. Bent's obsession with his mother was a sordid piece of news he didn't want to concern Liza with.

A knock on the door a short time later signaled Winkly's arrival.

"Mornin', guv'nor."

"Good morning to you," Alaistair said, rising and moving around the desk. "Whiskey?"

"No thanks." Winkly grinned. "Even the likes o' me don' drink this early in the day."

"You've reformed." Alaistair smiled briefly before sobering. "Any news?"

"Nothin' worth worryin' over. Bent appears to have stopped goin' to the brothel. At least for now, anyhow." He pulled off his wool felt hat and rubbed his brow. "Still and all, I don' like it. A man don' change his ways without it meanin' somethin'."

Alaistair pondered Winkly's words. "Do you think he's found someone else?"

Winkly frowned, his forehead crinkling. "Don' know, but kinda doubt it. Five years is a long time to go to one whore."

Alaistair nodded. "True. Where is he now?"

"At his house, and been there the last week wi'out any company of any sort, 'ceptin' some lady of Quality I seen go there twice. She don' stay long, so unless he's quick at his pleasure, they can't be lovers."

"Hmm." Alaistair paced the floor. "What does the woman look like?"

Winkly grinned. "Demandin'."

"I didn't mean *that*," Alaistair said impatiently.

Winkly's grin widened. "I know that, guv, but that's what she looks like. Demandin'. Got brown hair and big..." His hands mounded on his chest. "Wears a lot of green."

"Marie," Alaistair breathed. "What's she doing with Bent?"

"No good," Winkly replied for him. "No woman built like her would waste time with Bent if it weren't for mischief."

The skin on Alaistair's nape crawled. He didn't like Marie and Bent seeing each other. He didn't trust them; not with Bent's obsession with his mother and Marie's undisguised hatred of his wife. But just exactly what were they planning?

"Winkly, go back and keep an eye on Bent. I'll pay a visit to the woman. Something is going on here and it stinks." With that, Alaistair left the room, Winkly close behind.

"Right-o, guv," Winkly said.

The cold December wind blew into Alaistair's face moments later, as he waited for his stallion to be brought around. A walk would warm him up, but something drove him to speed. When the groom appeared with the horse, he leapt into the saddle and set off.

Ten minutes later, Marie's butler showed him to the drawing room. Never a patient man, Alaistair clenched and unclenched his hands as he waited for her.

"Excuse me, your lordship..." At the butler's voice, Alaistair whipped around to face the door. "Madam is not at home."

Alaistair's eyes narrowed. "Tell your mistress to get down here or I'll come to her, and I don't give a bloody damn if she's got ten men in her bed."

The butler's face remained impassive. "As you wish, m'lord."

Alaistair paced the room, nervous energy driving him to activity. Something was going on and he was determined to get to the bottom of it.

The second time the door opened, Marie stepped into the room. Her clothing and hair were disheveled, and her eyes glittered. It was obvious he'd come at a bad time.

"Why are you seeing Bent?" he demanded before she could open her mouth.

Warily, she took a step back. "Whatever are you talking about?" Surprise lifted her perfectly shaped chestnut eyebrows, but there was a faint line of worry between them that told Alaistair he had guessed right.

He closed in on her until he was close enough to see the fresh tooth marks on her exposed breasts. Marie always had liked her love play rough.

"Don't play games with me, Marie," he snarled. "I know you and Bent are seeing each other." With one finger, he flicked over the angry red splotches that marred the creamy swell of her bosom. "Did he give you these?"

She gasped, anger inflaming her cheeks. "Of course not. You're deranged."

Alaistair took another step closer. "Am I? Or are you?"

She looked away from the fury in his eyes.

He grasped her by the arms and made her face him. "Tell the truth, Marie, or I shall be forced to add to your colorful display."

Her eyes returned to his, the emerald irises brilliant. "You won't harm me, Saint. I know you too well."

"Won't I?" he asked very softly, his fingers tightening.

She stood her ground. "No. You're weak where women are concerned."

"And Bent's not?" He increased the pressure on her arms. When she refused to be cowed, he smiled cruelly and released her. Moving away, he said, "You're right, Marie. I don't believe in physical abuse. But there are other ways."

"You can't harm me," she said defiantly.

He turned to face her again. "Can't I? I can arrange it so that Wright will be the only man willing to share your bed and pay your bills—and you know it."

The threat hung between them, and Marie knew he was capable of what he said. He had entrée everywhere; women adored him and men admired him.

She licked her lips, pale without rouge on them. "What do you want?"

He sauntered back to her. "I already told you, and as you know, I don't like to repeat myself."

She attempted nonchalance. "Bent wants revenge on you."

"That's hardly something I don't already know. Continue, Marie," he ordered.

"That's all," she insisted, her voice breaking on the last word.

He was on her immediately, his fingers once more gripping her arms. "I swear, I'll ruin you."

Seeing the truth of his words in his gaze, she swallowed hard. "He...he's going to debauch your wife."

Alaistair flung her from him. "Bloody bastard." He stared at her, fury contorting his features. "And you're helping him." It took all his self-control not to strike her as she cringed against the wall. "Be glad you told me. And if anything happens to Liza, I swear you will pay with more than your reputation."

Without another glance at her, he stormed from the house. He hadn't a second to lose. He had to get to the cemetery and Liza. He didn't want her to be alone for an instant.

He raced through the London streets, narrowly missing several pedestrians. The wind cut him like a knife, slicing through his greatcoat and numbing him. He wished the fear gnawing at him could be numbed as easily.

Reaching the cemetery, he jumped from the horse and ran. The ground around Michael's grave was plowed up as though a fight had occurred. The flowers Liza brought every week lay scattered.

Alaistair looked around, forcing himself to remain calm and think. She'd taken a groom with her, hadn't she?

He studied the disturbed dirt and discerned tracks, as though something, possibly a body, had been dragged. He followed their direction.

The groom lay hidden behind a large cement slab. Alaistair examined the man. There was a swelling lump on his forehead, but he was still breathing.

After several tries, he managed to rouse him. "Where's her ladyship?" he asked, trying to keep the desperation out of his voice and failing.

The groom stared up at him, his pupils pinpricks in the pale sun. "Attacked...from behind." He gulped for air, his eyes closing. "Fought..."

Impatience clawed at Alaistair. "When?"

The groom's eyes opened. "First thing."

"Can you stand?" Alaistair asked, knowing he couldn't leave the man here in this cold, but also knowing he had to find Liza.

"Yes, m'lord." But when he tried to stand, his face contorted and his legs gave out. "Sorry, m'lord," he said in a voice barely above a whisper.

Alaistair suppressed the urge to yank the man to his feet. Never before had anxiety eaten away at him to such a degree, but he couldn't leave the groom.

Slowly, so slowly Alaistair's skin crawled, they made their way to the stallion, who stood where he'd been left, munching on a tuft of brown grass. Alaistair helped the groom onto the horse's back and headed home. There was nothing else he could do.

But he prayed. He prayed to catch Bent before he molested Liza. But even if he was too late, he knew Liza would survive. She was strong. And he would stand by her just as she'd stood by him throughout his nightmares. He would help her come to terms with whatever Bent did to her—after he killed the bastard.

It seemed an eternity before they reached his Town house. Simpson answered the door, his eyes widening as he assessed the situation.

"M'lord," Simpson said, slipping an arm around the groom, "I will see to him. Winkly is waiting for you in the library. He says it is urgent."

Alaistair didn't wait to hear more. "Winkly!" he yelled before reaching the door.

Winkly, hat in hand, came into the hall. "He's flown the coop, guv. Seems he's taken a hankerin' to go to his country house."

"We've no time to lose," Alaistair said, relief washing over him at the knowledge of Bent's destination. "He's got Liza."

"What?" Winkly's eyes opened in surprise before narrowing again. "Nasty business, that."

Alaistair bellowed for two horses to be saddled. "He's got two hours' start."

"But he's travelin' in a coach," Winkly added, following Alaistair to the stables.

Alaistair mounted his horse, his face grim. "We'll catch the cur, and when we do, I'll put an end to his misery."

LIZA PULLED HER CAPE closer with one hand and hung on to the carriage strap with the other, never taking her eyes off Bent, who sat opposite her. There was no telling what he was capable of doing, and she didn't intend to be taken by surprise.

He swilled wine from the bottle he held, his second in the last hour. His eyes were bloodshot, the skin around them red and swollen. She could barely make out the blue of his irises. His jowls hung loosely and his mouth was slack. With any luck, he'd pass out.

As though reading her mind, he said, "I can drink five of these things before I need help standing. This is only number three."

Disgust warred with apprehension in her. "What do you intend to do with me?"

A leer transformed his face from pathetic to diabolical. "What do you think?"

The cold in the carriage infiltrated her bones. She had to take a deep breath to steady her voice. "Alaistair will kill you."

Bent shrugged, took another gulp of wine and wiped his face on the sleeve of his greatcoat. "That's better than a horsewhipping. At least that'll put an end to it all."

Liza couldn't believe her ears. "You *want* to die?"

Opening the window, he tossed the empty bottle out before answering her. "Sometimes. But I want revenge on that bastard more. If not for him, Alicia would be mine now."

Pain contorted his features, and Liza almost found it within herself to pity him.

In hushed tones, she said, "You really love her."

He nodded. "And she'd be mine now if not for your husband." A thin cackle parted his puffy lips. "I'll make him pay for the last five years of suffering."

Bent's eyes seemed to glow red with hatred. Liza drew as far back into the seat as she could. Nothing good would come of talking to him.

She sensed the coach slowing down. "Are we stopping?" she asked, hope springing forth. Every delay put Alaistair that much closer, for she never doubted he would come after her.

Bent belched. "We're changing horses."

The carriage swayed to a halt as boys bounded from the inn's stables to unharness the four lathered horses that had brought them this far. Peering out, Liza wondered frantically how to leave a message for Alaistair.

"I need to relieve myself," she said, looking at Bent.

"There's a chamber pot under the seat."

"I can't use it with you in here."

"Suit yourself," he said. "But soon your fine sensibilities will be brought to heel."

Bile rose in Liza's throat. There was no doubt in her mind that he intended to rape her. She had to escape him.

As she pondered her situation, Bent rose and threw open the door. If only he would leave the vehicle for a moment. That's all it would take her to escape.

Instead, he opened his breeches and relieved himself in the yard for all to see. Liza's stomach churned as she realized how low he had fallen. She prayed that he would let her go when he was through with her. She'd survived Michael's suicide, she could survive whatever Bent had in mind for her as long as he released her afterward.

They were on their way before Bent could reseat himself. He fell back onto the squabs with a curse. "I'll have that blasted coachman's head for this," he growled, straightening his breeches. He caught her watching him. "Curious about what will soon be making you scream for more?" he asked. "Trust me—it'll be much larger then."

Liza turned away, unable to bear the smirk on his face. Her fingers shook and nausea threatened to overcome her. Surely Alaistair would catch up with them soon. He was on a horse while they were in a carriage. She had to leave him a sign.

Quickly, before Bent could fathom what she intended to do, she took her embroidered handkerchief from her pocket and tossed it out the window.

"Damn you!"

He reached for her, but it was too late. The small white square was already gone. He would have to stop the coach to retrieve it, something he chose not to do.

Liza sighed in relief.

"That'll do you no good," he said, teeth bared. "He's too far behind. All you've done is made it necessary for me to enjoy your favors *before* we reach my estate."

Shivers crawled up Liza's spine. Her feet were frozen from the winter cold that penetrated the coach, and she wished her mind were, too. Then she couldn't think about what he intended to do to her.

Bent began to talk, his tone almost conversational. "I love her, you know. I've loved her forever. And she loves me."

Liza glanced at him and saw that his eyes stared into nothing. He unearthed a fourth bottle of wine from beneath the seat and worked the cork out of the top. He took a long drink.

"She ran away with me because she loved me, not Rundell." His eyes screwed up. "We'd be on the Continent right now if not for your husband."

In shock, Liza realized he was crying.

"I'd do anything to have her back." His voice was little more than a whisper. "Anything."

Liza's chills intensified as she realized that he was not sane. She'd read of love making people insane but had never believed it. But Bent was living proof—and she was his prisoner. She had to bite her lip to keep her teeth from chattering.

"Harming me won't win her," Liza said softly, fighting to keep the tremor from her voice.

He focused on her and his eyes hardened. "Don't try to talk me out of this. She'll never be mine now anyway. I know that, no matter how much I try to deny it. And it's all your husband's fault."

His sour breath overpowered Liza, and she edged back far into her seat in an effort to escape its stench. It permeated every inch of the carriage, just as his madness penetrated to his very soul. She feared becoming sick and adding that stench to the already overpowering odor surrounding her.

Before she could expel the bile that rose to her throat, Bent rapped hard on the top of the coach. The vehicle slowed.

"Pull over," Bent ordered.

As the coach slowed, Bent reached into a leather side pocket on one of the walls and pulled out a pistol. Liza felt sick at the realization that all this time there had been a weapon at hand that she could have used. Now it was too late. He had it gripped in his pudgy fingers and was pointing it directly at her.

He smiled. "Yes, it's been here all the time. I wondered if you'd realize I must have a weapon somewhere, but you didn't." He laughed so hard he doubled over.

Liza stared, her eyes widening at this further evidence of his madness. *Where was Alaistair?*

Abruptly, Bent straightened. Coldly, he ordered, "Get out."

The coach had come to a complete stop now and the driver held the door open for her. She stepped down, her eyes beseeching his, but he refused to look at her. With a sinking feeling, she knew there'd be no help from that quarter.

Bent followed her, only to wince as the freezing wind whipped around him. Frowning, he looked around at the winter-brown trees. Even the bushes were a dull green. Clouds whipped the air above them.

Liza, wrapped in her wool cape, looked desperately for a way to escape. The area was deserted. No one traveled the road in front or in back of them.

"Don't do it," Bent warned from behind her, cocking the pistol. "I don't want to kill you, but I will."

She didn't doubt him for an instant. Liza swallowed, fear making her breathing difficult.

"You'll hang," she made herself say around the obstruction in her throat.

He laughed. "No one would hang a peer of the realm."

"Alaistair will kill you."

His voice flattened. "I've told you before, I've no fear of your husband. Or of death. It would be a welcome release."

Liza felt as though an ague held her in its grip.

Only one other time had Liza felt this helpless, and Alaistair had held her then. But he wasn't here now. She was alone. She had to do something. She had to escape.

Bent would kill her if she tried to flee, but if she stayed and allowed him to do what he would without a fight, she might survive. It wasn't a pleasant thought, but neither did she want to die. She had too much to live for. Alaistair cared for her. Given time, he might come to love her.

She forced her fear under control and turned to face her tormentor. The cold had turned his cheeks and nose a brilliant red. His eyes watered, either from the freezing wind or his tears, she couldn't tell.

Her voice was harsh. "Do what you will with me. But get it over with."

He took a step back in surprise before warning her, "Lord Alaistair will desert you after I'm through with you."

She stared him down. "No, he won't. He's too much a gentleman to do so."

Suddenly she knew her words to be the truth. Alaistair didn't love her, but he was grateful to her. And he knew what it was to suffer. He would stand by her through this. She trusted him.

Bent's nose was running and his lips were tinged with blue. Even all the wine he'd consumed couldn't warm him in this arctic wind.

Wiping at his nose, he said, "'Tis bloody cold out here. Get back in the coach. It's as good a place as any to do what must be done, and a sight warmer. At least this blasted wind doesn't penetrate there."

For good measure he waved the pistol at her. Liza moved slowly, knowing what was coming and knowing that she must submit, but dreading it all the same. Head high, she climbed into the coach through the open door, the servant still refusing to meet her eyes.

Bent followed her in. "Pull your skirts up and lie still," he said. "Try to stop me and I'll knock you out and fornicate with you while you're uncon- scious."

She was tempted. If she were unaware, his penetration would be blissfully beyond her memory. But pride kept her from provoking him. She wouldn't actively participate, but neither did she want him forcing himself on her while she was helpless. She did as he said.

Lying there, she forced herself to watch him dispassionately. He undid the front of his breeches and reached inside with one hand, the other still holding the pistol aimed at her. He was limp.

His eyes met hers. "Touch me."

She blanched.

CHAPTER NINETEEN

ALAISTAIR GALLOPED into the coaching inn's stable yard, reining his stallion so the animal reared in the air. "You, boy!" he shouted. "Has a coach been here to change horses?"

The boy eyed him dubiously. "Yes, sir, lots of them."

Alaistair groaned. He'd been afraid of that. He had no idea what Bent's coach looked like, and the child wouldn't know a coat of arms if he saw it.

Even though he knew where Bent's estate was, he wanted to catch the bastard as soon as possible. Bent didn't have to be at his estate to do harm.

"Have you seen a woman with red hair in any of them?" he asked.

"No, sir." The boy shuffled his feet. Carriages were arriving as they spoke and the horses needed to be changed.

"How about a large man with blue eyes and brown hair? Well dressed."

Winkly, holding his mount steady beside Alaistair's, added, "It'd be a private carriage, like the Quality travels in."

The boy's face lit up. "Yeah. I remember one o' them. The gent pissed from the door, right there." He pointed to a well-trampled spot. "Right prodigious, too."

In spite of his anxiety, Alaistair's lips twitched upward at the boy's admiration for such a vulgar skill. But a sense of urgency drove him. "Which way did it go?"

The stable boy waved in the general direction of north. "Same ways they all go."

It was the best they'd get from him, and Alaistair had to be satisfied with that. At least Bent was still on the move. It might keep him from doing anything to Liza.

Throwing the lad a Golden Boy, he wheeled his stallion and headed north. Winkly followed closely.

A hundred yards farther on, a flash of white caught Alaistair's eye. Pulling up, he dismounted and picked it up. It was a muddy handkerchief. Closer examination revealed Liza's initials.

"That's my girl," he said. "Still using your head." Jumping back in the saddle, he spurred his tired horse on. He had to catch Bent before the cur stopped for the night—or stopped for anything.

His nose and ears were numb from the cold, his fingers fast losing their dexterity. But those physical discomforts were nothing compared to his emotions.

This was Salamanca all over again. His heart pounded like the marching of thousands of feet. Sweat coated his back and brow in spite of the freezing cold.

If anything happened to Liza, he didn't know what he would do. He didn't think he wanted to live without her, she had become so much a part of his life.

But death wasn't what Bent planned. He would defile her and do it with relish. Alaistair's face twisted at the thought of his compassionate Liza pinned beneath that bastard's humping body.

Ravishment would devastate her, but she'd still be alive and he would cherish her. But death would take her from him, and he prayed to God she would not die.

In either case, he would kill Bent. That was a certainty.

LIZA STARED IN HORROR at Bent, towering above her like a mountain and blocking the feeble light from the carriage door. She couldn't do what he wanted, no matter what the consequences.

"I...I can't do that," she managed to say in spite of her clenched jaw.

"Damn you to hell," he growled. "I can't take you otherwise." He waved the pistol at her. "I'll kill you if you don't do as I say." His blue eyes were glassy. "I mean it. I've nothing else to live for."

She couldn't believe he was saying those things. She couldn't take him into her mouth. She couldn't! But neither did she want to die.

"You have your son," she whispered, not wanting to plead with him but hearing it in her voice. Somehow, she had to stay alive till Alaistair reached her. "He needs you."

Bent sneered. "You won't soften me. I mean to do this to you. That bastard you married will pay for ruining my life, for taking Alicia from me."

Liza inched backward on her arms and bottom, striving to put as much distance between them as the traveling coach allowed. It wasn't much. Her back came up against the opposite side and she felt the outline of another door.

Fool! Why hadn't she thought of this before? If only she could open it, she could tumble out. With luck, she might get away before he realized what she planned. If she could reach the marsh grass lining the road she had a chance—a small one, but better than the fate he offered.

Swallowing, she forced her expression to reveal nothing of her thoughts. "Alicia's gone. Don't ruin yourself this way."

His laughter was high and shrill, that of a man beyond reason. "I was ruined five years ago. Now I intend to destroy the man responsible." He took another step toward her and cocked the pistol. "Get on your knees and service me till I tell you to stop."

Liza pushed herself up the side of the carriage, her eyes on Bent the entire time. Her legs felt like gelatin, unable to support her weight as she squatted on them. Carefully, she felt behind her for the latch to the door.

She took several deep breaths and thought of reasoning with him again. One look at his ravaged face told her it would be useless.

"Sit down then," she said, her voice tight. "I'll kneel in front of you. It'll be easier on both of us."

His mouth split in a grin. "I see you realize the futility of fighting me." Ponderously, he turned and eased himself onto the seat.

Instead of settling herself between his open legs, Liza twisted the door handle and flung herself out the opening. She landed with a thud on the cold, hard ground.

Behind her, she heard Bent yelling. "Bloody bitch! I'll kill you for this!"

She didn't wait to hear more. Stumbling to her feet, she plunged into the ditch lining the road and ran for her life. But she got no more than thirty feet away, when he caught her and yanked at her hair, knocking her off balance.

"I have you now," Bent said, gasping for air, his face purple with rage. "You'll regret this."

He struck her with the back of his hand, sending her reeling into the marsh. Liza lay there, dazed, unable to distinguish between the sky and the ground. Vaguely, she heard a commotion in the distance, followed by shouting.

"Damn you to hell, Bent!"

It was Alaistair! Liza struggled to see, forcing her blurred vision to clear.

"Bloody bastard," came Winkly's lighter voice. "He struck her right good."

"Stay where you are, Alaistair. You, too," Bent said, aiming his pistol at Liza. "I'll kill her if either one of you comes any nearer." When Alaistair took a threatening step closer, he said, "I mean it. It matters not to me whether she lives or dies. It's you I want to make suffer."

Alaistair watched the man, noting the crazed light in his eyes, and realized the earl was beyond reasoning with. Bent was like a wild animal. Alaistair stopped moving and signaled for Winkly to do the same.

"Don't harm her, Bent, and I'll let you go."

Bent's laughter rent the cold, still air, his breath a cloud that rose into the sky. "Kill me, for all I care."

Alaistair took a calming breath. The tension riding him was worse than anything he'd ever experienced.

"You can't get away with this," he said when he was sure his voice would be calm. "And now that I'm here I won't let you rape her."

Bent sneered. "You can't stop me. All I have to do is keep this gun pointed at her. I can do anything I want, and you can't stop me for fear of losing her."

He moved nearer to Liza's prone figure, looming over her, the pistol pointed directly at her head.

"Pull up your skirts and spread your legs," Bent ordered. "What better punishment for your husband than to see me riding you and know there's nothing he can do to stop it?"

Liza's mind spun. She had to do something. Looking up, she realized he was still incapable of carrying out his threat. "You can't do it, Bent," she said clearly. "And I don't intend to help you. Kill me if you must, but know Alaistair will then kill you."

Bent's face twisted. Liza thought it was in anger, then realized it was pain as tears began to flow unchecked down his cheeks.

From his position, Alaistair noted the change in his adversary's countenance. "My God," he breathed, "he's crying."

Winkly stood silently, his pistol never wavering from the Earl of Bent's chest.

"Alicia," he sobbed, "you're not my Alicia, my love." He wiped his free hand across his eyes and glared at her. "It's your fault for not being Alicia. You have red hair and green eyes. You're not my Alicia." The tears flowed freely down his face, leaving rivulets of glistening pain in their wake. "My beloved Alicia," he whispered.

Seeing his chance, Alaistair lunged at Bent, felling him with one punch. The urge to pound the bastard into pulp made Alaistair hit him again even though the man was already down.

Then Liza's voice called him. He forgot the earl, forgot Winkly and fell to his knees by her. Gathering her into his arms, he held her tightly, crooning her name over and over.

"My love," he said, his voice ragged with emotion. "I thought I'd lost you. Oh God, I thought he'd kill you before he was finished, and I couldn't have borne the pain of that. Never in my life have I know such terror."

Liza gazed up into Alaistair's ravaged countenance and realized how tormented he had been by her abduction. She had to comfort him, reassure him that she was all right.

She stroked the black hair from his face. "I knew you'd come."

His arms tightened about her. "Has he hurt you?" He ran his hands over her arms, her legs.

Liza felt his anxiety in the corded muscles of his arms and her heart went out to him for all his suffering. "No, only bruised me. And frightened me, but he did nothing that won't heal, nothing I can't live with."

His eyes looked into hers, and quietly he said, "It doesn't matter to me if he violated you. I love you and nothing else is of importance."

Gazing into the dark depths of his soul, she understood. "He didn't. And I never thought you'd hold that against me. I know you too well to misjudge you again."

"My love, my life," he whispered, taking her mouth with his.

A pistol shot rang out behind them.

Alaistair started, sweat breaking out on his upper lip. But Liza clung to him, warm and trusting in his arms, and her presence calmed him. Together they turned around.

Bent lay on the ground, almost as Alaistair had left him, only now there was blood seeping from his chest. In one hand he still held his pistol, smoke seeping from the barrel. He'd shot himself. Winkly stood nearby, his face impassive, his gun at his side.

"My God," Alaistair said softly, rising with Liza and going to his enemy. Squatting down, he saw that Bent still lived, though the man's breathing was shallow and strained. "Why?"

Bent's eyes were haunted. "No...use. Can't have...Alicia." He grimaced and blood bubbled from his lips. "Life not...worth..."

Liza gazed down at him in horror. "He's dead! He took his life because he could never have your mother."

Alaistair rose and drew her tightly to him. "Even after what he intended to do to you, I can almost pity him."

She buried her face in his shoulder and shuddered, the freezing air finally penetrating the intense anxiety that had held her in its insensate grip. "Without your mother, life lost its meaning for him. I can almost understand."

Tears of relief and sorrow coursed down her cheeks, wetting Alaistair's coat as he held her tightly against his heart.

"Hush, my love," he murmured, stroking her long auburn hair as it fell down her back. "Don't cry for him."

She burrowed deeper into his warmth. "I . . . I'm crying for all of us."

"Shh," he soothed her. "Our sorrows are in the past, love."

Gently, he guided her over to where the two horses stood, munching on the marsh grass that lined the road. Untangling her fingers from the cape of his coat, Alaistair kissed her tenderly. Then he lifted her to the saddle and climbed up behind so that she rested against his chest, near his heart. He heard Winkly mount his own horse.

"I'll fetch the magistrate, guv'nor," Winkly said, turning his horse in the direction of a nearby town.

"Thanks," Alaistair said, using the reins to set his stallion on the road back to the inn.

Some distance on, Liza asked quietly, "What's to become of Bent's son?"

It was an easier question to answer than Alaistair had expected. "The boy has grandparents, his mother's parents, who have wanted custody of him since her death. Now they'll get him and he'll be better off for it.''

She nodded, unable to argue. But there was one last thing she had to know, and the asking of it took more courage than anything else in her life. Her stomach knotted and her throat dried, but she forced herself to twist around so that she could see her husband's face.

"Alaistair, when you found me, you..."

His smile, that wonderful warm smile he so seldom gave, transformed the hard lines of his face. "I called you my love." His arms tightened around her waist. "And I meant it. I think I've loved you from the start, but I knew so when Bent took you. The fear I felt for you, for what your life would be like after Bent finished with you, was worse than anything I've ever experienced. I knew that no matter what the cost, I had to reach you before he succeeded." He kissed her lightly on the lips. "That's when I knew I loved you. That's when I knew ours could never be a marriage of convenience."

EPILOGUE

LIZA RAISED HER GLASS in a toast to the New Year. "May we always be this happy."

Alaistair touched his glass to hers and added, "And may you always love me as I love you."

Happiness warmed Liza from the inside out. Taking a sip of her whiskey, she enjoyed its burning progress down her throat.

Lifting her glass for another toast, she added, "May all marriages of convenience end this way."

Alaistair's laughter rang through the room. He put his glass down and took hers as well. Without a by-your-leave, he swept her into his arms and carried her out the drawing-room door and to the staircase.

"Ahem." Timmens's voice stopped him. "I believe your bath is ready, m'lord."

Alaistair turned just in time to see the gleam of pleasure in the butler's rheumy eyes. "You always did have impeccable timing, Timmens."

Timmens drew himself up proudly. "I believe I've already explained that, m'lord."

"Just so," Alaistair murmured, smiling down into his wife's laughing eyes.

Without more ado, he carried Liza up the stairs to the new water closet he'd had installed in Thornyhold for their pleasure. Setting her down near the tub that was big enough for four, he started undressing her. Slowly, deliciously, he removed her clothing until she stood before him in all her glory.

"I love you," he murmured, lowering his lips to hers.

A long time later, the warm bathwater laving them, Liza opened her heavy-lidded eyes and asked, "Alaistair, whatever possessed you to build these rooms in the first place? Although—" she put one finger to his lips to keep him from speaking until she was through "—I've enjoyed both immensely—for different reasons."

His eyes were teasing. "You have? Then I shall have to have one installed in the London house."

Her face beamed. "Please do."

He chuckled, his chest vibrating against hers in the soothing water where they lay. "As to why I had them built—it was pure whim. The knowledge has existed since Elizabeth's time. One of her courtiers developed this."

"Thank goodness for courtiers," Liza murmured, no longer interested in his reasons as she gazed through the water to the heated place where their bodies still merged. He moved within her and she caught her breath on the words she longed to say, the only words that mattered. "I love you, Alaistair Gervase St. Simon. And I always shall."

From that point on, their future was rosy indeed.

1994 MISTLETOE MARRIAGES
HISTORICAL CHRISTMAS STORIES

With a twinkle of lights and a flurry of snowflakes, Harlequin Historicals presents *Mistletoe Marriages,* a collection of four of the most magical stories by your favorite historical authors. The perfect way to celebrate the season!

Brimming with romance and good cheer, these heartwarming stories will be available in November wherever Harlequin books are sold.

RENDEZVOUS by Elaine Barbieri
THE WOLF AND THE LAMB by Kathleen Eagle
CHRISTMAS IN THE VALLEY by Margaret Moore
KEEPING CHRISTMAS by Patricia Gardner Evans

Add a touch of romance to your holiday with
Mistletoe Marriages Christmas Stories!

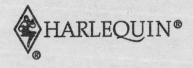

HARLEQUIN®

MMXS94

Take 4 bestselling love stories FREE

Plus get a FREE surprise gift!

Fifty red-blooded, white-hot, true-blue hunks
from every State in the Union!

Look for MEN MADE IN AMERICA! Written by some
of our most popular authors, these stories feature fifty
of the strongest, sexiest men, each from a different state
in the union!

Two titles available every month at your favorite
retail outlet.

In October, look for:

CHOICES by Annette Broadrick (Missouri)
PART OF THE BARGAIN by Linda Lael Miller
(Montana)

In November, look for:

SECRETS OF TYRONE by Regan Forest (Nebraska)
NOBODY'S BABY by Barbara Bretton (Nevada)

You won't be able to resist MEN MADE IN AMERICA!

This November, share the passion with *New York Times* Bestselling Author

Sandra Brown

(previously published under the pseudonym Erin St. Claire)

in

THE DEVIL'S OWN

Kerry Bishop was a good samaritan with a wild plan. Linc O'Neal was a photojournalist with a big heart.

Their scheme to save nine orphans from a hazardos land was foolhardy at best—deadly at the worst.

But together they would battle the odds—and the burning hungers—that made the steamy days and sultry nights doubly dangerous.

Reach for the brightest star in women's fiction with

MIRA™

MSBDO-R

Relive the romance.... This December,
Harlequin and Silhouette are proud to bring you

by **Request**™

Little
Matchmakers

All they want for Christmas is a mom *and* a dad!

Three complete novels by your favorite authors—
in one special collection!

THE MATCHMAKERS by Debbie Macomber
MRS. SCROOGE by Barbara Bretton
A CAROL CHRISTMAS by Muriel Jensen

When your child's a determined little matchmaker,
anything can happen—especially at Christmas!

Available wherever
Harlequin and Silhouette books are sold.

HARLEQUIN®   **Silhouette**®

HREQ1194